BY LEE CHILD AND ANDREW CHILD

The Sentinel
Better Off Dead

By Lee Child

Killing Floor
Die Trying
Tripwire
Running Blind
Echo Burning
Without Fail
Persuader
The Enemy
One Shot
The Hard Way
Bad Luck and Trouble
Nothing to Lose
Gone Tomorrow
61 Hours
Worth Dying For
The Affair
A Wanted Man
Never Go Back
Personal
Make Me
Night School
No Middle Name
The Midnight Line
Past Tense
Blue Moon

Short Stories

Second Son
Deep Down
High Heat
Not a Drill
Small Wars
The Christmas Scorpion

By Andrew Grant

Even
Die Twice
More Harm Than Good
RUN
False Positive
False Friend
False Witness
Invisible
Too Close to Home

Better Off Dead

LEE CHILD and ANDREW CHILD

 Delacorte Press | New York

Better Off Dead

A JACK REACHER NOVEL

Copyright © 2021 by Lee Child and Andrew Child

Published in the United States by Delacorte Press, an imprint of Random House, a division of Penguin Random House LLC, New York.

DELACORTE PRESS and the HOUSE colophon are registered trademarks of Penguin Random House LLC.

ISBN 9781984818508

Printed in the United States of America

Book design by Virginia Norey

For Jane and Tasha

Better Off Dead

Chapter 1

The stranger got into position under the streetlight at 11:00 P.M., as agreed.

The light had been easy to find, just like he'd been told it would be. It was the only one in the compound that was still working, all the way at the far end, six feet shy of the jagged metal fence that separated the United States from Mexico.

He was alone. And unarmed.

As agreed.

The car showed up at 11:02. It kept to the center of the space between the parallel rows of lockup garages. They were made of metal, too. Roofs warped by the sun. Walls scoured by the sand. Five on the right. Four on the left. And the remains of one more lying torn and corroded ten feet to the side, like something had exploded inside it years ago.

The car's lights were on bright, making it hard to recognize the make and model. And impossible to see inside. It continued until it was fifteen feet away then braked to a stop, rocking on its worn springs and settling into a low cloud of sandy dust. Then its front doors opened. Both of them. And two men climbed out.

Not as agreed.

Both the car's back doors opened. Two more men climbed out.

Definitely not as agreed.

The four men paused and sized the stranger up. They'd been told to expect someone big and this guy sure fit the bill. He was six feet five. Two hundred and fifty pounds. Chest like a gun safe and hands like backhoe buckets. And scruffy. His hair was coarse and unkempt. He hadn't shaved for days. His clothes looked cheap and ill-fitting, except for his shoes. Somewhere between a hobo and a Neanderthal. Not someone who was going to be missed.

The driver stepped forward. He was a couple of inches shorter than the stranger, and a good fifty pounds lighter. He was wearing black jeans and a black sleeveless T-shirt. He had on black combat-style boots. His head was shaved, but his face was hidden by a full beard. The other guys followed, lining up alongside him.

"The money?" the driver said.

The stranger patted the back pocket of his jeans.

"Good." The driver nodded toward the car. "Backseat. Get in."

"Why?"

"So I can take you to Michael."

"That wasn't the deal."

"Sure it was."

The stranger shook his head. "The deal was, you tell me where Michael is."

"Tell you. Show you. What's the difference?"

The stranger said nothing.

"Come on. What are you waiting for? Give me the money and get in the car."

"I make a deal, I stick to it. You want the money, tell me where Michael is."

The driver shrugged. "The deal's changed. Take it or leave it."

"I'll leave it."

"Enough of this." The driver reached behind his back and took a pistol from his waistband. "Cut the crap. Get in the car."

"You were never going to take me to Michael."

"No shit, Sherlock."

"You were going to take me to someone else. Someone who has questions for me."

"No more talking. Get in the car."

"Which means you can't shoot me."

"Which means I can't kill you. Yet. I can still shoot you."

The stranger said, "Can you?"

A witness would have said the stranger hardly moved at all but somehow in a split second he had closed the gap between them and had his hand on the driver's wrist. Which he pulled up, like a proud fisherman hauling something from the sea. He forced the guy's arm way above his head. He hoisted it so high the guy was raised up on his tiptoes. Then he drove his left fist into the guy's side. Hard. The kind of punch that would normally knock a man down. And keep him down. Only the driver didn't fall. He couldn't. He was suspended by his arm. His feet slid back. The gun fell from his fingers. His shoulder dislocated. Tendons stretched. Ribs shattered. It was a grotesque cascade of injuries. Each one debilitating in its own right.

But in the moment he hardly noticed any of them. Because his entire upper body was convulsing in agony. Searing bolts of pain shot through him, all stemming from one place. A spot just below his armpit, where a dense tangle of nerves and lymph nodes nestled beneath the skin. The exact spot that had just been crushed by the stranger's massive knuckles.

The stranger retrieved the driver's fallen gun and carried him over to the hood of the car. He laid him back, squealing and gasping and writhing on the dull paintwork, then turned to the other three guys and said, "You should walk away. Now. While you have the chance."

The guy at the center of the trio stepped forward. He was about the same height as the driver. Maybe a little broader. He had hair, cropped short. No beard. Three chunky silver chains around his neck. And a nasty sneer on his face. "You got lucky once. That won't happen again. Now get in the car before we hurt you."

The stranger said, "Really? Again?"

But he didn't move. He saw the three guys swap furtive glances. He figured that if the guys were smart, they'd opt for a tactical retreat. Or if they were proficient, they would attack together. But first they'd work one of them around to the rear. He could pretend to check on the injured driver. Or to give up and get in the car. Or even to run away. The other two could create a distraction. Then, when he was in place, they would all rush in at once. A simultaneous assault from three directions. One of the guys was certain to take some damage. Probably two. But the third might have a chance. An opening might present itself. If someone had the skill to exploit it.

They weren't smart. And they weren't proficient. They didn't withdraw. And no one tried to circle around. Instead, the center guy took another step forward, alone. He dropped into some kind of generic martial arts stance. Let out a high-pitched wail. Feinted a jab to the stranger's face. Then launched a reverse punch to the solar plexus. The stranger brushed it aside with the back of his left hand and punched the guy's biceps with his right, his middle knuckle extended. The guy shrieked and jumped back, his axillary nerve overloaded and his arm temporarily useless.

"You should walk away," the stranger said. "Before you hurt yourself."

The guy sprang forward. He made no attempt at disguise this time. He just twisted into a wild roundhouse punch with his good arm. The stranger leaned back. The guy's fist sailed past. The stranger watched it go then drove his knuckle into the meat of the guy's triceps. Both his arms were now out of action.

"Walk away," the stranger said. "While you still can."

The guy lunged. His right leg rose. His thigh first, then his foot, pivoting at the knee. Going for maximum power. Aiming for the stranger's groin. But not getting close. Because the stranger countered with a kick of his own. A sneaky one. Straight and low. Directly into the guy's shin. Just as it reached maximum speed. Bone against toe cap. The stranger's shoes. The only thing about him that wasn't scruffy. Bought in London years ago. Layer upon layer of leather and polish and glue. Seasoned by time. Hardened by the elements. And now as solid as steel.

The guy's ankle cracked. He screamed and shied away. He lost his balance and couldn't regain it without the use of his arms. His foot touched the ground. The fractured ends of the bone connected. They grated together. Pain ripped through his leg. It burned along every nerve. Way more than his system could handle. He remained upright for another half second, already unconscious. Then he toppled onto his back and lay there, as still as a fallen tree.

The remaining two guys turned and made for the car. They kept going past its front doors. Past its rear doors. All the way around the back. The trunk lid popped open. One of the guys dropped out of sight. The shorter one. Then he reappeared. He was holding something in each hand. Like a pair of baseball bats, only longer. And thicker and squarer at one end. Pickax handles. Effective tools, in the right hands. He passed one to the taller guy and the pair strode back, stopping about four feet away.

"Say we break your legs?" The taller guy licked his lips. "You could still answer questions. But you'd never walk again. Not without a cane. So stop dicking us around. Get in the car. Let's go."

The stranger saw no need to give them another warning. He'd been clear with them from the start. And they were the ones who'd chosen to up the ante.

The shorter guy made as if to swing, but checked. Then the taller guy took over. He did swing. He put all his weight into it. Which was bad technique. A serious mistake with that kind of weapon. All the stranger had to do was take a step back. The heavy hunk of wood whistled past his midriff. It continued relentlessly through its arc. There was too much momentum for the guy to stop it. And both his hands were clinging to the handle. Which left his head exposed. And his torso. And his knees. A whole menu of tempting targets, all available, all totally unguarded. Any other day the stranger could have taken his pick. But on that occasion he had no time. The taller guy got off the hook. His buddy bailed him out. By jabbing at the stranger's gut, using the ax handle like a spear. He went short, aiming to get the stranger's attention. He jabbed a second time, hoping to back the stranger off. Then he lunged. It was the money shot. Or it would have been, if he hadn't paused a beat too long. Set his feet a fraction too firm. So that when he thrust, the stranger knew it was coming. He moved to the side. Grabbed the ax handle at its midpoint. And pulled. Hard. The guy was dragged forward a yard before he realized what was happening. He let go. But by then it was too late. His fate was sealed. The stranger whipped the captured ax handle over and around and brought it scything down, square onto the top of the guy's head. His eyes rolled back. His knees buckled and he wilted, slumping limp and lifeless at the stranger's feet. He wouldn't be getting up any time soon. That was for sure.

The taller guy glanced down. Saw the shape his buddy was in. And swung his ax handle back the opposite way. Aiming for the stranger's head. He swung harder than before. Wanting revenge. Hoping to survive. And he missed. Again. He left himself vulnerable. Again. But this time something else saved him. The fact that he was the last of his crew left standing. The only available source of information. He now had strategic value. Which gave him the chance to swing again. He took it, and the stranger parried. The guy kept going, chopping left and right, left and right, like a crazed lumberjack. He managed a dozen more strokes at full speed, then he ran out of gas.

"Screw this." The guy dropped the ax handle. Reached behind him. And pulled out his gun. "Screw answering questions. Screw taking you alive."

The guy took two steps back. He should have taken three. He hadn't accounted for the length of the stranger's arms.

"Let's not be hasty." The stranger flicked out with his ax handle and sent the gun flying. Then he stepped closer and grabbed the guy by the neck. "Maybe we will take that drive. Turns out I have some questions of my own. You can—"

"Stop." It was a female voice. Confident. Commanding. Coming from the shadows near the right-hand row of garages. Someone new was on the scene. The stranger had arrived at 8:00 P.M., three hours early, and searched every inch of the compound. He was certain no one had been hiding, then.

"Let him go." A silhouette broke free from the darkness. A woman's. She was around five-ten. Slim. Limping slightly. Her arms were out in front and there was the squat outline of a matte-black pistol in her hands. "Step away."

The stranger didn't move. He didn't relax his grip.

The woman hesitated. The other guy was between her and the stranger. Not an ideal position. But he was six inches shorter. And slightly to the side. That did leave her a target. An area on the stranger's chest. A rectangle. It was maybe six inches by ten. That was big enough, she figured. And it was more or less in the right position. She took a breath. Exhaled gently. And pulled the trigger.

The stranger fell back. He landed with his arms spread wide, one knee raised, and his head turned so that he was facing the border fence. He was completely still. His shirt was ragged and torn. His entire chest was slick and slimy and red. But there was no arterial spray. No sign of a heartbeat.

No sign of life at all.

The tidy, manicured area people now called *The Plaza* had once been a sprawling grove of trees. Black walnuts. They'd grown, undisturbed, for centuries. Then in the 1870s a trader took to resting his mules in their shade on his treks back and forth to California. He liked the spot, so he built a shack there. And when he grew too old to rattle across the continent he sold his beasts and he stayed.

Other people followed suit. The shanty became a village. The village became a town. The town split in two like a cell, multiplying greedily. Both halves flourished. One to the south. One to the north. There were many more years of steady growth. Then stagnation. Then decline. Slow and grim and unstoppable. Until an unexpected shot in the arm was delivered, in the late 1930s. An army of surveyors showed up. Then laborers. Builders. Engineers. Even some artists and sculptors. All sent by the WPA.

No one local knew why those two towns had been chosen. Some said it was a mistake. A bureaucrat misreading a file note and dispatching the resources to the wrong place. Others figured that someone in D.C. must have owed the mayor a favor. But whatever the reason, no one objected. Not with all the new roads that were being laid. New bridges being built. And all kinds of buildings rising up. The project went on for years. And it left a permanent mark. The towns' traditional adobe arches became a little more square. The stucco exteriors a little more uniform. The layout of the streets a little more regimented. And the amenities, a lot more generous. The area gained schools. Municipal offices. Firehouses. A police station. A courthouse. A museum. And a medical center.

The population had dwindled again over the decades since the government money dried up. Some of the facilities became obsolete. Some were sold off. Others demolished. But the medical center was still the main source of healthcare for miles around. It contained a doctor's office. A pharmacy. A clinic, with a couple dozen beds. A pediatric suite, with places for parents to stay with their sick kids. And thanks to the largesse of those New Deal planners, even a morgue. It was tucked away in the basement. And it was where Dr. Houllier was working, the next morning.

Dr. Houllier was seventy-two years old. He had served the town his whole life. Once he was part of a team. Now he was the only physician left. He was responsible for everything from delivering babies to treating colds to diagnosing cancer. And for dealing with the deceased. Which was the reason for that day's early start. He'd been on duty since the small hours. Since he received the call about a shooting on the outskirts of town. It was the kind of thing that would attract attention. He knew that from experience. He was expecting a visit. Soon. And he needed to be ready.

There was a computer on the desk, but it was switched off. Dr. Houllier preferred to write his notes longhand. He remembered things better that way. And he had a format. One he'd developed himself. It wasn't fancy, but it worked. It was better than anything those Silicon Valley whiz kids had ever tried to foist on him. And more important in that particular situation, it left no electronic trace for anyone to ever recover. Dr. Houllier sat down, picked up the Mont Blanc his father had bought him when he graduated medical school, and started to record the results of his night's work.

There was no knock. No greeting. No courtesy at all. The door just opened and a man came in. The same one as usual. Early forties, tight curly hair, tan linen suit. *Perky,* Dr. Houllier privately called him, because of the bouncy way the guy walked. He didn't know his real name. He didn't want to know.

The guy started at the far end of the room. The cold storage area. The *meat locker* as Dr. Houllier thought of it, after decades of dealing with its contents. There was a line of five steel doors. The guy approached, examined each handle in turn, but didn't touch any of them. He never did. He moved on to the autopsy table in the center. Crossed to the line of steel trolleys against the far wall, near the autoclave. Then he approached the desk.

"Phone." He held out his hand.

Dr. Houllier passed the guy his cell. The guy checked to make sure it wasn't recording, slipped it into his pants pocket, and turned to the door. "Clear," he said.

Another man walked in. *Mantis,* Dr. Houllier called him, because whenever he looked at the guy with his long skinny limbs, angular torso, and bulging eyes he couldn't help but think of the insect. The large triangular burn scar on the guy's cheek and the way his three missing fingers made his right hand look like a claw added to the effect. Although Dr. Houllier did know this guy's real name. Waad Dendoncker. Everyone in town knew it, even if they'd never met him.

A third man followed Dendoncker in. He looked a little like Perky, but with straighter hair and a darker suit. And with such an anonymous face and bland way of moving that Dr. Houllier had never been inspired to find him a nickname.

Dendoncker stopped in the center of the room. His pale hair was almost invisible in the harsh light. He turned through 360 degrees, slowly, scanning the space around him. Then he turned to Dr. Houllier.

"Show me," he said.

Dr. Houllier crossed the room. He checked his watch, then worked the lever that opened the center door of the meat locker. He pulled out the sliding rack, revealing a body covered by a sheet. It was tall. Almost as long as the tray it lay on. And broad. The shoulders only just fit through the opening. Dr. Houllier pulled the sheet, slowly, revealing the head. It was a man's. Its hair was messy. The face was craggy and pale, and the eyes were taped shut.

"Move." Dendoncker shoved Dr. Houllier aside. He pulled the sheet off and dropped it on the floor. The body was naked. If Michelangelo's *David* was made to embody masculine beauty, this guy could have been another in the series. But at the opposite end of the spectrum. There was nothing elegant. Nothing delicate. This one was all about power and brutality. Pure and simple.

"That's what killed him?" Dendoncker pointed to a wound on the guy's chest. It was slightly raised. Its edges were rough and ragged and they were turning brown.

"Well, he didn't die of sloth." Dr. Houllier glanced at his watch. "I can guarantee that."

"He'd been shot before." Dendoncker pointed at a set of scars on the other side of the guy's chest. "And there's *that*."

"The scar on his abdomen?" Dr. Houllier glanced down. "Like some kind of sea creature. He must have been stabbed at some point."

"That's no knife wound. That's something else altogether."

"Like what?"

"Doesn't matter. What else do we know about him?"

"Not much." Dr. Houllier snatched up the sheet and spread it loosely over the body, including its head.

Dendoncker pulled the sheet off again and dropped it back on the floor. He wasn't done staring at the biggest of the dead guy's scars.

"I spoke to the sheriff." Dr. Houllier moved away, toward his desk. "Sounds like the guy was a drifter. He had a room at the Border Inn. He'd paid through next weekend, in cash, but he had no belongings there. And he'd registered under a false address. One East 161st Street, the Bronx, New York."

"How do you know that's false?"

"Because I've been there. It's another way of saying *Yankee Sta-*

dium. And the guy used a false name, too. He signed the register as John Smith."

"Smith? Could be his real name."

Dr. Houllier shook his head. He took a Ziploc bag from the top drawer of his desk and handed it to Dendoncker. "See for yourself. This was in his pocket."

Dendoncker popped the seal and fished out a passport. It was crumpled and worn. He turned to the second page. *Personal Information.* "This has expired."

"Doesn't matter. The ID's still valid. And look at the photo. It's old, but it's a match."

"OK. Let's see. Name: Reacher. Jack, none. Nationality: United States of America. Place of birth: Berlin, West Germany. Interesting." Dendoncker looked back at the body on the rack. At the scar on its abdomen. "Maybe he wasn't looking for Michael. Maybe he was looking for me. It's a good job that crazy bitch killed him after all." Dendoncker turned away and tossed the passport in a trash can next to Dr. Houllier's desk. "Observations?"

Dr. Houllier held out one of his special forms. The one he'd just finished filling in. Dendoncker read each comment twice then crumpled the paper and dropped it into the trash, on top of the passport.

"Burn those." He turned to the two guys he arrived with. "Get rid of the body. Dump it in the usual place."

Chapter 2

I first encountered the woman with the limp two days earlier. We met on a road outside the town with the dimly lit compound and the medical center where Dr. Houllier worked. The whole area was deserted. I was on foot. She was in a Jeep. It looked like it was ex-military. Old. Maybe Vietnam War era. Its stenciled markings were too faded to read. Its olive drab paintwork was caked and crusted with pale dust. It had no roof. No doors. Its windshield was folded forward, but not latched. The racks and straps for holding fuel cans and tools were empty and slack. The tread on its tires was worn way below the recommended minimum. Its motor wasn't running. Its spare wheel was missing. Not the kind of thing anyone would call a well-maintained vehicle.

The sun was high in the sky. I guess a thermometer would have said it was a little over eighty but the lack of shade made it feel much hotter. Sweat was trickling down my back. The wind was picking up and grit was stinging my face. Walking hadn't been part of my plan when I woke up that morning. But plans change. And not always for the better. It looked like the woman's plans had taken an unwelcome turn as well. A fair chunk of the Jeep's remaining rubber was now streaked across the faded blacktop from where she'd skidded. She'd gone right off the road and plowed into the trunk of a tree. A stunted, twisted, ugly thing with hardly any leaves. It wasn't going to win any prizes for appearance. That was for sure. But it was clearly resilient. It was the only thing growing taller than knee height for miles in either direction. If the driver had lost control at any other point she would have wound up in the rough scrub on either side of the road. Probably been able to reverse right back out. The landscape looked like a bunch of giants had shoved their hands under a coarse green blanket and stretched their fingers wide.

How the woman had hit that exact spot was a mystery. Maybe the sun had blinded her. Maybe an animal had run out, or a bird had swooped down. It was unlikely that another vehicle had been involved. Maybe she was depressed and had done it on purpose. But whatever had caused her accident, that was a problem for another time.

The woman was slumped over the steering wheel. Her left arm was stretched forward across the flattened windshield. Her hand was open like she was reaching out to the tree for help. Her right arm was folded into her abdomen. She was facing down, into the footwell. She was completely inert. There was no sign of bleeding. No sign of any other injuries, which was good. But there was also no sound of breathing. I figured I should check for a pulse or some other indication she was alive so I stepped in close to the side of the Jeep. I reached for her neck, slowly and gently. I brushed her hair aside and homed in on her carotid. Then she sat up. Fast. She twisted around to face me. Used her left hand to bat my arm away. And her right to point a pistol at my gut.

She waited a beat, presumably to make sure I wasn't about to freak out. She wanted my full attention. That was clear. Then she said, "Move back. One step only." Her voice was firm but calm, with no hint of panic or doubt.

I moved back. One step. I made it a large one. And I realized why she'd been looking down through the steering wheel at the floor of the vehicle. There was a piece of mirror wedged between the gas pedal and the transmission tunnel. She must have cut it to the right size and positioned it to give an early warning of anyone who approached her.

"Where's your buddy?" She glanced left and right.

"There's no one else," I said. "Just me."

Her eyes darted across to the rearview mirror. It was angled so she could spot anyone sneaking up behind her. "They only sent one guy? Really?"

She sounded half offended, half disappointed. I was starting to like her.

"No one sent me."

"Don't lie." She jabbed the gun forward for emphasis. "Anyway, it doesn't matter. One of you or a whole squad? You get the same deal. Tell me where Michael is. Tell me now. And tell me the truth, or I'll shoot you in the stomach and leave you here to die."

"I would love to tell you." I held my hands up, palms out. "But there's a problem. I can't. I don't know who Michael is."

"Don't . . ." She paused and glanced around again. "Wait. Where's your car?"

"I don't have a car."

"Don't get smart. Your Jeep, then. Your motorcycle. Whatever mode of transport you used to get here."

"I walked here."

"Bullshit."

"Did you hear an engine just now? Any kind of mechanical sound?"

"OK," she said after a long moment. "You walked. From where? And why?"

"Slow down." I tried to make my voice sound friendly and unthreatening. "Let's think this through. I could recount my day to you, minute by minute. In other circumstances I'd be happy to. But right now, are my travel arrangements that important? Maybe a better question would be: Am I the person you were waiting for? The person with information about Michael?"

She didn't answer.

"Because if I'm not, and the real guy shows up with me still here, your whole crashed car routine is never going to fly."

She still didn't respond.

"Is there some law that says only people you want to ambush can use this road? Is it off-limits to everyone else?"

I saw her glance at her watch.

"Look at me. I'm on my own. I'm on foot. I'm unarmed. Is that what you were expecting? Does it make sense to you?"

Her head moved an inch to the left and her eyes narrowed a fraction. A moment later I caught it, too. There was a sound. In the distance. A vehicle engine. Rough. Ragged. And moving closer.

"Decision time," I said.

She stayed silent. The engine note grew louder.

"Think about Michael," I said. "I don't know where he is. But if whoever's coming does, and you keep me here, you'll lose your chance. You'll never find out."

She didn't speak. The engine note grew louder still. Then she gestured toward the other side of the road. "Over there. Quick. Ten yards up there's a ditch. At an angle. Like a streambed. It's dried out. Get in it. Keep your head down. Stay still. Don't make a sound. Don't alert them. Don't do anything to screw this up. Because if you do . . ."

"Don't worry." I was already moving. "I get the picture."

Chapter 3

The ditch was right where she said it would be. I found it, no problem. I got there before the approaching vehicle was in sight. The streambed was dry. I figured it could provide adequate cover. But the bigger issue was whether to hide at all. Or to leave.

I looked over at the Jeep. The woman was back in position, slumped across the steering wheel. Her head was turned away from me. I was out of range of her mirror. I was pretty sure she wouldn't be able to see me. But even if she did spot me I doubted she would risk taking a shot. She wouldn't want to alert whoever was coming for her.

Leaving was the sensible option. There was no doubt about that. But there was a problem. I had questions. A whole bunch of them. Like who was this woman? Who was Michael? Who was coming after her? And would she really shoot someone in the stomach and leave them to die?

I checked the road. Saw a speck in the distance, shrouded in

dust. I figured I still had time so I picked up a rock from the floor
of the ditch. It was about the size of a cinder block. I positioned it
on the lip, between me and the Jeep. I found another, a little narrower and flatter. Rested it at an angle against the first one so that
there was a triangular gap between them. A small one. Just the right
size for me to squint through with one eye. High school physics at
work. The sight line opened up away from me like I was looking
through an invisible cone. It gave me a clear view of the Jeep and
the area around it. But the angle narrowed correspondingly in reverse so no one at that distance would be able to spot me watching
them.

The approaching vehicle emerged from its cloud. It was another
Jeep. Also ex-military. It was making steady progress. Slow and un-
hurried. Then, when it was close to the spot where I'd been when I
noticed the skid marks, it slewed a little to the side and stopped.
There were two men in it. A driver and a passenger. Both were
wearing khaki T-shirts. They had khaki baseball caps and mirrored
sunglasses. Some kind of an urgent conversation broke out between
them. There was a whole lot of gesticulating and pointing toward
the tree. That told me they hadn't expected anyone to be in place
before them. Or that they hadn't expected anyone with a matching
vehicle, which suggested they were from the same outfit. Or that
they hadn't expected either thing. I thought maybe they'd call the
new development in. Ask for updated orders. Or if they were smart,
withdraw altogether. But they did neither. They started moving
again, faster than before, then pulled in next to the driver's side of
the woman's Jeep.

"Unbelievable." The passenger jumped down and stood between
the two vehicles. I could see the grip of a pistol protruding from the
waistband of his cargo pants. It was knurled and worn. "Her?"

The driver looped around and joined him. He put his hands on his hips. He also had a gun. "Shit. Dendoncker's going to be pissed."

"Not our problem." The passenger took hold of his pistol. "Come on. Let's do it."

"Is she still alive?" The driver scratched his temple.

"I hope so." The passenger stepped forward. "We deserve a little fun." He reached for the side of the woman's neck with his free hand. "Ever done it with a gimp? I haven't. Always wondered what it would be like."

The driver crowded in closer. "I—"

The woman sat up. She twisted to the side. Raised her gun. And shot the passenger in the face. The top of his skull was obliterated. One moment it was there. The next it was a hint of pink mist drifting in the surrounding air. His empty hat fluttered to the ground. His body folded over backward. One arm was still stretched out and it swung around and slapped the driver on the thigh as he fell. His neck clattered into the open doorway of his Jeep.

The driver went for his gun. He grabbed it, right-handed. He started to pull it clear of his waistband. Got it about three quarters of the way out. Then he tried to bring it to bear. The move was premature. It was a sloppy mistake. The barrel was still trapped by his belt. His hand slipped off the grip. The weapon was left hanging loose and unbalanced. It pivoted around and fell. He tried to catch it. And missed. He leaned down, started to scratch around frantically in the dirt, then saw the woman's gun. Its muzzle was moving. Zeroing in on his face. He stopped himself. Jumped back. Dived for cover behind the woman's Jeep. Crawled forward a couple of yards until he reached the road then scrambled to his feet. He started to run. The woman swiveled around in her seat. She took a breath. Aimed. Then she pulled the trigger. The bullet must have come within an inch of removing the guy's right ear. He flung himself down to the left and rolled over twice. The woman climbed out of the Jeep. She moved around to its rear. That was the first time I noticed she favored her left leg. She waited for the guy to get back on his feet then fired again. This time the bullet almost took off his left ear. He threw himself down the opposite way and started to wriggle along on the ground like a snake.

"Stop." The woman sounded like she was running short of patience.

The guy continued to crawl.

"The next bullet won't miss," she said. "But it won't kill you, either. It'll sever your spine."

The guy rolled onto his back, as if that would protect him. He threw a couple of kicks like he was trying to swim. The effort was futile. It stirred up plenty of dust but only bought him a few more inches. His arms and legs went limp. His head flopped back against the ground. He closed his eyes. He lay there for a moment, breathing deeply. Then he sat up and held his hands out in front like he was warding off some kind of invisible demon.

"Let's talk about this." His voice was shrill and shaky. "It doesn't have to be this way. My partner. I'll pin it on him. I'll tell the boss he set the whole thing up. We got here, no one else showed, he pulled his gun on me—'cause he was the traitor all along—but I was faster. We've got the body. That's proof, right? What else do we need?"

"Get up."

"It'll work. I can sell it. I promise. Just don't kill me. Please."

"Get up."

"You don't understand. I had—"

The woman raised her gun. "Get up or I'll blow *your* leg off. See how you like being called *gimp*."

"No, please!" The guy scrambled to his feet.

"Move back."

The guy took a step. A small one.

"Farther."

He took another step. That left him out of range if he was dumb enough to try his luck with a punch or a kick. He stopped with his ankles pressed together and his arms clamped tight by his sides. It was a weird position. He reminded me of a dancer I saw busking on the street in Boston, years ago.

"Good. Now. You want me to let you live?"

"Oh yes." His head bobbed up and down like a novelty doll's. "I do."

"All right. I'm prepared to do that. But you have to do one thing for me first."

"Anything." The guy kept on nodding. "Whatever you want. Name it."

"Tell me where Michael is."

Chapter 4

The guy's head stopped moving. He didn't speak. His legs were still together. His arms were still by his sides. His posture still looked awkward.

"Tell me where I can find Michael. If you don't, I will kill you. But not quickly like your friend. No. Not like that at all."

The guy didn't respond.

"Have you ever seen anyone get shot in the stomach?" The woman made a show of taking aim at the guy's abdomen. "How long they take to die? The agony they're in, the entire time?"

"No." The guy shook his head. "Don't do that. I'll tell you."

Then I realized why the guy looked strange. It was his hands, still pressed against his sides. One was open. His left. But his right was clenched. His wrist was bent back. He was holding something and trying to conceal the fact. I wanted to shout a warning, but I couldn't. Breaking the woman's concentration right at that moment wasn't going to help her.

"Well?" A sharp edge had crept into her voice.

"So, Michael's whereabouts. OK. It's kind of complicated but he's—"

The guy's right arm snapped up. His fingers opened and a swirl of sandy grit flew right at the woman's face. She reacted fast. Her left hand came up in front of her eyes and she pivoted away on her good leg. She dodged the worst of the cloud. But not the guy himself. He launched forward, swatted her arm aside, and slammed his shoulder into her chest. He was only a couple of inches taller than her but must have been at least eighty pounds heavier. The impact sent her reeling. Her feet couldn't keep up and she tumbled over backward. She was still holding the gun. She tried to raise it but he followed in and stamped on her wrist. She clung on. He pressed his foot down harder. And harder still until she shrieked with frustration and let go of the weapon. He kicked it away then stepped across her body, one foot either side, and stood there looming over her.

"Well now, *gimp*. I'd say the boot's on the other foot but that would be cruel, as you only have one."

The woman lay still. I stood up. The guy had his back to me. He was less than fifteen yards away.

"My friend had a plan for you." The guy started to fumble with the front of his pants. "A kind of dying wish. I figure I should see it through. Once for him. Once for me. Maybe more, if I like it."

I climbed out of the trench.

"Then I'll kill you." The guy pulled his belt clear and tossed it away to the side. "Maybe I'll shoot *you* in the stomach. See how long it takes *you* to die."

I started down the slope.

"It could take hours." The guy started to unbutton his fly. "All night, even. Dendoncker won't care. And he won't care what condition you wind up in. Just as long as you're dead when I hand you over."

I forced myself to slow down. I didn't want to make a sound on the loose gravel.

The woman shifted her position a little then stretched her arms out on both sides. "So you know about my foot. Gold star to you for observation. But do you know much about titanium?"

The guy's hands stopped moving.

I reached the blacktop on the far side of the road.

"It's a very interesting metal." The woman braced her palms against the ground. "It's very strong. Very light. And very hard."

The woman whipped her right leg up, bent it at the knee, and drove her prosthetic foot toward the guy's groin. It connected. Front and center. Full power. No mistake. Nothing held back. The guy screamed and gasped and pitched forward. He landed face-down in the dirt. She rolled to the side and only just avoided getting crushed. She rolled a couple more times and retrieved the gun. Then she used both arms to lever herself up off the ground.

I stopped where I was, halfway across the pavement, one foot either side of the faded yellow line.

The guy rolled onto his side and curled into a ball. He was whimpering like a whipped dog.

"One last chance." The woman raised the gun. "Michael. Where is he?"

"Michael's history, you idiot." The guy was breathing hard. "Forget about him."

"He's history? What do you mean?"

"What do you think I mean? Dendoncker takes some poor schmuck in for interrogation, then . . . Want me to draw a diagram?"

"No need for a diagram." Her voice was suddenly flat. "But I do need to be sure."

"He was a dead man the moment he started swapping secret notes." The guy raised his head. "You know about Dendoncker. He's the most paranoid guy on the planet. He was bound to find out."

"Who killed him? You?"

"No. I swear."

"Then who?"

"I thought it was going to be us. Dendoncker told us to be ready as soon as he was done with his questions. We dropped everything. No one lasts very long when Dendoncker goes to work on them. You know that. So we were good to go. Then he told us we weren't needed after all."

"Why not? What changed?"

"I don't know. I wasn't there. Maybe Michael was too slow with his answers. Or too smart with his mouth. Or just had a weak heart. Anyway, Dendoncker stood us down. Then this morning he sent us for you."

The woman was quiet for a moment. Then she said, "Michael's body. Where is it?"

"Usual place, I guess. If there was enough of it left."

The woman's shoulders sagged a little. She lowered the gun. The guy curled back up. He reached for his ankle. Slowly and smoothly. He slid something out of his boot. Rolled onto his front. A second later he was on his feet. The sun glinted off whatever he had in his right hand. A blade. It was short and broad. He launched himself forward. His arm was high. He was swinging, horizontally. Trying to slash the woman's forehead. He wanted her eyes to fill with blood. So she couldn't see. Couldn't aim. She leaned back, bending sharply at the waist. Just far enough. He missed. He switched the knife to his other hand. Shaped up for another try.

This time she didn't hesitate. She just pulled the trigger. The guy went over backward. He dropped the knife, screamed, and clutched his gut with both hands. A dark stain spread across the fabric. She'd hit him in the stomach. Exactly like she'd threatened to. She stepped in close. She stood and looked down at him. Thirty seconds crawled past. No doubt the longest half minute of the guy's life. He was writhing and moaning and trying to stem the stream of blood with his palms and his fingers. She took a step back. Then she raised the gun. Lined it up on his head. And pulled the trigger. Again.

Some of my questions had been answered, at least. But now I had another one on my mind. Something much more urgent. The woman had just killed two people. I had watched her do it. I was the only witness. I needed to know what she was going to do about that. Her actions could be classed as self-defense, for sure. She had a solid case. I wouldn't argue against it. But she had no way of knowing that. Relying on a stranger's support was a gamble. And any trial she faced would come with its own risks. The skill of the lawyers. The disposition of the jurors. And she would inevitably spend months in jail before seeing the inside of a courtroom. An unappealing prospect in itself. And a dangerous one. Jails don't generally boost the life expectancy of anyone who gets locked up in them.

I stepped forward. There was no point going back. A couple of extra yards between us weren't going to make any difference. The gun she was holding was a Glock 17. One of the most reliable pistols in the world. It had a misfire rate of around one in ten thousand. Great odds from her side of the trigger. Not so good from mine. The magazine held seventeen rounds. She had fired five shots, to my knowledge. There was no reason to assume she hadn't started out with a full load. So she would have twelve bullets left. There was no way she would need even a quarter of that number. She was an excellent markswoman. She had demonstrated that. And she had shown no hesitation when a violent solution was called for. The two guys who were now on the ground had found that out the hard way.

I took another step. Then my new question was answered, too. And not in a way I expected. The woman nodded to me. She turned. Walked back to her Jeep. Leaned against its rear. Shrugged her shoulders. Sighed. Raised her gun. And pressed its muzzle against her temple.

"Stop." I hurried toward her. "You don't have to do that."

She looked at me with wide, clear eyes. "Oh yes. I do."

"No. You did what—"

"Get back." She held up her free hand, palm out. "Unless you want to wind up covered in blood and brains. I'll give you three seconds. Then I'm going to pull the trigger."

I believed her. I couldn't see any way to stop her. All I could think to do was ask, "Why?"

She looked at me like the answer was so self-evident it was barely worth the energy it would take to respond. Then she said, "Because I lost my job. I disgraced myself. I put innocent people in harm's way. And I got my brother killed. I have nothing left to live for. I'd be better off dead."

Chapter 5

Losing a job can be a blow. I know. I've had the experience. But the feeling pales into nothing beside losing a brother. Into less than nothing. I know. I've lived through that experience, too. And if you think you're responsible for your brother's death, the burden must be even heavier. Maybe too heavy to bear. Maybe there isn't a path back. I wasn't sure. But I hoped there was a way to survive. In this case, at least. I didn't know what shape it should take, but I hoped something could help this woman. I liked the way she stood up for herself. I didn't want her story to end with a self-inflicted bullet at the side of some lonely road.

I stood my ground and counted to three in my head. Slowly. The woman didn't pull the trigger. I didn't get covered in her blood and brains. I took that as a good sign.

"I heard what that was guy was saying." I waited a couple more seconds. My eyes didn't leave her trigger finger. "Michael's your brother?"

"Was my brother." The gun was still pressed to her head.

"You were looking for him?"

"That's what got him killed."

"You were looking for him on your own, is what I mean. You hadn't gone to the police."

"Was he on the wrong side of the law? Was he a criminal? That's what you mean. And the answer's yes. He was." She lowered the gun. "Gold star to you for figuring that out."

"And you?"

"No. Well, yes. Technically. By association. But only because I infiltrated Michael's group. I was trying to get him out of there. He wanted to leave. Straighten himself out. He got a message to me. You didn't know him. He was a good man. In his heart. That last tour changed him. What the army did was wrong. It derailed him. Left him vulnerable. Some other guys got their hooks in him. Took advantage. He made some bad choices. Clearly. Which is on him. I'm not making excuses. But it was a temporary thing. A blip. The real Michael was still in there somewhere. I know it. If I could have just gotten to him in time . . ."

"I'm not judging. I understand why you didn't go to the police before. But things have changed."

The woman didn't reply.

I said, "The guy who killed Michael? Get him arrested. Go to his trial. Give evidence. Put him away for the rest of his life."

She shook her head. "It wouldn't work. The guy who killed Michael is too careful. He won't have left any proof. Even if they believe me the police could look for months and not find any-thing."

"Maybe the police don't need to find anything. We could go visit the guy. I heard a name. Dendoncker?"

"That's the asshole."

"We could chat. I'm sure he would soon feel the urge to confess. With the correct kind of encouragement."

A small, sad smile spread across the woman's face. "I would love to go visit Dendoncker. Believe me. I'd be there in a heartbeat. But we can't. It's impossible."

"No such thing as impossible. Just inadequate preparation."

"Not in this case. Getting your hands on Dendoncker cannot be done."

"How do you know?"

"I've tried."

"What stopped you?"

"For a start, no one ever knows where he is."

"So make him come to you."

"Not possible. He only shows his face in one particular circum-stance."

"Then create that circumstance."

"I'm about to. But it won't help."

"I don't follow."

"He only breaks cover when someone who was a threat to him is dead. Even if he only thought they were a threat. Even if he only imagined it or dreamed it. He has them killed. Then he has to see the body for himself. It's like a paranoid compulsion he has. He won't take anyone's word. He won't trust a photograph or a video or a death certificate or a coroner's report. He only believes his own eyes."

I took a moment to think. Then I said, "So, two people."

"What?"

"If that's his M.O. it'll take two people to capture him. You and I could do it. If we worked together."

"Bullshit. You don't know what you're talking about."

"Actually, I do. I spent thirteen years catching people who didn't want to get caught. And I was good at it."

"You're serious?"

"Absolutely."

"You were a bounty hunter?"

"Guess again."

"Not a cop?"

"A military cop."

"Really? You don't look like one. What happened to you?"

I didn't respond to that.

The woman was silent for a moment, too. Then she said, "What difference does a second person make? I don't see it."

"All in good time. The question right now is: Capturing Dendoncker—is that worth living for?"

The woman blinked a couple of times then looked away toward the horizon. She gazed in silence for a whole minute. Then she looked me in the eye. "Stopping . . . Capturing Dendoncker. That would be a start, I guess. But two people. Working together. You and me. Why would you do that?"

"Michael was a veteran. You're one, too. I can see it in you. Too many of us have been lost already. I'm not going to stand by and watch another life get wasted."

"I can't ask you to help."

"You're not asking. I'm offering."

"It would be dangerous."

"Crossing the street can be dangerous."

She paused for a moment. "OK. But can we actually do it?"

"Sure."

"You promise?"

"Of course," I said. "Would I lie to a woman with a gun in her hand?"

Chapter 6

My fingers weren't literally crossed, but they might as well have been. I had no idea how to capture Dendoncker. And no intention of finding a way. I had no desire to get tangled up with a crazy person. He hadn't done anything to me, as far as I knew.

I guess the overall scenario carried a certain amount of intrigue. It sounded like the guy had come up with his own take on Catch-22. You could only get close enough to kill him by being in a condition that prevented you from killing him. It was ingenious. Almost a challenge, in itself. I was sure it could be done, if I thought about it hard enough. Gathered enough intel. Maybe deployed the right kind of specialized equipment.

The truth was, I had no interest in any of those things. But I wasn't about to tell the woman. I figured that the prospect of capturing her brother's killer was a lifeline I could use to pull her ashore. Probably the only thing I could use. It would be stupid to cut it before her feet were safely on dry land. Worse than stupid.

Criminal. I might not have been serious about capturing some guy I'd never met. But I meant every word about helping her. Suicide has claimed far too many veterans. One would have been too many. So if I could prevent there being one more, that's what I was going to do.

I planned to take things slow. Give her time to see that the police were her best option. I was going to deceive her, yes. In the short term. But better deceived than dead.

The woman pushed herself away from the Jeep and stood still for a moment, staring at the ground. She seemed smaller than before. Stooped. Deflated. Finally she looked up at me. She slid the gun into her waistband and held out her hand. "I'm Michaela. Michaela Fenton. And before you say anything—yes. Michael and Michaela. We were twins. Our parents thought it was cute. We didn't."

I shrugged. "I'm Reacher."

Her hand was long and narrow and a little cold. Her fingers curled around mine. She squeezed, and I felt a tiny shiver flicker up my arm.

"Well, Reacher." She pulled away, glanced to her left and right, and her shoulders seemed to sag even further. "These bodies. Guess we should do something with them. Any ideas?"

That was a good question. If Dendoncker had sent his goons after me I would have left their remains someplace he couldn't miss them. Like on his front lawn. Or in his bed. So that he was clear about the message I was sending. I don't like to leave any room for misunderstanding. But Dendoncker hadn't sent them after me. And if we were really out to capture him, a more subtle approach would be called for. Hiding the bodies would be the right move. Something that kept our cards close to our chests. But we were in the middle of the desert. The sun was high in the sky. Digging graves had not been part of my plans when I woke up that morning and I felt like I'd been flexible enough for one day.

I said, "One of them must have a phone. We'll call 911. Let the police handle it."

"Is that smart? These guys have obviously been . . . well, they didn't die of natural causes."

"It'll be fine."

"But won't the police send in a bunch of detectives? Forensic teams? The whole nine yards?" She paused for a moment. "Look, if I have to pay a price for what I did, I'm fine with that. I'll take what I deserve. In due course. But I don't want to wind up in jail while Dendoncker is out here, free. And I don't want some huge investigation getting in our way and stopping us from catching him."

My agenda was different. I hoped the police would send in a bunch of guys. As many as possible. I wanted them swarming around all over the place. It's not smart to try and snatch anyone with the law watching you. I was counting on Fenton to realize that. Just not yet.

"That's all part of the plan." I pulled what I hoped was a reassuring smile. "You said Dendoncker is paranoid. If he sees the police sniffing around he'll panic. Make a mistake. Something we can use."

"I guess." She didn't sound convinced.

I moved across to the guy she'd shot second and searched his pockets. He had a bunch of keys on a ring with a square plastic fob. One was for a vehicle. A Ford. Two looked like house keys. One was a Yale. It was new and shiny. The other was for a mortise lock. It was old and scratched. I figured it was for a separate building.

A garage, maybe. Or a storage shed. The guy also had a phone. And a wallet. It had no ID in it. No credit cards. But there was $200 in twenties, which I took. Spoils of war. Only fair.

The other dead guy's pockets yielded a similar haul. He had a keyring with the same kind of plastic fob. One of the keys was for a Dodge. Two were Yales. And one was a mortise, which was also old and scratched. He had a wallet with $120 in twenties. And a phone with a cracked case. I pressed the guy's thumb to its central button and held it there until the screen lit up.

"Where are we, exactly?" I asked Fenton.

She shrugged. "Everyone in town just calls it *The Tree*. Hold on a sec. I'll see what I can find." She pulled out her phone and prodded and swiped at the screen, then held it up for me to see. "Here you go. Map reference."

When the emergency operator came on the line I gave him the coordinates and told him I had seen two guys shoot each other during an argument. Then I wiped the phone clean of prints and tossed it away.

I asked Fenton, "Is your Jeep wrecked?"

"No. I didn't touch the tree. See for yourself."

I walked around to the front of her Jeep and looked. There was maybe room to slide a cigarette paper between the fender and the tree trunk, but no more. She must be one hell of a driver.

I said, "Good. We'll take yours. Leave the other one here."

"Why? An extra vehicle might be useful."

"True." The tainted Jeep certainly could be useful. As another juicy morsel for the forensic guys to get their teeth into. Not as transport. "But it's too big a risk. Dendoncker is bound to freak out when he doesn't hear from his guys. He'll send a search party. If either of us was seen with their Jeep, that would screw things up big-time."

"I guess."

I retrieved the guys' guns, plus a baseball cap and a pair of sunglasses. "I doubt the cavalry will arrive any time soon. But we should still get out of here."

"Where to?"

"Somewhere private. We have a lot to talk about."

"OK." Fenton made her way around to the driver's side of her Jeep and flipped up the windshield. "My hotel." She fired up the engine and shifted into Reverse, then sat with one foot on the brake and the other pressing down on the clutch. Both her hands were on the wheel. At the top. Pressed together at the twelve o'clock position. She was hanging on tight. Her knuckles were white. Veins and tendons began to bulge. She closed her eyes. Her chest heaved, like she was having trouble catching her breath. Then she regained control. Slowly. She relaxed her grip. She opened her eyes, which dislodged a couple of tears. "Sorry." She brushed her cheeks then switched her right foot to the gas pedal and raised the clutch. "I was thinking of Michael. I can't believe he's gone."

Chapter 7

Fenton pushed the Jeep hard. The aged suspension creaked and squealed. The motor rattled. The transmission howled. Clouds of dark smoke spewed out of the tailpipe. She worked constantly at the wheel, sawing back and forth, but she still struggled to keep us going straight. I tried to focus on the road ahead but after ten minutes she caught me glancing down at her right foot.

"IED," she said. "Afghanistan."

She meant *Improvised Explosive Device*. It was a term I objected to. It had become prevalent during the second Gulf War. Probably coined by some government PR guy to make the insurgents' weapons sound low-tech. Unsophisticated. Like they were nothing to worry about. To conjure the image of them being cobbled together by unskilled rubes in caves and cellars. Whereas the truth was the opposite. I knew. I was in a compound in Beirut, years ago, when a dump truck loaded with twelve thousand pounds of explosives burst through the barracks' gates. Two hundred forty-one US Marines and sailors died that day. Fifty-eight French paratroopers were killed in another attack nearby. And since then things have only gotten worse. The bomb makers now have access to complex electronics. Remote detonators. Infrared triggers. Proximity sensors. They've become experts in positioning. Concealment. And they've become even nastier. More ruthless. As well as nails and metal fragments designed to tear human flesh they routinely load their devices with bacterial agents and anticoagulants. Then even if their victims survive the initial blast they're still likely to bleed out or die of some hideous disease.

I pushed those thoughts aside and asked her, "Army?"

She nodded. "Sixty-sixth Military Intelligence Group. Out of Wiesbaden, Germany. But this didn't happen while I was in uniform. There was no Purple Heart for me."

"You joined a private contractor?"

She shook her head. "Not me. I have no time for those guys. Call me crazy but I don't think wars should be fought for profit."

"What, then? Not many civilians go to Afghanistan."

"I did. It's a long story. I'll tell you some other time. Meanwhile, what about you? What brings you from the Military Police to this particular place? On foot? Of all the roads in all the towns . . ."

"Also a long story."

"Touché. So I'm going to come straight out and ask you. Are you on the run? Are you some kind of fugitive?"

I thought about her question for a moment. About the last town I'd been to. It was in Texas. I'd left the previous morning. In a hurry. I ran into a little trouble there. It had resulted in a fire. A destroyed building. And three dead bodies. But no major risk of blowback. Nothing she needed to know about.

I said, "No. I'm not a fugitive."

"Because if you are, no judgment. Not after what you saw me do today. But stopping Dendoncker is important to me. It's all I have right now. And if we're going to do it, there are going to be risks. We have to trust each other. So I have to know. Why are you here?"

"No special reason. I'm on my way out west. A guy was giving me a ride. He had to turn around and go back east, so I got out."

"Got out? Or got kicked out?"

"Got out."

"In such a hurry you forgot to grab your luggage? Come on. What really happened?"

"I don't have any luggage. And I could have carried on riding with the guy. He asked me to. But I don't like turning around. I like to keep moving forward. So I got out."

"OK. First things first. No luggage? Really?"

"Why would I need luggage? What would I put in it?"

"I'm going to take a wild shot in the dark here and say, I don't know, you're on a cross-country road trip, so . . . clothes? Nightwear? Toiletries? Personal items?"

"I'm wearing my clothes. They have toiletries at hotels. And my personal items are in my pocket."

"You have one set of clothes?"

"How many does a person need?"

"I don't know. More than one. What do you do when they need to be washed?"

"Throw them away and buy more."

"Isn't that wasteful? And impractical?"

"No."

"Why not take them home? Clean them? Re-use them?"

"Laundry's not my thing. Nor are laundry rooms. Or houses."

"So you're homeless, in other words?"

"Call it what you like. The reality is, I have no use for a home. Not at the moment. Maybe I'll get one, someday. Maybe I'll get a dog. Maybe I'll settle down. But not yet. Not for a long time."

"So you do what? Just roam around the country?"

"That's the general idea."

"How? Do you even have a car?"

"Never felt the need."

"You prefer hitching rides?"

"I don't mind it. Sometimes I take the bus."

"You take the bus? Really?"

I didn't reply.

"OK. Back to the guy who was driving you this morning. Why his sudden one-eighty?"

"He wanted to buy some old British sports car. He'd been to Texas to buy a different one. But he backed out. The seller tried to rip him off. Something about numbers that didn't match. I don't know why that's a big deal. I'm not much of a car guy. So he was driving again. To someplace in western Arizona. He wanted to let off steam. So he wanted an audience. So he picked me up. Outside a motel near El Paso."

"Wait a minute. We're nowhere near the regular route west from El Paso."

"The radio said I-10 was snarled up. Some kind of multicar accident. So he took a bunch of smaller roads. Cut across the southwest corner of New Mexico. Made it all the way past the Arizona state line. Then his phone rang. It was his wife. She had a lead on another of these old cars. In Oklahoma this time."

"But you wanted to keep heading west. Why? What's out there for you?"

"The Pacific Ocean."

"I don't follow."

"Call it a whim. I was in Nashville, Tennessee. There's a band I like. I caught them at a couple of clubs, then when I was on my way out of the city this weird bird flew by. For a moment I thought it was a pelican. It wasn't, but it made me think of Alcatraz. Which made me think of the ocean."

"And you thought the ocean was somewhere up this road?"

"No. I got bored of waiting for another ride. I started to walk. And I saw a giant stone structure at the side of the highway with an arrow pointing this way. An obelisk. Or a monument. It was covered with carvings and fancy patterns. And it made me curious. I thought, if the sign's that elaborate, what will the town be like?"

"See for yourself," she said. "We're nearly there."

Chapter 8

We had been climbing gradually since we left The Tree
and just at that moment we crested the hill and the town came into
view. It was spread out below us, maybe half a mile away. I could
see clusters of buildings with pale stucco walls and terra-cotta
roofs. It was hard to make sense of the layout. It looked like the
place was made up of two rough ovals. They partially overlapped,
like a Venn diagram drawn by a kid with a shaky hand. The buildings in the segment to the left were lower. Mainly single level. Their
walls looked a little rougher. They were scattered around a little
more randomly. The ones in the other part were taller. Straighter.
More evenly laid out. The section in the center had buildings that
were taller still. I could see arches and curves and courtyards.
Maybe it was the municipal district. Maybe the bars and restaurants
were around there, too. If the place ran to that kind of thing.

On the far side of the town a row of tall metal ribs rose out of the
ground and extended east and west as far as the eye could see. They

looked solid. Permanent. Unwelcoming. They were set close together and their tips were pointed and sharp. I guessed the land beyond them belonged to Mexico. It looked pretty much the same as the land on the US side. The incline picked up again and there was a slope a few hundred yards long that was undeveloped, like a kind of no-man's-land. Then at the top of the rise the buildings began again. I could see another set of pale stucco walls and terracotta roofs stretching far into the distance.

"What do you think?" Fenton said.

"I think I'm missing something."

Dendoncker had just ordered Fenton killed. He had at least three others on his payroll. Fenton had talked about him like he was the second coming of Al Capone, only with added craziness. That meant he must be based someplace that could sustain a decent level of crime. Protection. Drugs. Prostitution. The usual staples, most likely. But this town looked like nothing more than a sleepy backwater. The kind of place you would come to get over insomnia. I'd be surprised if they'd ever even had a shoplifting problem.

I asked, "Was Dendoncker born here?"

Fenton didn't answer. She seemed lost in thought.

I asked her again, "Was Dendoncker born in the town?"

"What?" she said. "No. He was born in France."

"So out of the entire United States, maybe the entire world, he chose to settle here. I'm wondering why. What else do you know about him?"

"Not as much as I'd like." Fenton stared at the road ahead without speaking for a moment, then dragged her attention back to my question. "OK. His full name is Waad Ahmed Dendoncker. His father was German. His mother was Lebanese. He lived in Paris until he was eighteen, went to high school there, then was accepted by the University of Pennsylvania. He was a bright enough kid by all accounts. He got through his Bachelor's and stayed on to do a PhD in Engineering but dropped out after eighteen months. He went back to France, bounced around Europe and the Middle East for a couple of years, and then I lost his trail. I couldn't find any other trace of him until 2003, when he resurfaced in Iraq. He started working for the army as one of those general translator/fixer/facilitators. Then in 2007 the government started a program to bring a bunch of those guys over to the States to save them from reprisals. Dendoncker applied in May 2008. The vetting process is pretty thorough so he didn't get his visa until April 2010. The government set him up in a town called Goose Neck, Georgia, and got him a job in a chicken processing plant. He kept his nose clean. His attendance record was perfect. He traveled a fair bit, but only in the lower forty-eight, and he spent a lot of time in the library. Then after a year he quit and moved here."

Fenton took a left after the first couple of buildings on the outskirts of town and started to thread her way through a warren of meandering streets.

"I can understand him not wanting to chop up chickens for the rest of his life," I said. "But it doesn't explain why he picked this place."

"I have a theory." Fenton pulled through an archway and into a courtyard that had been converted into a parking lot. "Right after he arrived here Dendoncker set up a business. On the QT. He owns it through half a dozen shell corporations. That implies a strong desire for secrecy. So it follows that he wouldn't want his operation to attract a whole lot of attention. This place is perfect for that. It's on its own, tucked away at the ass-end of a single road, in or out. The population's been declining for years. The locals say it's turning into a ghost town. Plus there's no border crossing for miles. Official or unofficial. The fence is secure. There have been no reported breaches in more than ten years. So there's nothing for any department or agency to take an interest in."

"What kind of business did he set up?"

"Catering. A company called Pie in the Sky, Inc." Fenton stayed to the right and continued to the far end of the row of spaces. She took the final spot. It lay between a dull white panel van and a blank wall and she pulled all the way in so that the Jeep was pretty much hidden.

"So why would he need to stay out of the limelight? You think he's hiding from the health inspector?"

"It's not what he cooks. Or how. It's who for. It's a specialist company. It makes in-flight meals, but not for mainstream airlines. For private jets only. Dendoncker has contracts with half a dozen operators. His people pack up the food. Put it in those special metal boxes or trolleys, depending on the quantity. Take it to the airport. Load it right onto the plane. And retrieve the containers afterward. He provides the flight attendants, too."

The setup could be totally innocent, of course. People who fly on private planes need food and drink just the same as if they were stuck in coach on a 737. Dendoncker could have hidden his involvement because he has a bunch of ex-wives he owes money to. He could be shy about paying his taxes. Or the setup could be something else altogether. The kind of airports most private jets operate out of aren't like JFK or LAX. Security is minimal. For the passengers. And for the support services. I could see how that kind of setup could provide a guy like Dendoncker with certain opportunities. And why he would want to keep his comings and goings out of sight.

Fenton shut off the Jeep's motor. "He could be moving drugs. Diamonds. Weapons. Pretty much anything."

I asked, "Any proof?"

"Just suspicion at this point. But it's not unfounded. Take my first day on Dendoncker's crew. I got sent to cover for another woman. As a flight attendant. It was a last-minute thing. She was out sick. Or she knew what was in store. The whole experience was gross. There were two of us and four passengers. Rich assholes. They were constantly trying to grope us. Making suggestions about extra services we could perform. One guy was obsessed with my leg. Kept trying to touch it. I nearly took him to the bathroom and beat him to death with it. Not even the food distracted him. Or the drink. It was obscene. The most expensive stuff you can imagine. Caviar—Kolikof albino. Ham—Jamón Ibérico. Cheese—pule. Champagne—Boërl & Kroff. Brandy—Lecompte Secret. There was a ton of it. A dozen containers. Large ones. And here's the thing. We only used ten of them. Two went untouched."

"Maybe they over-ordered. Or Dendoncker was padding the bill."

"No. I was going to take a look inside the spare ones while the other woman was in the bathroom, but they had seals on them. Tiny things. Little blobs of lead on short skinny wires. Partly hidden by the latches. I almost didn't see them. So I checked the containers we did open. There were no broken seals on any of them."

"What happened to the sealed ones?"

"They got off-loaded at the destination airport. Two more got put on in their places. Same size. Same shape. Same kind of seals."

"What would have happened if you opened one *by mistake*?"

"I thought about trying that, but the plane flew back empty. No new passengers got on board, so there was no need to open any of the containers. And when I thought back to the outbound flight I realized something. It was the other woman who always picked which container we should open. At the time it seemed reasonable. I was new, she had experience, she knew where things were. But later it felt different, like she had been steering me away from the sealed ones. And it was the same basic picture with all the other flights I worked on. Different passengers. Different destinations. But there were always containers that weren't accounted for."

Fenton climbed out of the Jeep. She started toward a door at the center of the long side of the courtyard. I followed. I saw that the buildings on all four sides had originally been separate. Now they were joined together. Some were sticking out. Some were set back. But they were all the same height. The roof that connected them was continuous and uniform. It must have been added later.

Each original section of the building had a sign mounted on its front wall. I guessed they stated the initial occupant. There were lots of names. Lots of different businesses and services. A blacksmith. A cooper. A hardware store. A place to buy provisions. A warehouse. One whole side had been a saloon. Presumably the places had originally been independent but now their signs were all the same shape. They used the same colors. The same font. The doors and windows were laid out in different configurations but they were the same style. They used the same materials. They looked the same age. And each one had a glass rectangle mounted on the wall near the door, the size of a typical security keypad but with no buttons.

I said, "What is this place?"

"My hotel. Where I'm staying. Where we're staying, I guess."

I looked around all four sides. "Where's the office?"

"There isn't one. The place is unmanned. It's a new concept. Part of a new chain. They're in five cities. Maybe six now. I don't remember."

"So how do you get a room?"

"You book online. You don't see anyone. You don't interact with anyone. That's the beauty of it."

"How do you get a key? They send it in the mail?"

Fenton shook her head. "There isn't a physical key. They email you a QR code."

I said nothing.

"A QR code. You know. Like a two-dimensional bar code. You display it on your phone and the scanners by the doors read it. It's excellent."

"It is?"

"It is. Particularly if you happen to book with a false ID. And a false credit card. And a made-up email address. That way, no one can ever trace you."

"This isn't going to work for me. I don't have a false ID. I don't have any kind of a credit card. Or a phone."

"Oh." She shrugged. "Well, never mind. We'll figure that out later."

"There are cameras." I gestured to a pair of them. They were mounted on the wall near the Jeep's parking spot. A mesh cage protected them. "Someone could trace you that way."

"They could try. The cameras do appear to be working. But if anyone tries to access their files, they won't see anything. They'll just get snow. That's the beauty of the training they give you at Fort Huachuca. It's the gift that keeps on giving."

Chapter 9

Fenton fiddled with her phone then held its screen up to a scanner below a sign that read *Carlisle Smith, Wheelwright.* The door clicked open. I followed her inside. I couldn't picture any hard manual labor taking place in there now. The room was all pastel colors and throw cushions and nostalgic black-and-white photographs. Plus the standard hotel stuff. A bed. A couch. A work area. A closet. A bathroom. Everything you could need for a comfy night, except for a coffeemaker. There was no sign of one of those. But there was a suitcase, neatly squared away, sitting on its own by the door. Fenton saw me looking at it.

"Old habits." She wheeled the case across to the bed. "Always be ready to move." She turned to look at me. "I figured I would be moving again today. I hoped it would be with Michael. But really I knew. There was no chance. I was always going to be leaving alone. I just had to be sure. It wasn't a surprise. But still, back there, at The Tree, it hit me. Harder than I expected. Pushed me close to the edge for a second or two. I'm sorry you had to see that. It won't happen again. Now, let's focus. Come on. Make yourself at home."

I figured it was a minute after 3:00 P.M. I was hungry. Breakfast was a long time ago. I'd made an early start, back in El Paso. I didn't know if Fenton had eaten at all that day. But she must have burned plenty of adrenaline. I figured food would help both of us. I suggested we order some. Fenton didn't argue. She just pulled out her phone. "Pizza work for you?"

Fenton took the chair from under the desk and tapped away at her screen. I sat on the couch. I waited until she was done summoning up our food, then said, "I told you why I'm here. Now it's your turn."

She paused, like she was marshaling her thoughts. "It started with Michael's message, I guess. We were always close, like most twins are, but we lost touch. He wasn't the same. Not after he left the army. I guess I should explain that. He was in a thing called a *TEU*. A Technical Escort Unit. They're the guys who are experts in bomb disposal and chemical warfare."

"I've heard of them. If another unit is clearing an area and they find chemical ordnance, they call in a TEU."

"They're supposed to. But that doesn't always happen. A grunt doesn't always know what a chemical artillery round looks like. In Iraq the enemy didn't have any, remember. Not officially. So they're not marked properly. Or they're deliberately mismarked. Plus they look like other shells. Signal shells, especially, because they also have a separate chamber for the precursor material. And even if the guys know chemicals are involved they sometimes try to handle it themselves. They don't want to wait. With the best will in the world it can take twelve hours for a TEU to respond. Sometimes twenty-four. That's up to an extra day of exposure to enemy snipers and booby traps. And an extra day they're not clearing other areas. That leaves other caches for insurgents to find and raid, or for civilians to stumble across, maybe getting hurt or killed. So quite often Michael's team would arrive at a scene and find it contaminated. Like the first one they ever responded to. It was a brick chamber, underground. Some infantry guys literally fell into it. They busted through the ceiling. They started poking around, then got cold feet. The shells in there were old. They were in bad shape. The guys must have cracked one without realizing. It contained mustard gas. One of Michael's friends got exposed. It was horrible."

"Did he make it?"

"By the skin of his teeth. They medevaced him. The hospital induced a coma before the worst symptoms set in. That saved him a lot of agony. And probably saved his life."

"Did Michael get exposed?"

"Not on that occasion. But he did later. You see, however they come by chemical shells, the TEU has to dispose of them. If the area they're found in is inhabited, they have to move the shells before they can blow them up. And if there's some unusual feature, they have to recover them so they can be studied. That's what happened to Michael. He was transporting a pair of shells that the pointy heads wanted taken back to the Aberdeen Proving Ground. He had them in the back of his Humvee, heading to an RV with a Black Hawk. One of them leaked. It made him sick. He managed to get back to base but the medics wouldn't believe his symptoms were real. He had no burns. No blisters. No missing body parts. He was accused of malingering, or treated like a drug addict because his pupils had shrunk. Anything to put the blame on him, not the army. He had spasms. Chest pain. He couldn't stop vomiting. His whole

GI system was messed up. They finally sent him to Germany. To a hospital there. It took him weeks to recover."

"That's harsh."

"It was. The way they treated him was bad enough. But the real kicker? Michael, and his friend with the mustard gas, and a whole bunch of others who got hurt—the army refused to recognize them. There was no Purple Heart for them, either. You know why? The poison didn't leak out during an active engagement, so their injuries weren't deemed to have been caused by enemy action. It was like the army was telling them they did these awful things to themselves. And you know what? In the exact same circumstances, the Marines do decorate their guys. It just wasn't right. Michael was demoralized. He left the army at the end of his next tour. He drifted for a few years, and I guess he went off the rails. I kept trying to reach out to him. But then I had problems of my own." She patted her leg. "And I was busy with my work."

"What do you do?"

"I'm a lab technician. In a place near Huntsville, Alabama."

"That the job that sent you to Afghanistan?"

She nodded. "I went to supervise some sample collection. Stuff we had to bring back and analyze. My boss knew I was ex-army. He thought I'd be OK. I was out of action for a while, afterward. Surgery. Physical therapy. And then I was a bit down. A bit self-absorbed. But when I got Michael's message it shook me up. It was something I just couldn't ignore."

"What did it say?"

"'M—help! M.' It was handwritten on the back of a card from a place called the *Red Roan*. It's a café here, in town."

"So you dropped everything and came?"

"I dropped everything. But I didn't come here right away. Old habits die hard. First, I did some digging. I got in touch with his friends. Some contacts of my own. Tried to find out what he might have been into. Where he might have been. Everyone said they didn't know. A few promised to ask around. Then a buddy from the Sixty-sixth told me about a guy, kind of like an agent. If you were a vet and you wanted work, and you weren't too particular if it was legal, he could hook you up. I got in touch. Leaned on him. He admitted introducing Michael to Dendoncker. Indirectly. I pressed him some more and he admitted to placing a few guys with Dendoncker over the years. Sometimes Dendoncker just wanted anyone ex-military. Sometimes he wanted people with specialized skills. The guy recalled placing an ex-sniper who was an expert in .50 rifles. Michael got hired because he knew about land mines."

"Sounds like Dendoncker could be smuggling weapons."

"That was my first thought, too. So I came down. Poked around. But couldn't find any sign of Michael or smuggling rings or other kinds of criminals. I became desperate. That's when I got back in touch with the agent guy and asked him to hook me up with Dendoncker. I expected an argument, but he was super cooperative. Said I was doing him a favor. Dendoncker was in the market for another recruit. No particular MOS. Just had to be a woman. I was worried about what that could mean. But I figured my brother's life was on the line. So I said, all right. Set it up."

"And you got the job, just like that?"

"No. My background was already legit but I made up a few false references to embellish it a little. Then I had an 'interview.' With Dendoncker's sidekick. A huge, creepy guy. He took me out into the desert and had me prove I could shoot and strip down a gun and drive and so on."

"Didn't Dendoncker connect you with Michael? You have virtually the same name."

"No. We have different surnames. His was Curtis. Mine was, too, obviously. Then I got married. I took my husband's name. And I kept it after he was killed. In Iraq."

"I'm sorry."

"Don't be. It's not your fault."

Fenton looked away. I waited until she turned back to me.

I said, "Dendoncker wanted Michael because he knew about land mines?"

"That's what the guy told me."

"How's that connected to the catering business?"

"I don't know. My best guess is Dendoncker's some kind of procurer. He smuggles in whatever his customers want and sells it to them. He probably needs experts from time to time to evaluate the merchandise."

"But Michael stayed on?"

Fenton nodded.

"You didn't come in contact with him, even when you were on the inside?"

"No. I tried, but I had to be discreet. Then two days ago I saw a woman I recognized. Renée. She was working at Dendoncker's catering business, like me. With a different partner. She had different shifts. And she'd been there longer. She knew the lay of the land better."

"Where did you know her from?"

"I didn't know her. I'd seen her in photos. Ones Michael had of his old unit."

"She was at the place where the containers get loaded for the planes?"

Fenton shook her head. "No. At the Red Roan. The place Michael sent the card from. I followed her when she left. Cornered her at her hotel. She admitted Michael was in town and still working for Dendoncker. But on some special project. She swore she didn't know what it was. Just that it involved Michael doing tests in the desert from time to time."

"Land mines?"

"Maybe." Fenton shrugged. "So I asked this Renée to set it up for Michael and me to meet. She refused. Said it was too dangerous. She seemed genuinely terrified. So I asked her to at least give Michael a note for me. She agreed to that."

"What did you write?"

"I kept it simple. I said, 'I'm here. Contact me. I'll do whatever you need.' And I gave him an email address. One I'd set up specially. No one else knew it."

"This was two days ago?"

"Right. She said she might not be able to get the note to Michael right away. Then an email came this morning. I knew Michael was in trouble the moment I read it. I feared the worst. But I had to find out for certain."

"How did you know?"

"From the way the message was addressed. I had signed my note *Mickey*. That's what people who knew me as a kid call me. The email that came, which set up the rendezvous at The Tree? It was written to Mickey."

"So? Michael obviously knew you when you were a kid."

"You don't understand. When we were growing up we were always playing soldiers and spies. We started doing that thing from the movies where you only use the other person's real name if you're in danger. The note used my real name. So either Michael was in danger, or my note got intercepted and whoever replied didn't know our routine."

"What happened to the woman who took the note?"

"Renée? I don't know. I went to her room at the hotel this morning, as soon as I got the email. Some of her clothes had been taken from the closet. All her underwear was gone. So were her toiletries. I think something spooked her. After she gave Michael the note. I think she ran for her life."

Chapter 10

Fenton's phone pinged and a moment later there was a knock at the door. She whispered, "Pizza." I moved along the side of the bed where I'd be out of sight. I heard Fenton open the door and thank the delivery guy. Then she grabbed a towel from the bathroom, spread it on the bed like a tablecloth, and set down the giant square box.

We ate in silence. When we were finished I asked, "You said Dendoncker inspects the bodies. Where? At the scene? Or does he have them taken someplace?"

"He always does it at the morgue. He likes the bodies properly laid out and examined. The whole nine yards."

"Is the ME on his payroll?"

"I don't know. Could be, I guess."

"That means to pull this thing off we need to clear three hurdles. To convince Dendoncker that one of us is a threat to him. To make him believe that person was killed. And to persuade the ME to co-operate. That's a big ask."

"I came to the same conclusion." Fenton brushed a crumb from her chin. "I was thinking about it while we were eating. It is a big ask. But it's not impossible. And I have a way we can do one and two, if you play the role of the dead guy."

"How?"

"OK. First hurdle. Make Dendoncker believe you're a threat. That's easy. All you have to do is play the part of Mickey. Dendoncker's already sold. He sent two guys to ambush *him*. Those guys didn't come back so Dendoncker must be doubly convinced that Mickey's a problem by now."

I said nothing.

"Second hurdle. Make Dendoncker believe you're dead. That's harder, but still achievable. We do it by setting up another rendezvous with Mickey, which I will attend on Dendoncker's behalf. Then—"

"How do we set it up?"

"The foundations are already in place. Dendoncker must have gotten his hands on my note because he used the email address on it. But he didn't know I sent it or there would have been no need for the first rendezvous. He would have sent his guys straight after me. So, I'll write another note. The handwriting will be the same, which will seal the deal."

"Another note saying what?"

"That no one showed up today, so let's try again."

"He'll know that's not true. At the least he thinks his guys are missing. And if he has ears inside the police department he'll know they're dead."

"Of course he'll know. But that's not the point. He won't care if

Mickey is lying to him. All he'll want to do is eliminate the threat he represents as quickly and cleanly as possible. What's he going to do? Leave Mickey out there, free to come at him whenever he wants, because he didn't tell the truth? No. He'll jump at the chance to take him out. He'll agree to the rendezvous, and pull a double cross. Again."

"Say you're right. Say he agrees. Then what? He sends another couple of guys? Maybe more?"

"No. In the note I'll say Mickey knows he's not communicating with Michael. But he's willing to pay ten thousand dollars for information about Michael's whereabouts. And he will only deal with me."

"How will you get the note to Dendoncker?"

"I'll give it to his deputy. I'll ask to meet him. Tell him I was approached by a guy outside the Red Roan. I'll describe you. That'll be plausible because they must assume the last note was brought to Michael by Renée, since she's gone missing. And if they bite, they'll offer another rendezvous. We'll both show up. And I'll shoot you. At least that's what I'll report to Dendoncker."

I thought for a moment. "There's a big risk for you if they don't buy it."

"I don't think so." Fenton counted off on her fingers. "The scenario, with someone getting one of Dendoncker's crew to carry a note? A match. The handwriting on the note? A match. The email address for Dendoncker to reply to? A match. The note leading to a rendezvous? A match. The setup is plausible. I can sell it. I've done this kind of thing before, remember."

I didn't reply.

"OK," Fenton said. "Yes. There is a risk. But whether to accept it is my choice."

"That's fair. And getting them to set up a rendezvous might work. But what if they send someone with you? Or they have someone hidden, watching? You can't just report a shooting. We need to stage one. And we need it to look real."

"That's easy enough. I've done it before. In Kosovo, years ago. I was there on a mission. We needed leverage over a local gangster so we made him believe he'd killed a guy who we revealed was a US diplomat. All we had was fake blood in a special kind of bag, a detonator, a transmitter, and some tape. The army provided the supplies, of course, but I know where they came from. A store in New York. I could have the stuff shipped here. The only other prop is blanks and I already have some. I brought them with me. I didn't know what kind of things Dendoncker would have me doing and I thought I might need to avoid killing the wrong people."

The trick with the blanks and the fake blood could work. I knew, from experience. Only not in Kosovo. And not with a diplomat.

I said, "That leaves the ME. Could be a problem if he's loyal to Dendoncker. We'll have to tread carefully."

"That's true. Although I'm sure he could be convinced to take a sicky. Given the proper encouragement." Fenton winked at me. "But that's maybe best left until last. We should see if Dendoncker bites, first."

"We also need a wound that looks convincing. We need Dendoncker to believe it's real. Even if only for a minute."

"No problem there, either. When operatives go undercover they often use a false wound to hide a handcuff key or a blade. That way, they have it even if they get captured and stripped. It works, even if they get searched. Psychology 101. Humans instinctively avoid contact with wounds. You can get the stuff from the place that sells the fake blood. I'll add some to the order."

Fenton cleared away the empty pizza box and lifted her case onto the bed. She opened it and took a card and a pen from a pocket in the lid.

"This is the same kind I used before." She started to write. "I took a bunch, just in case."

After a minute Fenton put her pen down and showed me the card. There was a picture of a horse on one side. A red roan, I guessed. She'd written her message on the reverse, next to the café's address. It looked OK to me. I nodded. She put the card down, grabbed her phone, and tapped out a text.

"I said I've just been contacted by an angry stranger who asked me to carry a note to someone called Michael. Keep everything crossed."

The reply came within a minute. "All right," Fenton said. "That was Dendoncker's right-hand man. He wants to meet. He wants me to give him the note. We could be in business."

Fenton stood up and unfolded a jacket from her case. To conceal her gun.

I said, "Where are you meeting?"

"The Border Inn." She turned to the door. "My other hotel. It's a regular type place. I'm booked under my real name, but it's just for show. I never stay there. Don't worry. I'll be back soon."

The door closed behind her and the room was suddenly quiet. It felt empty, with just a hint of her perfume to remind me she'd been there. I went back to the couch and lay down. I wanted to play some music in my head. That always helps to pass time. I figured John Primer would fit the bill. He backed Muddy Waters until he died.

Then he backed Magic Slim for fourteen years until he died. John's music is as good as it gets. But try as I might, it wouldn't come. Because I was worried. About Fenton. That she would be able to sell our scam to Dendoncker's guy. Or worse, that she wouldn't be able to sell it. Then they'd kill her. If she was lucky.

I told myself to snap out of it. Fenton was ex–Military Intelligence. She'd have had extensive training in all kinds of black arts. She could no doubt convince anyone of anything. Only that thought made me more worried. I really knew nothing about her. Only what she'd told me. Which was what she wanted me to know. I got up and started to search the room. I didn't enjoy it. Even though she had invited me in, the old feeling of being a trespasser came back to me. I always used to feel it when I searched a dead person's place. I hoped it wasn't a premonition.

I went through her case. Everything was neatly folded or rolled. She had clothes. Toiletries. Extra ammunition for her Glock. A spare prosthetic foot. A blond wig. Glasses, with plain lenses. A field dressing kit. But nothing that said she'd lied to me. I checked under the mattress. Along the seams of the curtains. Under the couch. And still found nothing. I went to sit back down but stopped myself. The solution was obvious. I should leave. Walk out and never look back. That would leave the plan dead in the water. It needed two people. There was no way Fenton could do it alone.

I took a step toward the door. And stopped again. If Fenton couldn't get Dendoncker, what would she do? I pictured her with a gun to her head. Again. I didn't like that image. I didn't like it at all. So I went back to the couch and waited in silence.

* * *

There was no sound of a key in the lock. Just a subdued click, seventy-two minutes later. Then the door swung open and Fenton appeared.

"I think they bought it." She checked her phone. "No confirmation yet. But I made progress while I was waiting for the guy. I ordered the fake blood and the other stuff we'll need. I expedited the shipping. It'll be here in the morning. I just hope they don't want to meet tonight."

I agreed. But that wasn't all I hoped. We still had two hurdles to clear. I wanted it to stay that way.

Chapter 11

Fenton changed into blue silk pajamas and climbed into the bed. I kept my clothes on and stretched out on the couch. She pulled a mask over her eyes and lay still. But I don't think she went straight to sleep. Her breathing wasn't right. It was too fast. Too shallow. Too tense.

I kept my eyes open and stayed awake for hours, too. Something was bothering me. I couldn't put my finger on exactly what, but red warning lights were flashing away deep in my brain. They stopped me from settling. I guess I finally dozed off at around 4:00 A.M. I got woken up again at 7:00. By Fenton, calling my name. She was sitting up in bed. Her mask was pushed up on her forehead. Her hair was disheveled. And she was holding her phone at arm's length.

"Eleven P.M." Her voice was husky. "Tonight. They want to meet you. We've done it."

This was not the start to the day I was hoping for. I'd been awake for fifteen seconds and already we were down to only one hurdle.

I said, "You better reply. Remind them—just you, unarmed, and the deal is cash for information."

Fenton fiddled with her phone for a moment. A minute later it made a *ping* sound. "All right. They've agreed."

After another minute Fenton's phone made a different kind of noise. It was an incoming text. Fenton read it, then held her phone out for me to see. "Hook, line, and sinker. It's Dendoncker's deputy. Telling me to stand by for a job tonight."

Fenton lay back on her pile of pillows and went to work with her phone. "OK. I searched for MEs in this area. Only one name comes up. A Dr. Houllier. He seems to be the doctor for everything here. He's based at the medical center. The big building in the middle of the town. We'll wait for our delivery then head down there. It's due before noon. Should give us plenty of time."

"We can't both go." I sat up. "The delivery. Will it need a signature?"

Fenton nodded.

"You better do that. I'll go talk to the doctor."

Fenton did whatever was necessary with her phone to order some breakfast. I took a shower. I heard a knock at the door when I was getting dressed and when I came out of the bathroom I could smell coffee. It was sublime. There's nothing like the first cup of the day. Fenton had also ordered burritos. We ate in silence. Then I gathered up the paper plates, grabbed the sunglasses I'd taken from the guy at The Tree, and started toward the door.

"No gun?" Fenton looked worried.

"I'm going to an official building. There will be metal detectors."

"In this town? I don't think so."

"It's not worth the risk. And I don't need one. If the doctor's straight I'll persuade him to help. If he's in Dendoncker's pocket it'll take more than a gun to convince him."

I stepped out of the room and left the courtyard via the archway Fenton had driven through. It was a beautiful morning. Perfect for walking. The sun was bright but the temperature was comfortable. The last of the chill from the desert night was still to be chased away. The sky was so clear and so blue that if you painted it people would say you'd exaggerated the color. The streets were narrow and winding and the buildings that lined them seemed old and honest. Like they'd sprouted years ago along the paths that people had walked with their donkeys or mules or whatever animals they used to pull their wagons. There was no planning. No artifice. I could picture the people inside, getting on with their lives, looking after their families, doing their jobs. I looked up at the roofs. Some had TV antennas but I could see no cell masts. That just added to the impression of a place that progress had passed by. Probably nothing substantial had changed for decades. Nothing except the arrival of Dendoncker.

I found the medical center without any problems. It was a solid, muscular building made out of pale stone. Pride had gone into its construction. That was clear. Real craftspeople had been involved. You could tell from the attention to detail in the doorway and the windows and the lintels. Inside, an ornate rendering of the Staff of Hermes was set into the polished white floor. A large lamp shaped like the globe hung directly above it. The ceiling was domed. It was painted with scenes showing the history of medicine all the way from caves to hospitals, ending sometime pre-WWII. From its style the building could have been a courthouse or a library. But if you closed your eyes you would have no doubt you were in a hospital. The smell was unmistakable.

The reception area was unattended. There was a freestanding desk made out of rich teak. Its surface shone with years of polish. A laptop computer sat to one side, closed, along with a leather binder and a message pad. There was a directory in a frame on the wall. It was the old-fashioned kind with separate white letters pressed into the gaps between rolls of plush burgundy fabric. It made no mention of the morgue. Probably not the kind of place medical people like to advertise.

I went through a doorway to the side of the desk. It led to a corridor that was lined with plain wooden doors. They had numbers, but no names. There was a staircase at the far end. I went down. Partly because the directory had listed all kinds of wards and clinics and examination rooms on the upper floors. And partly out of instinct. It seemed fitting that the dead would be kept belowground.

I came out onto another corridor. It was bright. There were triple fluorescent tubes hanging from the ceiling at close intervals. But only one pair of doors. They were labeled *Morgue*. As I approached I could hear a voice. A man's. At first I thought he must have company. I couldn't make out all the words but when I picked up on the stylized way of speaking I realized it was just one person. He was dictating. Probably medical notes. Probably into a machine. I raised my hand to knock. But I stopped myself. It was time to face facts.

Nothing I could say to the doctor was going to make a difference.

I turned around and went back up the stairs and out into the street.

Chapter 12

I found my way to the Red Roan and walked past it. Just out of curiosity. It had a racing theme. It seemed incongruous, given its neighboring buildings. And unappealing, so I continued to a diner farther down the street. It was smaller. More down to earth. I ordered two black coffees to go and carried them back to the hotel. Fenton snatched the door open the instant I knocked.

"Well?" She let the door swing shut. "Tell me."

I handed her one of the cups. The bags of fake blood and miniature detonators and material to make imitation wounds were laid out on the bed. Her gun was there, too. There was a glass full of bullets on the nightstand.

"You switched to blanks?"

She nodded. "Yes. But the ME? How did it go?"

Blanks were better than live rounds in a situation like that. But they were still dangerous, close up. Pull the trigger when the muzzle is in contact with your head and the jet of gas it emits can be fatal.

I know. I investigated two cases in the army. One turned out to be a jackass playing the fool one time too many. The other was something else altogether.

I put my coffee down on the desk. "Michaela, there's something we need to talk about. This plan. It's not going to work. It's time we thought about a plan B."

"The ME wouldn't cooperate?" Fenton slammed her cup down on the nightstand so hard it sent coffee spurting out of the slot in the lid. "Why not? What was the problem? How hard did you lean on him?"

"I'm not going to lie. I didn't speak to the guy. There was no point. There are too many other holes in the plan. It's DOA. We need to find an alternative."

"You said yourself, there are three hurdles. The threat, the death, and the ME. I took care of one and two. I can't believe you chickened out of three. I knew I should have gone myself. Never send a man to do a woman's job. I'll go now. I'll take care of it."

Fenton reached for her gun. I stepped in her way.

I said, "It doesn't matter which of us talks to him. Or if neither of us does. The outcome will be the same. The guy's either on Dendoncker's payroll or he's not. He's well disposed to us, or he's not. We may need to persuade him, or threaten him, or bribe him. In any case there's no guarantee of a result. Even if he agrees to help, can we trust him? What if he changes his mind later? What if he gets cold feet? And say he does stay away, how will Dendoncker behave? Will he poke the body? *My body.* Prod it? Stab it? Chop part of it off? Shoot it?"

Fenton didn't reply.

"And Dendoncker's unlikely to come alone. How many guys will he bring? What weapons will they have? Who else will be in the building?"

Fenton shrugged.

"And if we do snatch him, what about afterward? We'll need time to encourage him to confess. Where would we go? How long would it take? Where's the nearest police station, when we're done?"

"I get the point." Fenton crossed her arms. "But it could still work."

"It could. Nothing's impossible. I'd give it a fifty-fifty chance of success. No more. With a high risk of collateral damage."

"I'll take those odds."

"I won't. Not when there are alternatives."

"There's no alternative. We must go ahead. OK. We'll swap roles. I'll tell them I'm sick. I'll play the part of Mickey at the rendezvous. I'll pretend to get shot. Let them take me to the morgue. I'll deal with Dendoncker myself when he shows up."

"That won't work. If you're sick they'll send others in your place. Who will kill you, for real, unless you kill them first. Neither of which would help."

"OK. So you go to the rendezvous, too. Lurk around in the dark until everyone shows up. Then shoot me with a blank before anyone else has the chance. They won't care who fired as long as I'm dead. Or they think I am."

"What happens when they check your pulse?"

Fenton was silent.

"Or if they give you a tap to the head, to make sure you're dead?"

Fenton opened her mouth, then closed it again without speaking.

I said, "Why not get Dendoncker thrown in jail? There's a federal agent I know. You can trust him. You could work with him. Stay undercover. Provide intel. Isn't that what you trained for?"

"That would take too long. We have to do it tonight. I'll find a way. With or without you."

"Why is this so urgent? The best way to honor Michael is to take the time to do it right. What about the vetting guys, for example. Who cleared Dendoncker for entry to the States? They must have plenty of muscle. And if they made a mistake, they'll want to put it right. To avoid embarrassment, if nothing else."

"This isn't just about Michael. It never was."

"No? Then who else is it about?"

"I don't know names. Innocent people."

"The vets in Dendoncker's crew?"

"No. Random strangers."

"Who? What kind of strangers?"

Fenton took a breath. "Reacher, there's something I didn't tell you. I know what Dendoncker's doing with those planes. What he's going to transport in them. Bombs."

"How do you know?"

"I know because Michael was making them."

Chapter 13

Fenton pushed the bags of fake blood aside and sat on the bed. She put her head in her hands. She rested her elbows on her knees. She was completely still for over a minute. Then she straightened up.

"I didn't lie to you, Reacher. I just didn't tell the whole truth."

"You better tell it now. If you want me to reconsider."

"OK. Rewind to when I left the army. I went into law enforcement. I joined the FBI. Became a Special Agent. Evidence processing was my specialty. I worked out of a couple of field offices, did well, and got assigned to TEDAC as a result. Do you know anything about it?"

"Not much."

"It's the Terrorist Explosive Device Analytical Center. Think of it as bringing forensics to the battlefield. It began during the second Gulf War. Our troops were taking a hammering. Someone got the idea of collecting evidence and sending it to Quantico. A team was put together to analyze everything that came in. They came up with ways to spot IEDs. To defend against them. Defuse them. Eventually they were able to identify the bomb makers. Sometimes right down to an individual. Sometimes to a factory. The recovered components tell a story. So do the techniques that are used. Even the way a wire is twisted can be significant. The team was so successful it expanded and moved to a new base in Alabama. Its scope expanded, too. Now it has a whole world mission, with no constraints on time. Information is shared with partners. Arrests have been made all over the globe with TEDAC's help. London. Berlin. Addis Ababa. All in the last few weeks. Evidence is being brought in from more places, and from further back in time. Material from Lockerbie, Scotland, is on its way, I heard. And Yemen. And some already arrived from Beirut, that big barracks bomb, all the way back in the eighties."

There was another weird echo from the past. I'd thought plenty over the years about the guy whose jawbone wound up in my abdomen. And the other Marines who died that day. But I hadn't dwelled too much on the physical evidence. I knew it was examined thoroughly at the time. Picked over and combed through by experts, with all the best tools and techniques available back then. I figured once all the clues and leads had been sniffed out anything left would have been disposed of. Cleaned up. Thrown away. Preferably set on fire. I never imagined it getting brought back to the States, so long after all the bodies.

She said, "There's an initiative to facilitate this kind of work. It's called *ICEP*. The International Collection and Engagement Program. I was part of it. Specialists are sent to partner countries to help with training. That includes Afghanistan. Because of my background, I got sent there. To a scene that hadn't been cleared properly. It plays into a classic AQ tactic. They hide a bunch of devices. Some obvious. Some, not so much. The rest is history. For my foot, anyway."

"That's why you moved to work in a lab?"

"Right. But I didn't leave the Bureau. I couldn't work in the field anymore so they let me retrain. I'm a bio recovery technician now. Or I was. I pulled prints, but mostly from older devices. I recovered hairs, and anything that could yield DNA. It was uneventful, dull, but sometimes very satisfying. Like a month ago. We had a case involving a guy who used to work for a Kuwait oil company. A lead came in claiming that he was an AQI sympathizer. Al Qaeda in Iraq. The Bureau set up a sting operation and they got him on tape boasting to an undercover agent about how he used to build bombs in a basement in Abu Ghraib. They cross-referenced dates and places, pulled a bunch of evidence that hadn't been processed yet, and guess what? I pulled his print from a fragment of a roadside bomb. Gold star for me. Life in prison for him. I was happy with that result. Unlike my last case. An unexploded bomb came in. That's the holy grail to us. Everything is intact. It's a feast of evidence. This was no different. There were a bunch of standout things. First, it was found within the United States, not brought here from somewhere else. Second, it had a GPS chip in it, which we figure was to let the terrorists know when their target was near so they could detonate. But as a backup. Because the third thing was, it also had a transponder."

"I don't know what that is."

"OK. It's like this. There are two parts. One sends out a radio signal. The other bounces back a reply. One was in the bomb. The other would be carried by the target. Presumably without his or her knowledge. I think it was supposed to be the primary trigger."

"What if something else sent a signal and triggered it?"

"They don't work that way. Each pair has a code. If the code doesn't match, nothing happens. Which is why I think it didn't go off. The other part of the transponder must not have come within range before the bomb was found. Which is fortunate. Because of all the lives that were saved. And because of the fourth thing in there. A fingerprint. Right on the transponder itself. It came to me for identification."

"Whose was it?"

"It was Michael's."

"What did you do?"

Fenton was silent for a moment. She looked at the floor. Then she looked at me. "I was shocked, obviously. I double-checked the print. I triple-checked it. But there was no mistake. It was Michael's."

"Could—"

"There's something else. I was also given the card from the Red Roan to examine. There was no writing on it. I made that part up, because I left the bomb part out. There was a condom in there, too. Still in its wrapper. I have no idea why. To make it look like random stuff had fallen in by accident, if one of Dendoncker's guys saw it, maybe? Anyway, I figured Michael was repenting. He wanted to stop. He wanted to get out. He knew where I worked. He knew what I did. He knew I'd find his print. It was so prominent. And that's rare. Current bomb makers wear gloves because they know the kind of things we can recover now. So, and I'm not proud of this, I panicked. I destroyed his print. And the transponder. And the card from the Red Roan. I deleted all records of them. And I quit. The rest you know. Everything else I told you is true."

"Did you find out anything more?"

She closed her eyes, then opened them and shook her head. "No. I never got to Michael."

I took a sip of coffee and weighed up what Fenton had told me. A bomb had been found with a transponder hooked up to it. A fingerprint. A business card. And a condom. But no note. Something wasn't adding up. I said, "The bomb. Where was it recovered from?"

"A private airfield."

"Was that the target?"

"Don't know."

"What size was it?"

"Small enough to conceal. Big enough to do a lot of damage. Depending on where it was detonated, if there were fewer than fifty casualties it would be a miracle."

"What if it exploded on a plane? If the plane was the target, not just the transport. If it blew up over a city. Or a shopping mall. Or a stadium."

"That's possible, but unlikely. The bomb we found was packed with shrapnel. That's an antipersonnel configuration. If a plane was its target we'd expect it to have a shaped projectile to ensure it could breach the fuselage or at least cause major system damage."

"That's something, I guess. What about the timescale, if they have other bombs?"

She shrugged. "Tomorrow. Next week. Next year. Can we afford to wait?"

"How many bombs did Michael make?"

She shrugged again. "Could be any number. Distributed anywhere in the country."

We were looking at hundreds dead, potentially. Maybe thousands. Dendoncker had the means. The opportunity. And there were plenty of groups out there with the cash to make it worth his while. All of a sudden fifty-fifty with a chance of collateral damage didn't look so bad. I drained my cup. "Wait here. I'm going for a word with the ME."

Chapter 14

I walked faster. The sun was hotter. The buildings seemed closer together. The empty sidewalks, narrower. The atmosphere was almost oppressive. I reached the medical center and went straight in. The foyer was just as it was before except that there was a woman at the reception desk. It was hard to say how old she was. Not far from being the wrong side of retirement age, I would guess. Her hair was silver and it was wound up in an elaborate series of braids. Her glasses were pointy at the temples like ones I'd seen in pictures from the 1960s. She had a discreet string of pearls and a neat, cream blouse. She glanced up when I approached but when she realized I was heading for the door that led to the basement she looked away. A benefit of Dendoncker's people doing business there, I guess. But I wasn't happy about being mistaken for one of his goons.

I paused in the lower corridor and listened at the door to the morgue. I could hear music. It was classical. Mainly piano. Something by Beethoven, I thought. I knocked and went in without waiting for an answer. Instantly I was hit by the stench. It was like an invisible wall. Made up of things I'd smelled before. Blood. Bodily products. Disinfectant. Preservative chemicals. But it was so strong it stopped me in my tracks.

Ahead of me there was a guy in the center of the room. He had white hair. A white lab coat. Metal-rimmed glasses on a chain. And a pronounced stoop. Behind him was a row of steel doors. Five of them. To the side, a desk. It held a computer, which was switched off. A stack of blank forms. And a fancy pen.

Right at the guy's side there was a metal table. It was made of stainless steel. It had raised sides, and a body was lying on it. A man's. It was naked. The top of its skull had been sawn off. Its rib cage cracked apart. Its abdomen cut open. Blood was running along the channels on both sides of the table and trickling down a drain. There was a trolley covered with tools. They were sharp and bloody. There was another trolley, covered with jars full of red and brown gelatinous things, and a scale. With a brain in its pan.

The guy took his glasses off and glared at me. "At least you knocked. That's something. Now, who are you? What do you want?"

He seemed like a straightforward guy, so I decided to take a straightforward approach. "My name's Reacher. You're Dr. Houllier?"

The guy nodded.

"I'm here to ask for your help."

"I see. With what? Is someone sick? Hurt?"

"I need you to stay away from work tomorrow."

"Out of the question. I've worked here for more than forty years and I've never missed a day."

"That's an admirable record."

"Don't blow smoke."

"OK. Let's try this. There's a guy in this town I believe you're acquainted with. Waad Dendoncker."

Dr. Houllier's eyes narrowed. "What about him?"

"Just how well acquainted are you?"

Dr. Houllier snatched up a scalpel, still slick with blood, and brandished it at me. "Cast an aspersion like that again and to hell with my oath. I'll cut your heart out. I don't care how big you are." He gestured to the body at his side. "You can see I know how."

"So you're not a fan."

Dr. Houllier dropped the scalpel back on the table. "Let me tell you a little about my history with Waad Dendoncker. Our paths first crossed ten years ago. I was here, working. The door flew open. And two of his guys barged in. No knock. No, *excuse me*. They didn't say a word. Not right away. They just handed me an envelope. Inside was a photograph. Of my brother. Outside his house. In Albuquerque. You see, I'm not married. My parents have passed. Donald was the only family I had. The guy told me, if I ever wanted to see my brother alive again, I had to go with them."

"So you went?"

"Of course. They put me in a crummy old army Jeep. Drove out into the desert. Maybe ten miles. It's hard to tell out there. They stopped when we reached a group of men. Dendoncker. A couple of his guys. And two others. No one told me explicitly but I worked out they were customers. There to buy hand grenades. They must have asked for a demonstration. A pit had been dug. Two people were in it. Both women. They were naked."

"Who were they?"

"No one I recognized. Later the guy who drove me said they

worked for Dendoncker. He said they'd disobeyed his orders. This was the consequence. Dendoncker threw in a grenade. I heard screams when it landed. Then an explosion. The others all rushed forward. They wanted to see. I didn't, but Dendoncker forced me. Believe me, I've seen injuries before. I've seen surgeries. Every kind of butchery you can imagine. But this was worse. What happened to those women's bodies . . . It disgusted me. I was sick, right there on the spot. I was worried that Dendoncker would expect me to deal with the remains, somehow. But no. A guy used one of the Jeeps. It had a snowplow blade on the front. He just filled in the hole. Dendoncker and his customers stayed there to talk business. The two guys who'd brought me took me back to the medical center. They told me that the next day, or maybe the day after, a body would find its way onto my slab. They said I was to process it, thoroughly, but not to keep any official record. And to be ready to answer questions."

"From Dendoncker?"

"Right."

"And if you didn't go along?"

"They said there'd be another pit. That they'd throw my brother in it. And make me watch when the grenade went off. They said they'd cut my eyelids off, to make sure I saw everything."

"The body they mentioned. It showed up?"

"Three days later. I couldn't sleep, picturing what kind of shape it would be in. In the end it was only shot. Luckily. For me, anyway."

"How many since then?"

"Twenty-seven. Mostly shot. Some stabbed. A couple with their skulls bashed in."

"Did Dendoncker come and see all of them?"

Dr. Houllier nodded. "He shows up every time. Like clockwork. Although he has calmed down a little. Originally he wanted a detailed analysis. Stomach contents. Residue on the skin and under the fingernails. Any indication of foreign travel. Things like that. Now he's happy with a brief report on the body."

"But he still wants to see them?"

"Correct."

"Why?"

"It could be one of several disorders. I'm not about to analyze him. It's not my field. And he gives me the creeps. Whenever he shows up I just want him out of my office as fast as possible."

I said nothing.

"Strike that. What I really want is for him to stop coming at all. But I can't make him. So I find a way to live with it."

"I have a way to stop him. All I need is this room."

"If you're going to stop Dendoncker, and you're going to do it in this room, someone's going to play dead. You?"

I nodded, then told him about the gunshot wound to my chest and the props we were going to use to make it look real.

"Where is this shooting going to take place?"

I told him the location that Dendoncker's guy had texted to Fenton.

"I see. And how are you going to get your body from there to here?"

I hadn't figured that out yet. When you're stuck with a plan full of holes, more have a habit of appearing.

"You don't know, do you?"

I said nothing.

"What time are you supposed to get shot?"

"It'll be a little after eleven P.M."

"OK. I'll bring you in myself."

"No. You can't be involved. Think of your brother."

"Donald died. Last year."

"Did he have a wife? Kids?"

"No kids. I don't like his wife. And she's sick, anyway. Cancer. Metastasized. If Dendoncker looked for her she'd be dead before he found out which hospice she's in. So. I'll give you a number for your sidekick to call me on. It's a direct line. It bypasses 911, which will make things easier."

"Are you sure?"

"Yes. Now, Dendoncker won't come until morning. That means you'll have to sleep here. He may have people watching the place and it wouldn't do for a dead man to be seen leaving and returning. I'll come in early and get you ready for the meat locker. You'll have a companion, I'm afraid, so I can't raise the temperature. But I can give you a mild sedative so you won't start shivering. I'll tape your eyes, too. Just in case. How long can you hold your breath for?"

I'd once gone for a little over a minute without breathing. But that was underwater. Swimming hard. Fighting for my life. This would be different. No exertion. Just the effort of keeping completely still.

"Ninety seconds," I said. "Two minutes, maximum."

"All right. I'll keep an eye on the time. I'll distract Dendoncker if he drags things out for too long. He's usually quick so I'm not too worried. Now, tell me. And you can be honest. After you stop him, what are you going to do with him?"

"Hand him over to the police."

A flash of disappointment crossed Houllier's face.

I said, "Does Dendoncker usually come alone? Or does he bring bodyguards?"

"Apes, I'd call them. Two. One comes in first to check the room. Then Dendoncker and the second guy follow."

"Weapons?"

"None visible."

"That's good. But even with your brother out of the picture there's still a risk. To you. You'd be much safer at home. Or out of town."

Houllier shook his head. "No. Dendoncker's had the upper hand for too long. I promised myself, if I ever could resist, I would. I only have myself to worry about, with Donald gone. It seems like now is the time."

"Thank you, Doctor. I appreciate that. But if you change your mind . . ."

"I won't."

"OK. Until this evening, then."

"One last thing, Mr. Reacher. I'm a doctor. I swore an oath to do no harm. You didn't. Specifically, where Dendoncker is concerned. I hope you take my meaning."

Chapter 15

I got into position under the streetlight at 11:00 P.M., as agreed.

The evening was chilly. I'd been in the compound for three hours to make sure I was alone. I wished I had a coat. I only had on a T-shirt. A yellow one. It was huge. It was baggy, even on me. But it needed to be. It needed room to conceal the bag of fake blood I had taped to my chest. I couldn't risk a coat hanging wrong and ending up with no bullet hole where there should be one.

The car showed up at 11:02. Its lights were on bright so I couldn't tell the make or model, but I could see enough to know it wasn't a Jeep. Not what I was expecting Fenton to be driving. If Fenton was driving. I couldn't see inside, either. A moment later the front doors opened. Both of them. Two men climbed out.

Not what we'd agreed.

Both the car's back doors opened. Two more men climbed out.

Definitely not what we'd agreed.

* * *

I sized the guys up. They were all between maybe six-one and six-three. Each around two hundred pounds. I didn't see anything to worry me. But I was mainly waiting to see if Fenton appeared from the backseat.

She didn't.

Either she'd been benched because Dendoncker opted for more firepower after losing two guys the day before. Or she'd been taken out of the game for good, if Dendoncker had seen through our ploy. I doubted any of the guys in front of me would know. Paranoid bosses don't generally share insights with their wet boys. So I decided on a different approach. Whittle down the numbers and persuade the last man standing it's in his interests to escort me up the food chain.

The last man standing wasn't going to be the driver. That was for damn sure. He stepped forward and immediately launched into a dumb routine designed to get me into the car. That wasn't going to happen. Not then, anyway. The guy realized he couldn't bluff me so he changed tack. He tried to use force. He pulled a gun. That's always a mistake when you're within arm's length. Or near it. Maybe he mistook size for slow. Maybe he was just stupid. Or overconfident. Either way I closed in fast, grabbed his wrist, and neutralized his weapon. Then I neutralized him with a quick, easy punch.

I retrieved the driver's fallen gun in case the other guys were smart enough to attack together. They weren't. The one in the center of the remaining trio was the next to try. He screamed like he thought that would frighten me, feinted a jab, then tried to land a punch in my gut. I blocked it and drove my middle knuckle into his biceps. I gave him the option to walk away. I figured that was only fair. He didn't take it. He rushed back in with a wild crazy punch aimed at my head. I let it flail past, then immobilized his other arm. I gave him another chance. He repaid me by trying to kick me in the balls. He didn't get close. I slammed my foot into his shin. Used his effort against him. The guy's ankle broke. At least one bone. Maybe more. He screamed and hopped around for a second, then fainted when the severed ends of his bone touched together. Now I was down to two.

These guys tried to raise their game. They fetched ax handles from their trunk. The taller of the pair led off with a monster swing. He missed by a mile. Then his buddy weighed in. He started jabbing. Two feints to begin with, then he went for my gut. But he telegraphed it. I grabbed the ax handle, wrenched it out of his hands, spun it around, and smashed it down onto the top of his head like I was chopping wood.

The final guy panicked. He took a couple of wild swings but there was no hope of him connecting. He must have figured that out because he went for his gun. But like the driver, he was too close. I knocked the gun out of his hand. I grabbed hold of his neck. I started to outline his options. Then I heard a voice ordering me to stop.

It was Fenton. She emerged from the cover of the row of garages to my right. Her arms were stretched out and she was holding her gun with both hands. She was trying to resurrect our plan. But the last guy was standing between us. That wasn't ideal. He was a witness now. He wouldn't believe I'd been shot if Fenton's bullet would have had to pass through him to hit me. I could have thrown him aside but that would have been suspicious, too. It would be more realistic to pull him closer. Use him as a shield.

I looked at Fenton. Glanced down at my chest. Figured she could see the right area. Or close enough, anyway. Taking the shot was the best bet under the circumstances. I willed her to do it. I saw her inhale and exhale. I braced myself for the sound. I felt a flick on my chest first, then cold dampness. I threw myself back. I've seen plenty of people get shot dead. Some crumple and end up like they're asleep. Some fly through the air and end up in a contorted heap. I aimed for somewhere in the middle. I pushed my arms out wide, kept one knee raised, and snapped my head right back.

"Didn't need me, huh?" Fenton was coming closer. "Don't worry. There's no rush. You can apologize in your own sweet time. Just make it good."

"What the hell did you do?" The guy sounded mad. "Dendoncker wanted him alive. He had questions."

Fenton paused for a moment. "Dendoncker wanted *him* alive? Huh. Well, if I hadn't shown up this guy would have been the only one who was alive. Those three idiots are down and you weren't far behind."

I felt fingers on my neck. They were long. Slim. A little cold. I felt myself shiver.

"Anyway, he's dead. No point crying about it." Fenton reached around and pretended to check my back pockets. "Like I thought, no cash. It was a setup from the start. What an asshole. OK, I'll call 911 and get the body picked up. You can call it in to Dendoncker. Throw me under the bus if you want. On one condition. You load up your buddies. I have a long walk back to my car after the ambulance shows up."

Chapter 16

I've spent more nights than I can count in weird, uncomfortable places but never until then in a morgue. It was actually less uncomfortable than I expected. Physically, anyway. Dr. Houllier brought me a bedroll, a sleeping bag, and an eye mask like you get on commercial flights. He left me to sleep, then came back in at 6:00 A.M. He brought me some coffee and while I drank it he got busy making the simulated gunshot wound for my chest out of the special clay. He made sure to get the size just right. The shape. The ragged edges. The colors, which were a mixture of angry red and congealed brown. When he was happy he stuck it onto me. Then he gave me my shots. One in each arm. Each leg. My chest. And my stomach. He cleared away my bedding and hid it behind the right-hand fridge door. Then he checked the clock on the wall.

"OK. It's time."

He opened the center door and pulled out the sliding rack. I took my clothes off. He hid them along with the bedding. I lay down. He threw a sheet over me and stuck my eyelids down with some kind of tape.

He said, "Good luck. Try not to trash my morgue when Dendoncker gets here."

He pulled the sheet up over my head and pushed the rack into the refrigerator. All the way. I heard the door shut. I could sense the light being shut out. I could feel the darkness. The skin between my shoulders began to prickle. I hate enclosed spaces. Always have. It's something primal. I forced myself to picture the void all around me. Behind the doors the refrigerator was a single unit. Not individual compartments. There was plenty of room. I began to feel better. Until I remembered the chopped-up body. I wondered which side it was on. Part of me wished I could see. Most of me was glad I couldn't.

I'd been inside for close to an hour when the refrigerator door opened. There was no notice. I suddenly sensed light. The rack rolled out. Smoothly and gently. The sheet was pulled back from my face. I heard a voice. It was nasal, and it gave hard edges to the word *"Move."* The sheet was whipped off the rest of the way. I heard it settle on the floor. Then the nasal voice spoke again. I guessed it was Dendoncker. He questioned what had killed me. Dr. Houllier replied. There was talk of my older wounds. The scars they'd left. What might have caused them. What else they knew about me.

Sixty seconds without a breath. Uncomfortable. But manageable.

The sheet covered me again. My body. Then my face. But before I could inhale it was torn back off. There was a debate about my pretend fake ID. My real ID. My real name. Questions and answers, back and forth. Then I felt Dendoncker come closer. I couldn't see him but I knew he was staring at me.

Ninety seconds without a breath. I needed air. Badly. My lungs were starting to burn. My body was desperate to move.

I heard Dendoncker make a comment about my looking for him, not Michael. So he was narcissistic as well as paranoid. A charming combination. No wonder he didn't play well with others. I heard papers rustle. More questions. Then talk about burning my passport. Dumping my body. Dendoncker's voice was louder and sharper, like he was giving orders. It sounded like he was wrapping things up.

Two minutes without a breath. My lungs were done. I took a huge gulp of air. Pulled the tape off my eyes. And sat up.

There were four people in the room. All men. All with their mouths open in shock. There was Dr. Houllier, at his desk. Two guys in suits, maybe in their forties, near the door. And one in the center, facing me. He looked like he was in his sixties. He had an angular face, with a burn scar on his left cheek. It was triangle-shaped. He had bulging eyes. Abnormally long arms and legs. Three fingers were missing from his right hand. He was using his thumb and remaining finger to pinch the bezel of his watch. I said, "Dendoncker?" He didn't react. I jumped off the tray. He fumbled in his jacket pocket. Produced a gun. A revolver. An NAA-22S. It was a tiny little thing. Less than four inches long. I took it from him, tossed it into the refrigerator, and shoved him toward the back corner of the room. I wanted him well away from the door. I wanted no chance of him sneaking out while I was dealing with his goons. Both were approaching me. A pale-suited, curly-haired one on my left. A dark-suited, straight-haired one on my right. There was two feet between them. They were reaching under their jackets. Going for their guns. But they never got the chance to draw. I moved toward them, fast. Pulled back both fists. And punched them both in their jaws, simultaneously. Maybe not the hardest blows ever. I felt like the sedative shots had affected me a little. Taken a few percent off the total. Not that it mattered. My forward motion combined with their movement toward me made it like they'd walked into the front of a truck. They landed together in a tight tangle of arms and legs. They weren't moving. I turned to check on Dendoncker and saw him standing in the corner. I had a momentary impression of a stick insect in a cage at the zoo.

I heard a sound. Behind me. From the door. It was flung open like a gas main had blown someplace nearby. A guy stepped through. I got the impression he had to turn sideways to fit, he was so broad. And he was tall. Six feet six, minimum. I would guess at least three hundred and fifty pounds. He had no hair. His head was like a bowling ball. His eyes and mouth and nose were small and pinched and they were all crammed together at the front. He had tiny protruding ears. Shiny pink skin. A black suit with a white shirt and no tie. Which was a shame. Ties can be useful for strangling people.

The guy started moving forward. He had a weird stomping, staccato motion like a robot. As he came closer his steps turned into kicks and his arm swings turned into punches. He was steady and repetitive and relentless, like he was doing a martial arts demonstration. It was mesmerizing. No doubt devastating if one of his blows connected. And deadly if more than one did.

I stepped back to buy a little time. Dendoncker tried to scuttle past. I grabbed him and threw him behind me. I didn't look to see where he landed. There was no way I could risk taking my eyes off the human bludgeoning machine that was closing in on me. Dendoncker tried to creep by on the opposite side. I shoved him back again. The huge guy was still coming. I figured he wanted to toy with me for a while, then back me up against the wall or into the corner and then pummel the life out of me when I could retreat no farther. He didn't seem worried about keeping out of range of anything I could throw at him.

I took another step away. Then I launched myself the opposite way off my back foot and darted around him. I jabbed him in the kidney on my way past. It was a decent blow. It would have floored a lot of people. This guy showed no sign of even noticing it. He took another step then went into some kind of elaborate turning routine. His arms crossed and recrossed and finally opened the opposite way. He pivoted on the balls of his feet. He pushed off the floor and threw another kick but I was already moving. I had turned faster. Pushed off the floor harder.

I charged, head down, before his next kick. Below his next punch. I slammed into his chest, hard enough to throw him back despite the difference in weight. He staggered. I tried to line up a punch before he could recover. I was thinking, his throat. This was no time for gentlemanly conduct. But before I could launch anything the guy's legs connected with the fridge rack. It was still extended. He toppled back onto it. The force was enough to release the latch and it started sliding. He had landed at an angle so he wouldn't fit through the door. His head slammed into the frame. Not hard enough to knock him out. But enough to stun him. For a moment. And a moment was all I needed.

I followed in and scythed my elbow down into the side of his head. I used all my strength. My full weight was behind it. It was a perfect connection. His arms and legs bounced up like a bug's then flopped down and dangled off either side of the rack. His tongue lolled out of his mouth. I waited a moment, to be sure. Then I turned to check on Dendoncker.

There was no sign of him. Aside from Dr. Houllier and the three unconscious guys, the room was empty.

"She was so quick." Dr. Houllier's voice was flat. "A woman. With a limp. She put a gun to Dendoncker's head. Dragged him out of here. She left this."

Dr. Houllier passed me a grocery store bag. Inside was the shirt I was wearing before swapping it for the baggy yellow one, which by then was ruined, and a single sheet of paper. I unfolded it. There was a handwritten message:

Reacher, I'm sorry. I was late to the rendezvous because Dendoncker sent me on a bullshit errand. And I didn't set out to use you. I hope you don't feel that way. But I have a feeling things could get very ugly, very soon, and there are lines I can't ask you to cross. I'm glad we met, even briefly. I hope you make it to the ocean soon.

xoxo

PS—You saved my life. I'm grateful, and I will never forget.

Chapter 17

I screwed the note into a ball and tossed it into the trash. Peeled the fake bullet wound off my chest. Pulled the shirt Fenton had brought over my head. Crossed to the right-hand refrigerator door. The one where Dr. Houllier had stashed my clothes. Opened it and got dressed the rest of the way. And then retrieved my passport from his trash can.

"Where are you going?" Dr. Houllier said. "Wait a minute. What are you going to do about the woman? And Dendoncker?"

The way I saw it I had two choices. I could let Fenton go. Or I could try to find her. And I couldn't see any point in finding her. I had no doubt she could handle herself when she was up against one old frail guy. Or numerous strong young guys, if that was how things shook out. I had no doubt she would do whatever she saw fit to stop Dendoncker's bombs. She had the contacts. She just needed information. How she got it was up to her. Maybe she would cross a line. Maybe a whole bunch of lines. But that was her call. I wasn't

100

her conscience, and I wasn't her priest. My nose was a little out of joint, the way she'd blindsided me. But at the same time I had to say, *Nicely played*. The truth was, I liked her. I wished her the best.

"I'm not going to do anything about either of them," I said. "If Fenton wants to handle things from here, I'm happy to let her."

"Oh." Dr. Houllier scratched the side of his head. "Then, what about these apes? You can't leave them on my floor. Especially not that big one. I treated him after one of his victims bit him and his arm got infected. He's called Mansour. He's a psychopath. What will he do when he wakes up and finds me? It's obvious I helped you."

"Don't worry. I'll take the trash out when I leave. You won't see these guys again."

I started with the guy Dr. Houllier had called Mansour. I checked his pants pocket and found what I was looking for straightaway. His keys. A big bunch on a plastic fob. With one kind in particular. A car key. The logo molded into the plastic grip said *Lincoln*. I hoped it was for a Town Car. They're spacious vehicles. Plenty of room for passengers. Conscious or unconscious. Alive or dead. That fact was established almost immediately after the first model rolled off the production line. They'd been popular with people who appreciated that quality ever since. People like me, at that moment.

I figured I could tie the three guys up. Load them in. Dump the car. And call 911. I bet they all had pretty substantial records. Although I wasn't impressed with the way the police had responded to my report of the bodies by The Tree. I hadn't seen a single uniformed cop in the town. Or a detective. Or a crime scene truck. It made me think of a conversation I had recently with a guy in Texas. He had a theory. He said that in remote regions any officer sent to deal with something messy like a bunch of dead bodies must be on his boss's bad side. Which meant he wouldn't be looking to carry out a thorough investigation. He'd be looking to get the case closed, quickly and tidily. To get back in his boss's good graces. And to make sure someone else would get sent the next time there was a problem out in the sticks.

Maybe the guy had been right. Maybe I'd be better off dumping the car somewhere farther away. At the side of the highway. Or in a bigger town. Or a city. I didn't want to invite extra work. But I did want the right result. And on top of that, I was hungry. Making plans on an empty stomach is a bad idea. It can distort your priorities. I figured I should grab something to eat, then decide.

I said, "It's been a busy morning. I could use some breakfast. Want to join me?"

Dr. Houllier pulled a face like he'd smelled something vile. "Eat? Now? No. No thank you. I couldn't."

I tried to slip Mansour's keys into my pocket but the bunch got all snagged up. It was big. And heavy. When I tried to streamline it, one key in particular stood out. A mortise. It was similar to the ones the guys had been carrying yesterday.

I said, "Which place around here has the best coffee?"

Dr. Houllier blinked a few times. Then he shrugged. "You could try the Prairie Rose. I've heard theirs is good. Turn left out of the main exit. Walk a hundred yards. You can't miss it."

"Thanks. I'll do that." I glanced around the room. "Have you got anything I could use to tie these guys up?"

Dr. Houllier thought for a moment. "Wait here. I have an idea." Then he hurried out through the door.

I used the time to work my way through Mansour's other pockets. I found his wallet. He had cash, but no ID. Nothing with an address. I tried his phone. It asked for a Face ID. I had no idea what that was but on a whim I held it level with the guy's nose. After a second its screen unlocked. There was no record of any calls being received. Or made. There were no texts. And no contacts. Nothing to help me, so I took his gun and moved on to the guys in the suits. They had a similar range of stuff. Guns, wallets, phones, and keys. Including plastic fobs. And a mortise key. The keys were scuffed and scratched. I held them up next to one another. The teeth lined up. They were a perfect match. I tried Mansour's. It matched just as well. I figured the keys must be connected to Dendoncker's operation in some way. I was curious, but the question didn't need to be answered. Dendoncker was at the wrong end of Fenton's Glock. His crew was heading to jail. And I would be on my way out of town as soon as I had eaten.

The door swung open. There was no knock, but it was pushed gently this time. Dr. Houllier appeared in the gap. He was clutching a bunch of packages. They were identical. Wrapped in clear packaging. And they were slippery. He tried to pass one to me and the whole lot fell and went skittering across the floor. I helped him gather them up and saw they were crepe bandages. They each had a manufacturer's logo and a sticker indicating their size. Four inches wide by five feet long.

"They're elasticated," Dr. Houllier said. "They'll stretch, but they shouldn't break. They're full of polyurethane fibers. They're added to the cotton. It makes them strong. In most places they're used to immobilize limbs. After a sprain, normally. Here we need them for snakebites. You have to bind the area around a wound really tight to stop the venom from spreading."

I opened one of the packets and tried to break the material.

"If you double it up it'll be even stronger," Dr. Houllier said.

I used the first bandage to tie Mansour's ankles. I checked the knot and figured Dr. Houllier was right. It should hold. I secured

Mansour's hands behind his back. Then I did the same with the guys in the suits. Dr. Houllier watched me work and when I was done he scooped up the pile of empty wrappers and dumped them in the trash. I dropped the guys' guns and wallets and other stuff in the clinical waste bucket.

I said, "If I was a secretive person and wanted to get in and out of the building without being seen, how would I do it?"

"Through the ambulance bay. The way I brought you in last night."

"I was in a body bag last night. You could have brought me down the chimney for all I could see."

"Oh. Of course. Well, it's all the way at the rear of the building. It's on its own. It has a separate entrance from the street. There's a gate but it's not locked, and you can't see in from the outside. The doors are automatic, and the corridor bifurcates before you get to the ER. One branch leads to an elevator, which comes straight down to the basement. As long as a casualty isn't incoming at that moment no one would have a clue you'd been there."

"Security cameras?"

Dr. Houllier shook his head. "It's been proposed a couple of times, but never acted on. Privacy issues. That's the official line. But there's also the question of budget. That's the real reason, if you ask me. Come on. I'll show you."

I followed Dr. Houllier out of the morgue and along to the far end of the corridor. He hit the call button for the elevator. We waited side by side, in silence. The doors jerked open after less than a minute. The elevator car was spacious. It was broad and deep and lined with stainless steel. We rode up one floor then stepped out and followed another corridor around to a pair of tall glass doors. They slid apart as we approached and dumped us out into a rectangular courtyard. A series of red lines was painted on the flaking asphalt. I figured they marked the route for ambulances. One arc to turn, and another to reverse into the unloading zone. There was ample space for two emergency vehicles. And tucked in next to the wall on the right side, facing away from the entrance, there was a lone sedan. A Lincoln Town Car.

I clicked a button on Mansour's key fob and the car's blinkers flashed. The locks in all the doors clunked open. It was the old style, square and severe. It was black. *Ubiquitous black*, the official name in the brochure should have been. And as a bonus it also had blacked-out windows. Maybe because of the climate. Maybe because of Dendoncker's paranoia. Or maybe just because he thought it looked cool. I didn't know. And I didn't care. Because it meant no one would be able to see inside. The town seemed pretty quiet. It was unlikely the ER would be overrun by a spate of wounded citizens at that time of day. I figured I could safely leave the car where it was for a half hour or so.

I locked the Lincoln and Dr. Houllier led the way back to the morgue. He helped me wrestle Mansour onto a gurney. I hauled him along the corridor and into the elevator and around to the ambulance bay. I continued across to the back of the car. Popped the trunk and half lifted, half rolled the guy inside.

I made a second trip and returned with the curly-haired guy in the pale suit. He was easier to maneuver. I wheeled him up close to the side of the car and slid him onto the backseat like a plank. Then I fetched the straight-haired guy in the dark suit. I tried to lay him on top of his buddy but he slipped off and fell facedown in the footwell. I left him there and returned the gurney to the morgue. I thanked Dr. Houllier for his help. Said goodbye, and headed for the medical center's main entrance.

Chapter 18

The Prairie Rose was as easy to find as Dr. Houllier had promised. It was still in the central portion of the town, right on the edge, in a building with two floors. It was also built around a courtyard. That seemed to be the fashion in the area. The café was on the ground floor. There was some kind of office above it and a store on either side. The interior was simple and square. There were twelve tables. Three rows of four, evenly lined up, each with four chairs. The furniture was solid and durable. The silverware was plain and functional. Nothing stood out, either good or bad. There were no flowers. No ornaments. No knickknacks. No other customers. I liked the place.

I took a seat at the table on the end of the right-hand row. After a couple of minutes a waitress pushed through the door from the kitchen. She was wearing a pink gingham dress with a frilly white apron and a pair of New Balance sneakers. They were also pink. She looked like she was in her sixties. She had no jewelry. Her hair was less elaborate and it was gray rather than silver, but something about her reminded me of the medical center receptionist. A sister, maybe. Or a cousin. She flipped over a cup and filled it with coffee from a glass jug, then looked at me and raised an eyebrow. I ordered a full stack with extra bacon and an apple pie. She raised her eyebrow a little higher but she didn't pass any other kind of judgment.

There were four copies of the same local paper jammed into a rack on the wall near a pay phone. I took one and leafed through it while I waited. It was light on news. Every other page either had a new poll, or the result of a previous poll. I guess the publisher thought reader interaction was more important than reporting. Or maybe it was cheaper. One thing they didn't skimp on was the graphics. There were pie charts. Bar charts. Scatter grams. Other kinds of diagrams that hadn't even been invented when I was in high school. All in bright, vivid colors. Addressing all kinds of topics. Should there be an armadillo sanctuary nearby? Should the border fence be repainted? Were there enough recycling facilities in the town? Should the community try to attract wind and solar power? Or oppose it?

I was on the last page of the paper when my food arrived. The *Police Blotter*. A fancy name for an account of all the crimes committed in the area recently. I read it carefully. There was no mention of Dendoncker. Or smuggling. Or planes. Or bombs. Just a few minor misdemeanors. Most of them were pretty tame. And most resulted in an arrest for public intoxication.

I ate my last morsel. I drained my coffee. I was waiting for a refill when the door to the street opened. A man walked in. I recognized him. He was the fourth guy from the previous night. Under the streetlamp. Who had tried to bludgeon me. And who had seen me get shot to death. He didn't seem very surprised by my resurrection.

He just walked straight up to me. He was wearing the same clothes. He hadn't shaved. And he was holding a black trash bag.

There was something inside the bag. It was at least nine inches long, and heavy enough to keep the plastic sides taut. I gripped the edge of the table. I was ready to shove it into his legs at the first hint of a weapon. But the guy didn't draw. He stood and sneered. Raised the bag. Gripped the lower edge with one hand. Flipped it over. And sent an item crashing onto the table.

It was a single piece, but it had three distinct sections. A socket. Shaped with carbon fiber. The kind of size that would fit a residual limb. A shank. Shiny, made of titanium. And a boot. Just like the kind Fenton had been wearing the last time I saw her.

"Follow me, or the woman will be missing more than part of her leg." The guy turned and headed for the door. "You have thirty seconds."

I stood and pulled a roll of bills out of my pocket. I peeled off a twenty and dropped it on the table. Ten seconds had passed. I picked up Fenton's foot. Walked to the door. Another ten seconds had gone. I waited nine more then stepped outside. The guy was still there. He was standing next to a car. A medium-sized sedan. It was dusty. I figured it was the same one they'd used the previous night. In daylight I could see it was a Chevy Caprice. An ex–police vehicle. The searchlight on the driver's door was a dead giveaway. Its paint was wavy and dull so I figured it had also spent time on taxi duty.

The guy grinned and opened the passenger door. He stepped back and gestured for me to climb in. I approached. Slowly. I switched Fenton's foot to my right hand. Stepped into the gap between the guy and the car door. Then I grabbed the back of his head and smashed his face into the car roof. His mouth hit the edge of the doorframe. Some of his teeth were knocked out. I couldn't see how many. There was too much blood. I took his gun from his waistband. Hauled him around. Jabbed him in the solar plexus, just hard enough to knock the wind out of him. I pushed him into the car. Folded him into the seat. Closed the door. Checked that no one was watching. Moved around to the other side. Racked the seat all the way back. Climbed in. Stretched across and grabbed the guy by the throat. And squeezed. I felt his larynx begin to collapse. His eyes bulged. His tongue flopped out of his mouth. But he couldn't make a sound.

I said, "Here's how this is going to work. I'm going to ask a question. I'll give you a moment to think. Then I'll relax my grip just enough for you to speak. If you don't, I'll choke you to death. Same goes if I don't like your answer. Are we clear?"

I paused, then eased the pressure on his throat.

"Yes." His voice was a scratchy gasp. "Crystal."

"The woman got taken. How?"

"Dendoncker has a GPS watch. With a transmitter in it. He triggered an emergency signal. We caught the woman before she got out of the building. We brought Dendoncker to safety. That's priority one. When the others didn't return, Dendoncker sent me after you."

"Where's the woman now?"

"Don't know."

"Is this really how you want to go? Here? Now?"

"I don't know. I swear."

"Where's Dendoncker?"

"Don't know."

"Then where were you supposed to take me?"

"To the house. That's all I was told to do."

"Address?"

"I don't know the address. It's just 'the house.' That's what we call it."

"So you get me to this house. Then what?"

"I send a text. Someone will come for you."

"This house. Is it far?"

"No."

"In the town?"

"Yes."

"OK. You can show me. We'll go there together. Then you can send that text."

Chapter 19

I heard a sound. From farther up the street. A vehicle engine. I looked around and saw a car moving toward us. Not fast. Not slow. Just cruising around. Looking for trouble. It was a Dodge Charger. Its hood and fender were black. It had a bullbar on the front and a slimline lighting rig on the roof. Clearly the police. Probably local. Possibly state. Either way, their timing sucked.

I let go of the guy's neck, dropped my arm into my lap, and made my hand into a fist. "Make any kind of a move . . ."

"Don't worry." The guy pulled a road atlas out of the gap next to his seat. He opened it wide and held it up so that it covered his face. "From fry pan to fire? I'm not stupid."

The police car drew closer. It slowed down. Came alongside us. And stopped. Two cops were inside it. They weren't looking at me. Or the guy with the bleeding mouth. Yet. They seemed more interested in the Chevy. They weren't young. They might have had a vehicle like it, once. Maybe even that actual one. Cops used to say the

Caprice was the best patrol car ever. Maybe they were nostalgic. Maybe they were bored. I just hoped they weren't suspicious. They sat and stared for a minute. Two. Then the driver lit up their roof bar and sped away into the distance.

I reached for the guy's neck. He closed the atlas. Raised it. He had both his hands behind it. The cover was shiny. It was slippery. My hand slid off its surface. I wound up grabbing his shoulder. He jabbed at my eye with the corner of the map, then wriggled free. He scrabbled for the handle. Got the door open. Dived out. Rolled over on the sidewalk then scrambled up and started to run.

I jumped out and followed him. The guy was fast. He was well motivated. I'd made sure of that. The gap between us was growing. He reached a cluster of buildings. Another courtyard arrangement. The windows facing the street were all boarded up. The guy should have kept on running. I would never have caught him. And I couldn't have risked a shot. Not in a residential area. But he didn't keep going. The lure of potential cover was too strong. He bolted through the archway. And disappeared.

I covered the remaining ground as fast as possible and stopped just before the entrance. I didn't want to risk presenting a silhouette. He could have had a backup weapon. I crouched and peered around the corner. I saw a bunch of disparate buildings like the ones that had been made into Fenton's hotel. Only these had two stories. They were joined together and boarded up with solid wooden panels, like a fence. There was a scaffold tower in each corner, leading to the roof. The process of conversion was under way. But there was no buzz of activity. No sound at all. The work had stalled. Maybe it had been abandoned altogether. Maybe the market had crashed. Maybe tastes had changed. I had no idea how the economics for that kind of development worked.

I craned my neck a little farther and I spotted the guy. He was standing alone in the center of the courtyard, just looking around. I guess the place was not what he had hoped for. There was no way out. And nowhere to hide. He moved a couple of feet to the left, then to the right, like he couldn't decide which way to go. I straightened up and stepped through the arch. He heard me and turned around. His face was pale and the blood from his mouth was flowing faster. The price of exertion, I guess.

"Do what I tell you and you won't get hurt." I kept my voice calm and even.

The guy took one step toward me then stopped. His eyes were flicking from me to the arch, back and forth, over and over. He was figuring the distance. The angles. Weighing the odds of getting past me. Then he turned. He ran for the scaffold tower on the right. He started to climb. There was no way I was going to follow him up. He was lighter. Far more nimble. He would reach the top long before me. There was no doubt about that. So I would emerge with my head exposed and no way to defend myself. He could have a weapon already. He could find something to use as one. A scaffolding pole. A hunk of masonry. A roof tile. Or he could just keep things simple and kick me.

Following him up was definitely out of the question. But so was letting him get away.

I ran to the tower on the left. I started to climb. Quickly, but carefully. I had to keep an eye on the guy in case he turned and went back down. I saw him make it to the top. He scrambled off the tower and disappeared. I made myself go faster. I got to the roof. Stepped out onto it. And steadied myself. The surface was slippery. The terra-cotta tiles were old. They seemed brittle. I didn't know if they could take my weight. The guy was almost at the far side. He must have been hoping there was another tower with access to the street. I doubted there would be one. I went after him. I tried to move smoothly. And I tried to be quiet. I didn't want him to bolt back the way he came before I was in a position to block him. He made it to the edge of the roof and peered over. I drew level. He turned toward me. His face was paler still.

I said, "Come on. You're out of options. It's time to go down. Take me to the house. Then I'll let you walk away."

"Do you think I'm crazy?" The guy's voice was shaking and shrill. "Do you have any idea what Dendoncker does to people who betray him?"

He seemed on the verge of panic. I figured I would have to knock him out and carry him down. I would have to calibrate the punch very carefully. That would be the critical part. I didn't want to wait too long for him to come around afterward. I moved a yard closer. He turned away. And stepped off the roof. He didn't hesitate. Just plunged straight off the edge.

I figured there must be a tower there after all. Or a ledge. Or a lower building. Then I heard a sound. It was like a wet hand slapping a table in a distant room. I got to the edge and looked over. The guy's body was lying on the ground, directly below. One leg was twisted. One arm was bent. And a deep red halo was spreading around the remains of his head.

I crossed to the tower and hustled down to the courtyard. I went through the archway. Worked my way around the perimeter of the site. And finally found a route through to the far side of the buildings. The guy was lying there on the sidewalk, completely still. There was no point checking for a pulse. So I went straight to his pockets.

I found nothing with an address or an ID. But he did have a phone. It had survived the fall. He said he was supposed to send a text when he got me to The House. Which gave me an idea. If I could come up with a good enough reason, I could change the location of the rendezvous. To somewhere that gave me an advantage. And to somewhere I could find. I used the guy's fingerprint to unlock the screen. But the phone was empty. There were no contacts. No saved numbers. No messages to reply to. Nothing I could use. And there was nothing else in his pockets. I was at a dead end. So I wiped the phone with my shirt. Dialed 911 through the material. Tapped the green phone icon. Dropped the phone on the guy's chest. And made my way back to his car.

I started with the glove box. I found the insurance and registration right away. They were the only two pieces of paper in there. Both showed the name of a corporation. Moon Shadow Associates. It was based in Delaware. Presumably one of the shell companies Fenton had mentioned. But whether it was or not, it didn't help me.

I found the page the town was on in the atlas. Nothing was circled. There were no marks. No addresses scrawled in the margins. No phone numbers written down. I tried the door pockets. The floor, front and back. The trunk. Under the carpet and around the spare wheel. There was nothing. No receipts from drugstores or gas stations. No carryout menus or to-go cups from a coffee shop. The car was completely sterile.

I climbed in behind the wheel, trying to figure out where to look next, and something hit my thigh. It was the guy's keys. They were hanging down from the ignition. One was a mortise. It was scratched and worn. I compared it with the one on Mansour's keyring. It was identical. I'd thought it might be for a garage, or a store. But now I had another theory as to what it would unlock. And, I realized, another person to worry about. Ever since the guy had dumped Fenton's foot on my table at the Prairie Rose, I'd been completely focused on finding her. But the guy had known where to find me. That was clear. And there was only one way he could have found that out.

Chapter 20

I knocked on the morgue door and went straight in. Dr. Houllier was there. Alone. He was on the floor, slumped against his autopsy table. His head was on his chest. Blood was dribbling out of one nostril and the corner of his mouth. His lab coat was hanging open. Its buttons had been ripped off. His tie was stretched and askew. He'd lost one shoe. His right wrist was fastened to the table leg with a cable tie. I stepped toward him and he raised his head, then turned away. Fear flashed across his face. Then he recognized me and turned back.

"Are you all right?" He sounded breathless. "Did that ape find you? I'm so sorry. I had to tell him where you went."

I said, "You did the right thing. I'm fine. But what about you? Are you hurt?"

Dr. Houllier dabbed at his face with his free hand. "It's nothing serious. Yet. The ape said he was going to get you, then come back for me." He shivered. "And take me to Dendoncker."

"That guy won't be coming back." I crossed to the autoclave and picked up a scalpel. Then I went back to the table, cut the cable tie, put the scalpel in my pocket, and helped Dr. Houllier to his feet. "But others might. Do you have a car?"

"Yes. Of course. Would you like to borrow it?"

"Where is it?"

"Here. In the staff parking lot."

"Good. I want you to get in it. And drive out of town. Directly out. Don't go home. Don't stop to buy anything. Can you do that?"

Dr. Houllier touched his face again. "I've worked here for more than forty years . . ."

"I know. You told me. But you have to think about your patients. You can't help them if you're dead. These guys are serious."

Dr. Houllier was silent for moment. Then he said, "How long would I have to stay away?"

"Not long. A day? Two? Give me your number. I'll call you when it's safe to come back."

"I guess the world won't stop spinning if I go away for forty-eight hours." He crossed to his desk and scrawled a number across the bottom of one of his forms. "What are you going to do?"

"Things you're better off not knowing about. They'll conflict with your Hippocratic Oath. That's pretty much guaranteed."

Dr. Houllier retrieved his shoe, dropped his ruined lab coat in the trash, straightened his tie, and led the way to his parking spot. A Cadillac was sitting in it. It was white. Maybe from the 1980s. It was a giant barge. It looked like it should have been in a soap opera, with cattle horns on its hood. Dr. Houllier climbed in. I watched him drive away then found my way back to the ambulance bay. The Lincoln was still there, exactly where I left it. I was relieved. Ever since I found Dr. Houllier on the morgue floor, a worry had been nagging at the back of my mind. I figured there was a chance Dendoncker's guy had come across it when he was looking for me.

I opened the back door. The guys in the suits were awake. Both of them. They started wriggling. Trying to get out. Or trying to get me. And also trying to speak. I couldn't understand what they wanted to say. I guess their jaws were messed up. I took the scalpel out of my pocket and held it up so they would be clear what it was. I tossed it behind the guy in the darker suit's back, on the floor, where he could reach it. I threw Mansour's keys in after it. Then I closed the door and went back inside. I hurried to the main entrance. Passed the woman with the pearls. Crossed under the globe and the dome and emerged onto the street. I looped around the outside of the building to the place where I'd left the Caprice. It was in a gap between two smaller, municipal-style buildings diagonally opposite the ambulance bay's gate. I pushed a dumpster in front of it. It wasn't great cover but it obscured the car a little. It was better than nothing.

It took me four and a half minutes to get from the Lincoln to the Chevy. After another nine I saw the ambulance bay gates twitch. They began to slide open. I started the Chevy's motor. As soon as the gap between the two halves was wide enough the Lincoln burst out onto the street. It turned right, so it didn't pass in front of me. I waited two seconds. That wasn't nearly long enough, but it was as long as I could risk in the circumstances. I swung around the dumpster and turned to follow.

The conditions were terrible for tailing anyone. I was in a car that might well be recognized. There was no traffic to use as cover. I had no team members to rotate with. The streets were twisty and chaotically laid out so I had no option but to keep close. Which was easier said than done. Whoever was driving the Lincoln knew where he was going. He knew the route. He knew when to turn. When to accelerate. When to slow down. And when he didn't have to.

I was pushing the Chevy as hard as I could but the Lincoln was still pulling away from me. It took a turn, fast. I lost sight of it. I leaned harder on the gas. Harder than I was comfortable with. The car pitched on its worn springs and the tires squealed as I barreled around a bend. A cardinal error when you're trying to avoid drawing attention. I made it around another tight curve. The tires squealed again. But the noise didn't give me away. Because there was no one to hear it.

There was no sign of the Lincoln. Just empty pavement leading to a T-junction. I leaned on the gas harder still, then slammed on the brakes. The tires squealed again and I stopped with the hood sticking out into the perpendicular street. There was a little store in front of me. It sold flowers. A woman was tending to the window display. She glared at me then retreated from sight. I looked right. I looked left. There was no trace of the Lincoln. There were no signs to suggest that one way led to a more popular destination. No marks on the pavement to indicate one way carried more traffic. No clue to tell me which way the other car had gone.

I knew I was facing west. So if I turned left, the road would take me south. Toward the border. Which was another dead end. If I turned right, it would take me north. It would maybe loop back to the long road past The Tree. To the highway. Away from the town. Away from Dendoncker and his goons and his bombs. But also away from Fenton.

I turned left. The road opened out. Stores and businesses gave way to houses. They were low and curved and roughly rendered. They had flat roofs with the ends of wide, round beams protruding from the tops of their walls. Their windows were small and they were set back like sunken eyes in tired old faces. All the houses had some kind of porch or covered area so the owners could come outside and still be protected from the sun. But no one was outside just then. No people were in sight. And no black Lincolns. No cars at all.

Soon a street branched off to the right. I slowed and took a good look. Nothing was moving. There was a gap, then a street branched off to the left. Nothing was moving anywhere along it, either. There was a longer gap, and another street to the right. Something blinked red. All the way at the far end. A car's brake lights going out after the transmission was shifted into Park and the motor was shut off. I made the turn and crept closer. The car was the Lincoln. It was at the curb outside the last house on the right. A truck was stopped halfway along the street, next to a telegraph pole. It was from the telephone company. No one was working nearby so I pulled in behind it. I saw the three guys climb out of the Lincoln. Mansour had been driving. They hurried up the path. His keys were still in his hand. He selected one. The mortise, I guessed. Unlocked the door. Opened it. And they all disappeared inside.

I pulled out, looped around the truck, and stopped behind the Lincoln. The walls of the house it was by were bleached and cracked by the sun. They were painted a deeper shade of orange than its neighbors. It had green window frames. A low roof. It was surrounded by trees. They were short and twisted. There were no buildings beyond it. And none opposite. Just a long stretch of scrubby sand with a scattering of cacti leading up to the border. I took out the gun I'd captured and made my way up the path. The door was made from plain wooden planks. They looked like flotsam washed up on a desert island. The surface was rough. It had been bleached almost white. I tried the handle. It was made out of iron, pitted with age and use. And it was locked. I stood to the side and knocked. The way I used to when I was an MP. When I wasn't asking to be let in. When I was demanding.

Chapter 21

There was no response. I knocked again. Still nothing.
I took out the keys I'd found in the Chevy after the guy jumped off
the roof at the construction site. Selected the mortise. Stretched out
and slid it into the lock.

The key turned easily. I worked the handle and pushed the door.
Its hinges were dry. They screeched in protest. No one came running. No one shouted a challenge. No one fired into the gap. I
waited for ten seconds, just listening. There was nothing but silence. No footsteps. No creaking floorboards. No breathing. Not
even a ticking clock. I stood and stepped through the doorway. My
plan was to shoot Mansour on sight. I had no desire to repeat our
death match. And I would shoot either of the others if they went for
a gun. Then I'd make the final one talk. Or maybe write, if his
speech was unintelligible due to his injured jaw. And finally I'd
shoot him, too, in the interest of evening the odds.

It was cool in the house. The temperature was maybe fifteen degrees lower than outside. Whoever built the place knew what they were doing. The walls were thick. Made out of some incredibly dense material. The structure could absorb an immense amount of heat. That would make it comfortable in the day. And it would release the heat during the night, making it comfortable then, too.

The place also smelled musty. Of old furniture and possessions. It must have been a weird residual effect because there was nothing in the house. No chairs. No tables. No couches. And there were no people visible, either. The room I had stepped into was large and square. The floor was wooden. It was shiny with age and polish. The walls were smooth and white. The ceiling was all exposed beams and boards. Ahead there was a door. The top half was glass. I could see it led out to a terrace. It was covered, for shade. There was a kitchen to the right. It was basic. A few cupboards, a simple stove, a plain countertop made of wood. There were two windows set into the long wall on the right. They were small. And square. But even so they reminded me of portholes on a ship. There were three doors in the wall to the left. They were all closed. And in the center of the floor there was something strange. A hole.

The hole was more or less circular. Its diameter was probably about eight feet, on average. Its edges were rough and jagged like someone had smashed their way through with a sledgehammer. The top of a ladder was sticking out. About three feet was visible. It was an old-fashioned wooden thing, angled toward the door I'd just come through. I approached it, treading softly, trying to make no noise. I peered into the space below. The floor was covered with tiles. They were about a yard square. The walls were roughly boarded. There was a furnace. A water tank. And a whole bunch of pipes and wires. The pipes were lead. The wires were covered with cloth insulation. Anyone who lived there would be lucky not to get poisoned or electrocuted. The heating equipment looked newer, though. And large. Maybe too large for the original trapdoor. Maybe that's why someone had busted through the floor.

I walked around the hole. The full 360 degrees. I wanted to get a good look into all four corners of the cellar. No one was there. There was no one in the kitchen. I tried the first door in the left-hand wall. I kicked it open and ducked to the side. The room was empty. I guessed it had been a bedroom, but I couldn't be sure. There was no furniture. And no people. The next door led to a bathroom. There was a tub. A toilet. A basin. A medicine cabinet with a mirrored front, set into the wall. A drip from a dull metal faucet landed on a stained patch on the porcelain before trickling down the drain. It was the only thing I'd seen move since I entered the house. But I still had one room left to check. It was the farthest from the entrance. The most natural place to take shelter. Ancient psychology at work. I kicked the door. I guessed I'd found another bedroom. It was larger. Farther from the street. More desirable. But just as empty.

There was nowhere else three guys could hide. There was no second floor. There were no other rooms. No closets. But there was one place I hadn't checked as thoroughly as the rest. One place I hadn't actually set foot in. I crossed to the edge of the hole in the floor. Looked down again. Still saw no one. I reached for the top of the ladder. Felt beads of sweat start to prickle across my shoulders. I didn't like the thought of disappearing belowground. Of the ladder breaking. Leaving me trapped. I pictured the Chevy, sitting outside. Its tank was three-quarters full. I could leave the place far behind. Never look back. Then I pictured Fenton. Dendoncker. And his bombs.

I took a breath. Swung my left foot onto one of the rungs. Gradually transferred my weight. The ladder creaked. But it held. I swung my right foot over, two rungs down. Made my way to the bottom. Slowly and smoothly. The ladder wobbled. It flexed. But it didn't collapse.

I moved so that my back was to the wall and scanned the space. I was wasting my time down there. That was clear. There was nowhere one guy could hide, let alone three. The only cover came from the furnace and the water tank and I'd already seen them from above. No one was lurking behind either of them. I gave each one a good shove. Neither gave way. Neither was concealing a secret entrance to any kind of subterranean lair. I checked the walls for hidden exits. Examined the floor for disguised trapdoors. And found nothing.

I crept back up the ladder. And crossed to the exit to the left of the kitchen. The door was locked. I tried the key. It opened easily. Beyond it another path snaked away to the street on the other side of the house. There was no sign of the three guys. And no sign of a car. I slammed the door. I was mad at myself. The guys weren't meeting anyone there. And they weren't hiding. The place was a classic cutout. Designed to throw off a tail. As old as time itself. You go in one side. You come out the other. The guys must have had a vehicle stashed somewhere. They were probably gone before I was even out of the Chevy. And gone with them, any immediate hope of finding Fenton.

Chapter 22

Losing contact with Dendoncker's guys was a setback. A major one. That was a fact. There was no denying it. There was no disguising it. And there was no point dwelling on it. What had happened, happened. I could rake over the coals later, if I felt there was anything to gain from it. But just then, all that mattered was picking up the scent. I had no idea where they had gone. They had a whole town to hide in. A town they knew a lot better than I did. Or they could have gone farther afield. Fenton said Dendoncker was paranoid. I had no idea what kind of precautions he might take. I needed to narrow my options. Which meant I needed intel. If any was available.

I drove fast all the way to the arch that led to the courtyard at Fenton's hotel. The spot directly outside her room—the old wheelwright's shop—was free. I dumped the Chevy and jumped out. The next problem was getting the door open. There was no physical key. No lock to pick. Just some weird code that showed up on a phone.

Her phone. Even if I had it I wouldn't know what to do. So I went old school. I turned my back to the door. Scanned all four directions. Saw no one on foot. No one in any vehicles. No one at any windows. I hoped what Fenton had said about knocking out the security cameras was right. Then I lifted my right knee and smashed the sole of my foot into the door.

The door flew open. It banged against the internal wall and bounced back. I turned and nipped through the gap before it closed. Inside, I saw Fenton's bed was made. The cushions had been straightened on the couch. And her suitcase was again sitting on the floor next to the door.

I crossed to the window and closed the curtains. I took the chair from the desk and used it to wedge the door. It wouldn't withstand a serious attempt to get in but should at least stop the door swinging open in the breeze. I carried her case to the bed. Then I picked up the room phone and dialed a number from memory.

My call was answered after two rings. The guy at the other end was on a cell. His voice was echoey and disembodied but I could make out his words well enough.

"Wallwork," he said. "Who's this?"

Jefferson Wallwork was a special agent with the FBI. Our paths had crossed a little while ago. I helped him with a case. Things had worked out, from his point of view. He said he owed me. He said I should call if I was ever in a bind. I figured this counted.

I said, "This is Reacher."

The line went silent for a moment.

"Is this a social call, Major? Only I'm kind of busy."

"It's not Major anymore. Just Reacher. I've told you before. And no. This is not social. I need some information."

"There's this thing now. It's called the Internet."

"I need specialized information. A woman's life is on the line."

"Call 911."

"She's a veteran. She also worked for you guys. She got her foot blown off for her trouble."

I heard Wallwork sigh.

"What do you need to know?"

"She worked at a place called TEDAC. The Terrorist Explosive Device Analytical Center. Do you know it?"

"I know of it."

"She got wind of a plot to distribute bombs, here in the United States. There's the potential for a lot of people to get killed. The guy behind it is named Dendoncker. Waad Ahmed Dendoncker."

"What kind of bombs?"

"I don't know. Ones that explode."

"How many?"

"Don't know. Too many."

"Shit. OK. I'll get the right people on it."

"That's not all. The woman's missing. I believe Dendoncker's holding her. I believe he's planning to kill her. So I need all the addresses associated with him, and his business. It's called Pie in the Sky, Inc. You'll need to dig deep. He owns it through a whole bunch of shell companies. One's probably called Moon Shadow Associates."

"This woman. What's her name?"

"Michaela Fenton."

"Last known whereabouts?"

"Los Gemelos, Arizona. It's a small town, right on the border."

"She's out there undercover? From TEDAC? That's not SOP.

The nearest field office should be handling it. What's going on? Where's her partner?"

"She doesn't have a partner. She left the Bureau. This is more of a personal initiative."

Wallwork was silent for a moment. "I don't like the sound of that. The last former agent I know who went down the *personal initiative* route is now in federal prison. His ex-partner tried to help. It got her killed."

I said nothing.

"All right. I'll try. But no promises. TEDAC's not the kind of place you mess around with. It's locked down tighter than a bull-frog's ass. They deal with some seriously sensitive shit. Ask the wrong person the wrong thing, it's not just the end of your career. You don't just get fired. You can wind up in jail."

"I get that. Don't do anything to jam yourself up. Here's another angle you could try. I suspect Dendoncker is using his business as a front for smuggling. I don't know what, or who for."

"OK. That might help. I have a buddy in the DEA. Another at ATF. I'll tap them up. When do you need this by?"

"Yesterday."

"Can I get you on this number?"

"You should be able to. For a while, at least."

I hung up the phone, made sure the ringer was on, and turned to the bed. I unzipped Fenton's case and flipped it open. Everything was neatly folded and rolled, just like before. A hint of her perfume floated up. I felt even more intrusive than I had two nights ago. I pulled her stuff out. There was the same combination of clothes and toiletries and props for changing her appearance. I found nothing new. No notes. No files. No "if you're reading this . . ." letters.

The guns I'd taken from the guys at The Tree were missing. And she'd taken a couple of other things. The extra ammunition for her Glock. And her field dressing kit. That made sense given what she'd been planning. Everything else in her case was familiar. Including a stack of cards from the Red Roan. Like the one she said she found in the dud bomb, along with her brother's fingerprint. And a condom. Something about that had sounded off-key when she told me. It still didn't ring true. I couldn't place why. It was like a discordant hum at the back of my mind. Faint, but there.

I started to replace Fenton's belongings and I uncovered her spare foot wrapped in a shirt. A thought hit me when I saw it. I felt a sudden surge of optimism. I rushed out to the car and grabbed the limb Dendoncker's guy had dropped on the table at the Prairie Rose. I brought it inside the room. Compared it with the one from the suitcase. Both had sockets made of carbon fiber. I ran my fingers around inside them, tracing the shape. The contours felt identical. Both had titanium shafts. They were the same length. The only thing that was different was the shoe. One was a boot. The other a sneaker. Not enough to prove that Dendoncker's claim to be holding her was a bluff.

I shook off the disappointment and finished repacking Fenton's case. I did it as neatly as I could. Replaced it by the door, ready to take to the car. Then I searched the rest of the room again. I checked every hiding place I had ever come across. Every trick I had ever heard of anyone using to conceal stuff. And I found nothing. I was left alone with Fenton's foot lying in the center of the bed and a digital clock on the nightstand. Its cursor was flashing despondently. It was counting the seconds. Seconds that Fenton may not have to spare.

I got brought back to the present by a sound. The phone, chirping away on the desk. It was Wallwork.

He said, "Mixed progress. The smuggling? I got nowhere. My DEA guy quit last week. And my ATF buddy is out sick. Long term. He got shot. But I do have better news about TEDAC. An old supervisor of mine transferred there. He trusts me. He'll help if he can. I reached out. He hasn't gotten back to me yet. But he will."

"Addresses?"

"I turned up a bunch. All with connections to this Dendoncker guy's business. Most seemed like shells. I think you were right about that. I did find one that seemed legitimate. It's in the town you mentioned." He recited a unit number and a street name.

"Where is that in relation to the town center?"

I heard Wallwork's computer keys rattle. "A mile west. It's a straight shot. Only one road goes out that way. It looks like Dendoncker's is the only building on that road."

"OK. Anything else?"

"Not within five hundred miles. And nothing that isn't a lawyer's office or a PO Box."

"How about Dendoncker personally?"

"That's where things get stranger. There's no record of him owning any property anywhere in the state. I checked with the IRS. He does pay taxes. His returns are handled by his accountant. I found the address on his file."

"Tell me."

"It won't do you any good. I looked on Google Earth. It's a vacant lot. I'm trying to trace the owner, but so far it's just another bunch of shell corporations."

"Is Dendoncker married? Is there anything in a wife's name?"

"There's no record of a marriage. Nothing about this smells right,

Reacher. My advice is to walk away. I know you won't, so at least be careful."

"There's one more place you could check." I gave him the address of the house I followed the Lincoln to.

Wallwork paused while he jotted the details down. "OK. Will do. I'll get back to you the moment I learn more."

Chapter 23

I thanked Wallwork before I hung up the phone but I was just being polite. The truth was his information was no use to me at all. Not in the short term, anyway. I figured his contact within TEDAC could bear fruit, in due course. He might help get an angle on Dendoncker's bomb plot. But my immediate concern was Fenton. Wallwork had only turned up one solid address for Dendoncker's business and I could tell from the location that it was one Fenton already knew about. It wasn't the place I was looking for now. That was obvious. It was too public for Dendoncker. His other employees went there whenever they had a flight to service. Fenton had been there for the same reason. And that was while she was actively searching for her brother. She would surely have found him if he was there. Which meant Dendoncker must have another site he used for his wet work. Maybe more than one. It depended on the scale of his operation. And I had an idea how to tap into that. It wasn't a sure thing. Far from it, in fact. But it was better than sitting around waiting for the phone to ring.

The Red Roan was busier than it had been when I passed by the day before. The lunchtime rush was still in full swing. There were two couples sitting outside. They were at round tables, perching on spindly metal chairs with brightly colored cushions and off-white parasols. Another pair of tables had been pushed together at the edge of the patio. Nine people were crowded around them. They were all different ages. Smartly dressed. I guessed they were colleagues. Probably worked locally. Probably celebrating something.

Not the people I was looking for. I was sure about that.

A pair of tall double doors was standing open at the center of the bar's façade. There was a hostess station to the right, just inside. It was unattended so I crossed to a U-shaped booth on the far side and slid around until my back was against the wall. The room was a broad rectangle. The bar and the entrance to the kitchen were at one end. The space between the booths and the windows was filled with square tables. They were scattered around apparently at random. Each had a potted cactus on it. The walls were roughly rendered with some kind of pale sandy material. They were covered with oversized paintings of horses. Some were being ridden by cowboys out on the plains, rounding up longhorns. Some were racing. Some were standing around, looking disdainful. There were ten other people in the place. Two couples. And two groups of three.

Not the people I was looking for. I was fairly sure of that.

Fenton had an advantage when she saw Michael's friend in there. She recognized her from a photograph. I didn't know any of Michael's friends. But I figured I had an advantage of my own. Experience. I was used to spotting soldiers in bars. Particularly when they were up to things they shouldn't have been.

A waiter approached. He was a skinny kid in his mid-twenties. He had curly red hair tied up in a bun on top of his head. I ordered coffee and a cheeseburger. I wasn't particularly hungry but the golden rule is to eat when you can. And it gave me something to do aside from flicking through a copy of the same paper I had read at breakfast while I waited for more customers to arrive.

I sat and watched for thirty minutes. Both couples paid their checks and sauntered out. One of the trios followed suit. Another couple arrived. It was the receptionist from the medical center and a guy in baggy linen clothes. He had white hair, neatly combed, and a pair of open leather sandals. They took a square table at the end of the room farthest from the bar. They were followed in by a group of four guys. They were wearing shorts and pale T-shirts. They were thin and wiry and tanned. They had probably worked outside their whole lives. They were probably regular customers. They took the table nearest the bar. The waiter brought them a tray of beers in tall frosted glasses without needing to be asked. He stood and chatted with them for a couple minutes then turned and smiled at the next customers who came in. Two women. One was wearing a yellow sundress. The other had cargo shorts and a Yankees T-shirt. They would both be in their mid-thirties. Both had brown hair down to their shoulders. Both looked fit and strong. They moved with easy confidence. And they had purses large enough to conceal a gun.

Maybe the people I was looking for.

The women took the booth two away from mine. The Yankees fan slid in first. She continued all the way around until her back was against the wall. Like mine. Her head and body were perfectly still but her eyes were constantly moving. Flitting from the entrance to each occupied table to the bar to the kitchen door. Then back to the entrance. Round and round without stopping. The woman in the sundress slid in after her. She glanced at the drinks menu then dropped it back on the table.

"White wine," she said, when the waiter approached. "Pinot Grigio, I think."

"That'll work," the Yankees fan said. "Bring the bottle. Don't spare the horses."

The women waited for their drinks to arrive and I watched them out of the corner of my eye. They leaned in close together. They were talking, but too softly for me to make out what they were saying. No one left the bar. No one else came in. The waiter dropped off their wine. There was a picture of an elephant on the label. The bottle was slick with condensation. He wiped it down with a towel. He tucked the towel into his apron pocket, then poured two glasses. He tried to strike up a conversation. The women ignored him. He soldiered on for another couple of minutes then gave up the attempt and drifted back to the bar. The woman in the sundress sipped her wine. She looked at her friend and started talking again. She was gesticulating with her free hand. The Yankees fan drained her glass in two mouthfuls and poured herself another. She wasn't saying much but her eyes never stopped moving.

I slid out from my booth and approached theirs. I wound up standing where the waiter had been.

I said, "Sorry for the interruption but I have a problem. I need your help."

The woman in the sundress put her glass down. Her hands rested lightly on the table in front of her. The Yankees fan switched her glass to her left hand. Her right started hovering over her purse. I waited a beat. I needed to see if it disappeared inside. It didn't, so I sat down. I leaned in and lowered my voice. "I'm looking for a friend. His name is Michael. Michael Curtis."

Neither woman's expression changed. The Yankees fan's eyes didn't stop scanning the room.

I said, "He's in trouble. I need to find him. Fast."

"What's his name again?" the woman in the sundress asked.

"Michael Curtis."

The woman shook her head. "Sorry. We don't know him."

"I'm not with the police," I said. "Or the FBI. I know why Michael's here. I know what he's doing. I'm not looking to cause him any trouble. I've come to save his life."

The woman shrugged. "I'm sorry. We can't help you with that."

"Just give me an address. One place to look."

"Have you got a hearing problem?" The Yankees fan's eyes were finally still. They locked on to mine and didn't move. "We don't know this Michael guy. We can't help you find him. Now go back to your table and stop bothering us."

"One location. Please. No one will ever know it came from you."

The Yankees fan reached into her purse. She rummaged around for a moment. Then her hand reappeared. She was holding something. Not a gun. A phone. She glanced down and it came to life. She tapped it. Tapped it again three times. Then held it up for me to see. The digits 911 were glowing on its screen. "Do I make the call? Or do you leave us alone?"

I held up my hands. "Sorry to have bothered you. Enjoy the rest of your wine."

I slid back into my booth and pretended to read some more of the paper. The Yankees fan put her phone away and drained the rest of her drink. She picked up the bottle and topped off her friend's glass. Then she poured the rest for herself. The receptionist from the medical center and her companion got up and left. The four guys ordered another round of beer. No one else new arrived. The waiter approached the women's table. They waved him away. The Yankees fan finished her wine. She slid out of their booth and followed the sign to the restrooms. The woman in the sundress stood up, too. She made her way in the opposite direction. Toward me. She stopped in front of my booth. She put her palms down on the table and leaned forward until her head was as close to mine as she could get without sitting. "The Border Inn." Her voice was so quiet I could barely hear the words. "Do you know it?"

"I could find it."

"OK. Room 212. Twenty minutes. Come alone. It's about Michael." She straightened up and made it halfway to her seat. Then she doubled back and leaned toward me again. "When my friend comes back don't say a word. This is just between you and me."

Chapter 24

The Border Inn was on the southeast edge of the town. It was a wide building. Two stories high with a flat roof tucked away behind a balustrade. Its name was sketched out in faded neon letters. At first the façade looked very plain. Then I realized I was approaching from what was originally its rear. The entrance was on the far side, facing the border. That wall was covered with all kinds of fancy carvings and symbols. The outline of a row of letters and numbers was still visible near the top. They spelled out *Grand Central Hotel 1890*. That must have been the place's original name. Whoever designed it must have expected the town to spread south. Not north. Now it seemed like it had been built the wrong way around.

The entrance opened into a wide rectangular lobby. There were dark wood panels on the walls. Most had cracks and peeling varnish. There were terra-cotta tiles on the floor. Some were plain. Some had intricate patterns in shades of orange and brown. A chandelier hung from the ceiling. It looked like real crystal. It was cut into elaborate shapes but the pieces were dull and cloudy with age. And dust. More than half the bulbs were out. Maybe they were broken. Or maybe that was some kind of economy measure.

The reception desk was directly opposite the main door. It was five yards wide and also made of dark polished wood. A guy was behind it. He had his boots up on the counter. They were long, pointy things made of snakeskin. There were holes in the soles. The guy had faded jeans. A blue paisley-pattern shirt. A black leather vest. It was unfastened. His arms were folded across his chest. A wide-brimmed hat was pulled down over his face. He looked like he was fast asleep. I didn't disturb him. I didn't need to. I knew where I was going so I crossed to the corridor that led to the stairs.

Room 212 was at the end of the second-floor corridor on the south side of the building. Its door was standing open half an inch. A skinny paperback book was down at floor level, stopping it from closing all the way. I peered through the gap. Saw nothing unusual. Just coarse brown carpet. The end of a bed with a floral comforter cover. The edge of a window with matching curtains. No people. No weapons. But still obviously a trap. It would have been safer to walk away. But playing it safe wasn't going to help Fenton. I needed information, and the only source I knew of was behind that door.

I stood to the side and knocked.

"Come in." It was the woman from the Red Roan. I recognized her voice.

So far, so good.

I pushed the door and stepped into the room. The woman was in the corner to my left. The room was large enough and the gap between the door and the frame was narrow enough that I hadn't seen her from the corridor. She was still wearing the yellow sundress.

And now she had a gun in her hand. A Beretta M9. A weapon she would be very familiar with if I was correct about who she was. She was aiming it right at my chest.

She had planned the setup well. She was too far away for me to grab the gun without giving her ample time to pull the trigger. My only move was to dive back through the door. But she would be expecting that. There was no guarantee I would be fast enough. Plus I didn't know where her friend was. She could have the corridor covered by now. And I needed whatever information she could give me. Whether she was in a sharing mood or not.

I pushed the book aside with my foot. Let go of the door. And raised my hands to chest height.

"To the bed." The woman gestured with the gun.

I moved across.

She said, "See the pictures?"

There was a stack of photographs on the pillow. I picked it up. There were five of them. Four-by-sixes. Color. Of five different men. All in Hot Weather ACUs.

"Show me which one's Michael," she said. "Then we'll talk."

I shuffled through the images. Slowly and carefully.

"Show me the wrong one and the vultures are going to be well fed tonight." She still had the gun leveled on my chest.

Two of the men were African American. One was Hispanic. The other two were Caucasian. Like Fenton. That narrowed the odds. One out of two is better than one out of five. But still not close enough for comfort. I pictured Fenton's face. She wasn't Michael's identical twin. That was obvious. And I'd never seen him. I had no idea how similar they looked. But I had nothing else to work with. I compared the two guys' eyes to what I remembered of Fenton's. Their noses. Mouths. Ears. Hair color. The shape of their heads. Their height. Then I thought about what I'd do if I wanted to catch someone in a lie.

I tossed all five pictures back onto the bed.

"What kind of game are you playing?" I kept my eyes on her trigger finger. "Michael's not in any of those pictures."

The woman didn't lower the gun. "Are you sure? Look again. Like your life depends on it. Because it does."

"I don't need to. His picture's not there."

"OK. Maybe it isn't. How do you know him?"

"Through his sister. Michaela."

"His older sister?"

"His twin."

"Who joined the *chair force*?"

"Army intelligence."

The woman lowered the gun.

"All right. I'm sorry. I had to be sure. Please, sit."

Chapter 25

I lowered myself onto the bed. The woman came out of the corner and crossed to the other side of the room. She perched on the edge of an armchair that looked like it had been made in the fifties. And not cleaned since the sixties. The gun was still in her hand.

She said, "I'm Sonia."

"Reacher. How do you know Michael?"

"We met in the hospital. In Germany."

"Army hospital?"

She nodded. "Why do you think Michael's in trouble?"

"Why do you?"

"I never said I did."

"Then why are we having this conversation?"

Sonia didn't reply.

"My guess is that you haven't heard from Michael in three days. Maybe four."

She didn't answer.

"Add the fact that Renée is missing, too, and you're starting to panic. Rumors are starting to fly. That's why you met your friend for that liquid lunch. It's why we're here now."

"All right. I am worried. I can't reach Michael. It's not like him to drop out of sight like this. If it was just Renée who was missing that would be one thing. But both of them?"

"I need to know where Dendoncker could have taken him."

"Dendoncker? Why would he have taken Michael anywhere?"

"Michael was done working for Dendoncker. He wanted out. Dendoncker got wind of that. He didn't take it very well."

"That's not possible."

"That's what happened. Michael got a message to his sister. He asked for her help."

"No." Sonia shook her head. "You've got this ass backward. Michael isn't working for Dendoncker. Dendoncker is working for Michael."

"Michael's running a smuggling operation?"

"No. That's entirely Dendoncker's action. Michael just needs access to some of his equipment. And some raw materials."

"Why?"

"How's that relevant?"

"Do you want to help him or not?"

Sonia sighed and rolled her eyes. "There's a certain item Michael needs to build, OK? And transport. Secretly. And securely. Dendoncker has the infrastructure. Michael arranged access to it."

"OK. So, aside from the place west of town, what other premises does Dendoncker have?"

"I don't know. I don't work for him. I'm just a friend of Michael's."

"Where does Dendoncker live?"

"Nobody knows. Mexico, maybe? Michael mentioned something like that once. But I have no real idea."

"Where does Michael live?"

"He has a room here. But he doesn't use it much anymore. I guess he mostly sleeps at his workshop."

"Where's that?"

"I don't know. I never went there."

"But it's where he makes the bombs?"

Sonia was immediately on her feet. "How do you know about that?"

I stood as well. She still had a gun in her hand. "It's why he sent an SOS to his sister. He was in over his head. He knew it was wrong. He wanted to stop before it was too late."

"No." Sonia shook her head. "That makes no sense. Look, Michael was no angel. I'm not pretending otherwise. He started down a bad path. The operation is his shot at redemption. He believes in it one hundred percent. There's no way he wanted to stop. No reason he would want to. It's perfect. And it needs to be done."

"No reason? Maybe the penny dropped that killing innocent people is something that never needs to be done."

"What are you talking about? No one is going to get killed. He's a veteran, for God's sake. Not a murderer."

"He's plotting to detonate a whole bunch of bombs. You're looking at hundreds of casualties."

"No." Sonia almost laughed. "You don't understand."

"Then explain it to me."

"I can't."

"You can. You mean you won't. So I guess you don't want my help." I took a step toward the door.

"Wait. All right. Look, Michael's made a few prototypes. Sure. But he's only building one final device. He's using adapted signal shells. They emit smoke. That's all. A few people might get sore eyes but nothing worse than that."

"He's aiding Dendoncker's smuggling ring. And helping to sell illegal weapons. Just so he can plant a single smoke bomb? I don't buy it."

Sonia sighed and slumped back into her chair. "Dendoncker is a bad man. I give you that. I wasn't happy when Michael went to work for him. Far from it. But Michael was in a dark place then. Look, if Michael wasn't helping him, Dendoncker would find someone else. And it's a small price to pay in the greater scheme of things."

"To pay for what?"

"Success. For Operation Clarion. That's what Michael named it." Sonia leaned forward. "Picture this. It's Veterans Day. There are services and ceremonies all across the country. And at one of the biggest venues, at eleven minutes past eleven, the whole place fills with smoke. Beautiful red, white, and blue smoke. It'll be a sensation. Everyone who sees it in person will ask, why? Everyone who sees it on TV will ask also. It'll be all over the Internet. And Michael will be there to answer. I'll be by his side. The Pentagon won't be able to ignore us anymore. And the government won't be able to lie anymore."

"Lie about what?"

"Chemical weapons. Everywhere we fight. But in Iraq in particular. The Pentagon put together a report when the war was declared over. They sent a stuffed shirt to the Senate to answer questions about it. The official line was that only a very small quantity of chemical rounds were found and the risk they posed to our troops was minor. Which is bullshit. And we know it's bullshit not only because we were the ones getting poisoned and burned and sick. But because at the same time the data for the report was getting cooked, the army issued new instructions. For treating troops exposed to chemical agents. Detailed instructions. Which stated there was a continuing and significant risk to our deployed forces."

"So they knew?"

"Damn right they knew. But they lied. And why? Because of the shell cases. You need special ones. M110s are the most common. They look just like conventional M107s. More so when they're corroded or deliberately mislabeled. But inside they have two chambers. They hold two separate compounds. Each inert on its own. But lethal when they mix. And where did the Iraqis get the shells from? The United States and our allies. Powerful corporations. The government turned a blind eye to it. A classified report Michael saw said hundreds of thousands were sold. The politicians were in danger of getting embarrassed. So they threw us soldiers under the bus to save their own asses. And we're not going to stand for it. Not anymore."

"This kind of shell. Michael's using it for the smoke bomb?"

"Correct. Appropriate, don't you think? Kind of poetic?"

"Are you sure we're only talking about a smoke bomb? If the shells look the same, is there any way he could be making regular explosive ones on the sly?"

Sonia leaned farther forward. "I should slap you for that. Or shoot you. Yes, I'm sure. You think I'm an idiot? The shells look similar to a layperson. But not to me. Michael's done three separate tests. Out in the desert. In different wind conditions. I witnessed all of them. Do you think I'd be here talking to you if I'd been ten feet from an artillery shell when it went up?"

"I guess not. So when you do it for real, how will he set off the bomb?"

"The primary will be a timer. The secondary will be cellular."

"So Michael will be at the venue?"

"Correct. He'll drive out. I'll join him there."

"Where?"

"That was a secret. Even from me."

"When was Michael planning to leave?"

"Tomorrow. Which makes it even stranger that Michael's dropped off the radar now."

"Where does Dendoncker keep the equipment Michael was using? The raw materials?"

"I have no idea. Why are you so obsessed with this? Dendoncker isn't holding Michael. That would make no sense."

"You said Michael has a room here. Do you know the number?"

Sonia nodded to the wall behind me. "It's next door."

"We should take a look."

"There's no need. I already did."

"When?"

"A couple of days ago." Sonia looked at the floor. "I wasn't snooping. I'm not a bunny boiler. Michael didn't call me when he said he would. I was worried."

"What did you find?"

"Nothing out of the ordinary. His bed was made. His toiletries were in the bathroom. His clothes were hanging in the wardrobe. His duffel was there. So was his go-bag. Nothing was missing. Not as far as I could tell."

"Does Michael have a car?"

"He has two. A personal vehicle. And an old Jeep issued by Dendoncker. They're both still outside. Both as clean as whistles."

I said nothing.

"Now do you see why I'm worried? If Michael left under his own steam he must have felt some major heat coming down not to take any of his stuff or his car. In which case why wouldn't he call me? Let me know he's OK? Or warn me if I was in danger, too?"

"We should take another look in his room."

"Why? I told you what's there."

"A fresh pair of eyes never hurts. And we're not going to find Michael by sticking around here talking."

Chapter 26

Sonia sighed and rolled her eyes. She scooped up her purse from the floor and tucked the gun inside. "Fine. Come on."

She locked the door to her own room with a big solid key. It was on a heavy brass fob that was shaped like a teardrop. She dropped it into her purse, started down the corridor, and took out another key. This one was made of thin shiny metal, and it was on a flimsy plastic fob stamped with the name of a local drugstore. She used it to unlock the next door we came to. She pushed the door all the way open, took one step inside, and stopped in her tracks. She clamped her hand over her mouth, but she didn't make a sound. I moved up alongside her and stopped still, too. The room was a mirror image of hers. It was an efficient use of space. The bathrooms were half depth, so they fitted neatly next to each other, and kept the plumbing sounds away from the beds. But while Sonia's room was immaculate, this one looked like a tornado had ripped through it. The bed was on its side. The mattress was torn open in a dozen places and clumps of gray fibrous material were hanging out. The wardrobe was facedown on the floor. Shredded clothes were heaped up next to it. The chair was on its side. Its cushion was ripped. The curtain pole had been wrenched off the wall. The curtains had been sliced and left in ribbons on the floor.

Sonia said, "Who did this? What were they looking for? I don't understand."

"Does Renée have a room here?" I asked.

"Yes. At the other end of the corridor. You don't think . . . ?"

"I don't know. But we should find out."

Sonia closed Michael's door and led the way to room 201. She tried the handle and shook her head.

She said, "It's locked. Wait here. I'll go down to reception. Borrow a passkey."

I shook my head. "No. I don't want to involve anyone else. Have you got a knife in your bag? Or tweezers?"

Sonia rummaged in her purse and pulled out a little knurled black case. She opened it and revealed a whole array of small shiny tools. I guessed they had something to do with nails, but I had no idea what most of them did. She held out the set. "Take your pick."

I selected a pair of needle nose tweezers and a thin wooden rod. It was like a lollipop stick with a chamfered end. I bent the bottom of one leg of the tweezers to ninety degrees then crouched down and went to work on the lock. It was old and plain. But solid. From the days when things were built to last. It probably rolled off the line in a big, dirty factory in Birmingham, Alabama. One of thousands used all across America. Probably millions. Probably used all over the world. It was a quality item, but not overcomplicated.

I felt for the tumblers and found them right away. Easing them aside was another story. I figured the lock hadn't seen a great deal of maintenance over the course of its life. It was stiff. It took more than a minute to force it to turn. Then I stood, opened the door, and looked inside. The scene was almost identical to the one in Michael's room. But nothing like what Fenton said she had seen there.

The bed and the wardrobe and the chair and the curtains had been tipped over and ripped open. The only real difference was that the heap of ruined clothes on the floor were women's, not men's. The find was no big surprise. It wasn't conclusive. But it was consistent with the theory that Renée was suspected of smuggling Fenton's note to Michael. You could understand Dendoncker wanting to have both their rooms searched. He'd have wanted to see if there was any other illicit communication between them. Or anyone else.

There was nothing to suggest I needed to change tack. But nor was there anything to help figure out where Fenton was. Maybe if I had access to a forensic lab I could have found something. Some microscopic trace of rare dirt or sand. Some telltale fibers. DNA, even. But with the resources available, which basically meant my eyes and my nose, there was no point wasting effort sifting through the wreckage. It was frustrating, but those were the facts. Time was passing and I was running out of places to look.

I turned to leave and almost knocked Sonia down. She had crept up close behind me and was standing stock-still. Her eyes were wide and her mouth was hanging open.

"I don't understand." She stepped around me. "It looks like the same people did this. But why? What are they looking for? And where are Michael and Renée?"

I said nothing.

"Are they involved in something together? Wait. Are they . . . ?

No. They can't be. They better not be." Sonia strode farther into the room and kicked Renée's ransacked heap of clothes up into the air.

I said, "You and Michael? Were you . . . more than friends? Is that why you have a key to his room?"

Sonia turned to look at me. Her face was drained and raw. "It's nothing official. We aren't married or engaged or anything like that. We haven't told many people. But, yes. We found each other in that hospital. We saved each other. He's everything to me. I can't even think about someone stealing him away . . ."

This was not the scenario I had expected to walk into. I imagined I'd be dealing with a bunch of worthless, conscience-free mercenaries. The kind of people I'd happily pump for information then leave to rot when their half-assed scheme crashed down around their heads. Instead I found myself feeling sorry for this woman. Maybe she was naïve. But that isn't a crime. I guess she'd been duped by a guy who came into her life at a vulnerable moment. He must have been pretty persuasive. Even when he was off the rails.

I figured under the circumstances I should level with Sonia. There was no way to avoid it. Not without being unnecessarily cruel. But there was a problem. My death message skills were universally considered to be subpar. They were so bad the army had sent me for special remedial training. Years ago. It hadn't helped very much. Since then my preference had been to break bad news in public places. People are less likely to break down or freak out in front of an audience. I found bars and restaurants and cafés are the best. The whole process of ordering food and having it delivered and cleared away provides natural punctuation. It helps reality to sink in. I thought about the Red Roan. I thought about taking Sonia back there. It was very tempting. But I decided not to. It would take time to get there. Just then time was not my friend. And it certainly wasn't Fenton's.

I took hold of Sonia's elbow and eased her out into the corridor. "Come on. We better go back to your room. There are some things I need to tell you."

Chapter 27

Sonia took the chair. She perched at the front of it. Her whole body was rigid. She was wound up tight. I could tell she was a hairsbreadth away from fight-or-flight. I sat on the edge of the bed and faced her. I kept one foot on the floor near her purse. Her gun was still inside it. There's a reason the expression *don't shoot the messenger* is a thing.

I said, "I want to start with good news. There was nothing between Michael and Renée. That's for certain."

"Was nothing?"

"I'm getting to that. First we need to back the truck up a little."

I talked her through the whole story. All the way from Fenton receiving Michael's message to her botched attempt at snatching Dendoncker. Including the part where Dendoncker's guy told Fenton Michael was dead. Sonia was silent for a moment when I got to the end. Her eyes flickered from side to side as she joined the dots.

Then she said, "Michael got caught with the note from his sister? That's how everything turned to shit?"

"That's the way I see it."

"So Dendoncker had Michael killed?"

I nodded.

"No. I don't believe it."

I said nothing.

"And Renée?"

"I think she saw it coming. I think she got away."

"But not Michael? Are you sure?" Sonia's voice was on the edge of cracking up. "Like, totally beyond any doubt? No matter how tiny?"

"I didn't see his body. But I heard one of Dendoncker's goons swear that Dendoncker had killed Michael. And he had nothing to gain by lying."

Sonia got up and crossed to the window. She turned her back and pulled the curtain around her. "I don't know what to do with this. I can't believe he's gone. This must be a mistake."

I didn't know what else I could say.

Sonia disentangled herself from the curtain and spun around to face me. "If you knew Michael was dead, why didn't you tell me right away?" Her eyes were damp and red. "Why string me along? Why all that bullshit about wanting help finding him?"

"I didn't know what your deal was then." I held up my hands. "I might not be able to help Michael. But I can still help his sister. Maybe. If I can find her."

"You still bullshitted me." Sonia shuffled back to the chair and slumped down. "I just can't deal with this. What should I do now?"

"Leave town would be my advice. Now I have to get going. But first I need to ask you a question. It's going to sound insensitive. The timing's awful. But it could be important."

"What is it?"

"In the message Michael sent his sister, along with the card from the Red Roan there was something else. A condom. That seems weird to me. Does it mean anything to you?"

"No. Michael wouldn't have a condom. We didn't use them. And he would never send one to his sister. That's gross."

"It got in there somehow."

"Someone else must have put it in."

"I don't think so."

Sonia shrugged. "Maybe Michael was trying to tell her something. Like, to be careful. To take precautions. He did love cryptic messages. He was always leaving them for me. I generally didn't understand them, to be honest. I had to ask him to explain."

A condom as a warning to take precautions? It was possible. In the sense that it couldn't be positively ruled out. But it didn't seem likely. And as an explanation it didn't feel right. The voice at the back of my brain still wasn't satisfied.

Chapter 28

I guess the guy with the worn-out boots wasn't as heavy a sleeper as he'd made himself out to be.

His feet were no longer up on the reception counter when I got to the foyer. He was no longer lounging back in his chair. There was no sign of him at all. But two other guys were hanging around. Two of the guys from the previous night. The only two still able to walk. *They* were waiting for *me* this time. That was clear. They both puffed up a little when they saw me. Then they moved. The guy who'd been driving stepped in front of the double exit doors, which were closed. And locked, presumably. The guy I'd hit with the ax handle slunk around in the opposite direction. He wound up blocking the way back to the corridor. He needn't have bothered. I had no intention of going that way.

The men were wearing the same kind of clothes as before. Black T-shirts. Black jeans. Black combat boots. But now the driver's left arm was in a sling. And they each had a small backpack slung over one shoulder. Both packs were made out of ballistic nylon. Desert sand color, scuffed and stained and well used. And weighed down with something bulky.

The driver said, "Down on the floor. On your front. Hands behind you."

"Again?" I said. "Really?"

"Get down. Do it now."

I didn't move. "Were you dropped on your head when you were a baby? Was your boss? Because honestly, I'm worried. Virtually every creature on the planet has the ability to learn from experience. But not you, apparently. What happened last time you tried this? When you had three buddies to help out. Not just one."

"Oh, we learn." The driver nodded. The other guy swung his pack off his shoulder. He pulled back its flap and took out its contents. A full-face respirator. It was black with a butyl rubber coating; drooping, doleful triangular eyepieces; and a round filter case mounted on the left side. It looked like an M40 field protective mask. The kind that had been used by the US Army and the Marine Corps since the 1990s. Not the newest design in the world. Not the most comfortable. But effective. The guy pulled it over his head and tugged on one of the straps.

The driver held his pack between his knees, opened it, and took out an identical mask. He fumbled to put it on with one hand then stood still for a moment. It made him look like a depressed insect. Then he took out another item. A silver canister. It was about the size of a can of baked beans, and it had a ring and a lever sticking out of the top.

"Ever heard of CS gas?" The guy's words sounded muffled and tinny through the voice emitter at the front of the mask.

I'd more than heard of CS gas. I'd experienced it. Years ago, on the final day of a training module. A dozen of us were locked in a room with an instructor. The instructor placed a CS canister on a metal table in the center of the space. He pulled the pin and tossed it in the air. He was already wearing his mask. An older model. An M17, which was the standard in those days. We had to wait until the pin hit the ground. Then we had twenty seconds to get our masks on. We all made it. That part of the exercise was fine. The next part wasn't. We had to remove our mask and shout out our name, rank, and number. One at a time. And we could only put our mask back on when the instructor nodded. That was bad. Really bad. But it was even worse if the instructor didn't like you. If he pretended he couldn't hear you. If he made you repeat your information. He made one guy repeat his three times. Between each attempt he left a pause. Each one felt like an hour. To us. They must have felt like a year to the poor guy. The front of his smock was soaked with tears and snot and drool by the time we staggered out into the fresh air. He quit the program about ten minutes later.

"Well, we call this *DS gas.*" The guy held the canister up higher. "Dendoncker Special. It's like CS on steroids. It burns your eyes so bad you go blind if you don't get saline in time. And your nose? Your throat? Your lungs? Pain like you will not believe. I promise you."

I said nothing.

"Last chance," he said. "Get down on the floor. Do yourself a favor. Because if I have to use this, the game changes. You're going to have to crawl across to me. Lie at my feet. Beg me to save your eyesight."

I stayed still. "That's never going to happen."

"Come on, man." The other guy's voice sounded like a robot's. "This is science we're talking about. You can't fight it. You've got to respect the chemistry."

"Chemistry's fine." I still had the gun I'd taken from the guy outside the café. I was tempted to use it. That would solve the immediate problem. But a shot would be heard. And I had no desire to attract attention. Not just then. What I had in mind called for privacy. So I moved slowly to my left. Just until the driver was directly between me and the exit. "But me? I always preferred physics."

"I warned you." The driver flicked away the little clip that held the pin against the curved handle. He switched the canister to his left hand. Curled his right index finger through the ring. And gave it a tug.

It didn't budge.

I guessed this was the guy's first time. Arming a grenade is harder than it looks in the movies. The locking pin is made of surgical steel. One leg is bent at a steep angle. It needs to be. No one wants to be on the wrong end of an accidental discharge. The guy adjusted his grip. He raised his right elbow. Maybe he thought that would give him improved leverage. I didn't wait to see if he was right. I just pushed off my back foot, hard, and started to run. As fast as I could. Straight ahead. Directly toward him. I covered half the distance. Three-quarters. Then I threw myself forward.

My shoulder sank into the guy's midriff. It knocked him off his feet. We clattered together into the doors. A combined 450 pounds. And the effect of my weight was multiplied by the speed I'd gained. The old lock was no match for that. Not even close. The doors burst open. One swung around and crashed into the wall. The other came right off its hinges and cartwheeled away. The two of us landed on the ground. Him underneath, on his back. Me, on top. I was crushing his chest. I felt some of his ribs shatter on impact. Maybe a collarbone, too. Maybe both of them. But those injuries didn't matter. He would never feel the pain. Because his shoulders wound up level with the lip of the top step leading down to the street. My bulk pinned his torso in place. But his head continued to move. It swung around another five inches. Then the back of his skull hit the concrete. It split open like a watermelon. Something sticky sprayed up across my face. The guy twitched. Just once. And then he was still.

Chapter 29

Half a second later I felt a weight on my back. A couple
of hundred pounds. Then an arm snaked around my neck. It was
the other guy. He must have followed me out. Seen his opportunity,
with me practically on the ground. Dived on top of me. Sandwich-
ing me between him and his buddy. He kept stretching until the
angle of his elbow was wrapped around my throat. Grabbed hold of
his wrist with his other hand. Pulled back. Jammed his knee into my
spine for extra leverage. He was using all his strength. Straining like
a fisherman fighting to land the catch of his life. I reached around
behind me, scrabbling for his head, but he was leaning too far back.
That was smart. He'd anticipated the danger and was staying out of
harm's way.

He was going after me. I was going after him. Neither of us was
giving an inch. Neither of us was close to a breakthrough. He must
have sensed the deadlock. That suited me fine. If he was looking for
a battle of endurance he'd picked the wrong opponent. That was for

damn sure. He must have sensed that, too, because he started rocking back and forth, trying to ratchet up the pressure. That certainly raised his game. I was suddenly finding it hard to breathe. I flexed the muscles in my neck but I could still feel my windpipe starting to give way. Pain ripped through my larynx. My lungs began to burn. I needed to tip the scale in my favor. Fast.

I dipped my right shoulder and pushed down toward the ground at the side of the body I was still straddling. Lifted my left shoulder. Felt the guy on my back adjust his balance. He was trying not to slide off. Compensating by leaning the other way. The instant he moved I corkscrewed in the opposite direction. Jammed my left shoulder down. My right shoulder up. Twisted at the waist. Drove my right knee into the ground and heaved myself up. The pair of us pivoted to the left. We teetered for a moment as the guy realized what was happening and tried to fight the momentum. To reverse the motion. But he was too late. And he was still clinging to my neck.

We flipped over. Together. He was underneath this time. On his back. I was on top. Also on my back. He was pinned down. But he was still trying to strangle me. He hadn't given up. The opposite. He was trying to squeeze even harder. I guess desperation was setting in. He probably couldn't breathe very well himself with my weight on his chest. And he couldn't get his head clear. The ground was stopping him. I stretched around. Felt his mask. It was facing away from me. Toward the street. The angle was impossible. Then I realized he must have pushed it up onto the top of his head. He must have wanted to see better, but to be ready if the canister of gas erupted. I tore the mask off. Dropped it. Slid my hand down his forehead. Found the bridge of his nose. Pressed my thumb into his right eye. Poked my index finger into his left. And started to press.

I didn't press too hard. Not at first. He kept trying to crush my throat. I increased the pressure. He whimpered. Thrashed his head from side to side. Trying to break contact. But he didn't let go. I pressed harder. Harder still. I figured I was no more than a fraction of an inch away from his eyeballs bursting or popping out. I would normally consider that a satisfactory result. But under the circumstances, I had to be careful. His presence was a bonus. I didn't want to waste it. I needed him capable of answering questions. So I didn't increase the force any further. I kept my finger and thumb steady. I arched my back. Pushed my other hand between our bodies. Moved it down, toward his groin. Grabbed hold. Started to squeeze. And twist. Harder. Tighter. Until he screamed and let go of my neck.

I jumped straight to my feet before he could change his mind or try something else. I stamped on his abdomen. Not too hard. Just enough to immobilize him for a moment. Then I gathered up his gun and his mask and the gas canister. It had slipped out of the other guy's hand and rolled onto the top step. The pin was still in place. I picked up his backpack. Checked inside. He had a bottle of water. A coil of paracord. Some kind of tool. And a bundle of zip ties. The tool was in a tan leather case. It was like a folding pen-knife, with a whole bunch of extra blades and screwdrivers and scissors. The ties were heavy-duty. There were half a dozen. I put the knife and the ties in my pocket. I put the gun in the backpack. Then I prodded the guy in the ear with the toe of my shoe.

"That your car?" I gestured to the far side of the street. A Lincoln Town Car was parked by the curb. It was black. It looked like the one the three guys had driven away from the morgue.

He craned his neck around to see what I was pointing at, then nodded.

"Where's the key?"

He pointed at the body lying next to him.

"Get it."

"No way." All the color drained out of the guy's face. "He's dead. I'm not touching him."

"If you won't get the key, you're no use to me." I jabbed him in the ear again, a little harder. "Want to wind up like him?"

The guy didn't reply. He just rolled onto all fours, stretched across his buddy's body, pulled the keys out of his pants pocket, and held them up for me to see.

"Good. Now pick up the body. Put it in the trunk."

"No way. I'm not carrying him."

"His body's going in the trunk. Either you put it in there, or you join it in there. Your choice."

The guy shook his head, scrambled to his feet, and trudged down the steps. He grabbed his buddy's hands and pulled. He made it to the sidewalk and a gun rattled free. He tried to pounce on it. But he was too slow. I pinned the gun down with one foot. And kicked him in the head with the other. Not too hard. Just a warning. Which worked. He went back to dragging the body. It left a trail of dark, congealing blood across the street. I waited until he was halfway to the car then scooped up the gun and added it to the stuff in the backpack.

The guy popped the trunk. He struggled to lift the body. It was heavy. Its head and limbs were flopping around all over the place. Eventually the guy hauled it into a sitting position. Propped its shoulder against the fender. Moved in close behind it. Wrapped his arms around its chest. Heaved it up. And posted it in headfirst. He slammed the trunk immediately, as if that would prevent him being pushed in, too, and spun around. His eyes were wide. He was breathing hard. His forearms were smudged with blood.

I said, "Unlock the doors."

The guy prodded a button on the remote. I heard four almost simultaneous clunks as the mechanisms responded.

"Put the keys on the trunk."

The guy did as he was told.

"Get in. Driver's seat."

I collected the keys, followed him, and moved in close so he couldn't close the door. I took a zip tie from my pocket and dropped it in his lap. "Secure your right hand to the wheel."

He hesitated, then looped the tie around the rim. Fed the tail through the tie's mouth. Pulled until the first of the teeth started to engage. Slid his wrist through the gap. And tightened the tie half-way.

I said, "Tighter."

He took up half the remaining slack.

I leaned across, took hold of the loose end, and pulled it hard. The plastic bit into his wrist. He grunted.

I said, "Left hand on the wheel."

He rested it at the ten o'clock position. I took another tie and fastened it. I grabbed his elbow and tugged. He grunted again. His hand wouldn't slip through. I figured it was secure enough. So I closed the door and climbed into the seat behind him.

I said, "Where's Dendoncker?"

The guy didn't answer.

I pulled the guy's mask over my head and made a show of adjusting the straps. Then I placed the canister of gas on the armrest between the front seats.

"DS gas, your friend said. Before he died. Like CS gas on steroids. Am I getting that right?"

The guy nodded.

"I don't believe him. I think this is a dummy. A prop. I think you guys were trying to bluff me. I think I should pull the pin. See what happens."

The guy started thrashing around in his seat, sticking his elbow out, trying to knock the canister out of my reach. "No!" he said. "Please. It's real. Don't set it off."

"Then answer my question."

"I can't. You don't get it. Dendoncker—you don't cross him. Nothing's worth doing that."

Chapter 30

I tapped the gas canister. "This stuff makes you blind, right? Keeping your eyesight—that sounds worth it."

The guy shook his head. "I had a friend. We worked together for five years. For Dendoncker. My friend used to go to Walmart, once a month. The nearest one's like a hundred miles away. They have some special drink he liked. Chai, he called it. From India. Dendoncker thought that was suspicious. He had my friend tailed. The guy following him saw someone in the store at the same time who looked like he might have been a Fed."

"Looked like a Fed, how?"

"He wasn't definitely a Fed. But he might have been one. That was enough for Dendoncker. And at the same time he was looking to sell a bunch of .50 cal sniper rifles. To some drug lord. From Mexico. There's a big demand for those things down there. A lot of money to be made. The buyer wanted a demonstration before he would part with his cash. So Dendoncker got my friend. Had him tied to a pole a few hundred yards away in the desert. Naked. Made the rest of us watch. Through binoculars. The rifle worked fine. The drug guy—he was a terrible shot. He fired a dozen rounds. Hit my friend in the leg. In the shoulder. Clipped him in his side, by his gut. He wasn't dead. But Dendoncker left him there. Sent someone to collect his body a couple of days later. I saw it. It made me puke. His eyes had been pecked out. Snakes had bitten his feet. Something big had taken chunks out of his legs. I tell you, I swore right there and then, there was no way I was ever going to let anything like that happen to me."

I tapped the canister.

The guy tried to twist around and face me. "Another time Dendoncker was selling land mines. To another drug lord. He was building a giant new compound. Wanted to fortify it. He also asked to see the merchandise in action. To prove it worked. Dendoncker had a bunch planted in some remote spot. Then he made a guy, I can't even remember what he was supposed to have done, walk through it. He made it ten feet. And that was the end of him."

"When I'm done with Dendoncker, he'll be in no position to hurt anyone. That's for damn sure." I tapped the canister again. "But this stuff? In this enclosed space?"

The guy leaned forward and banged his forehead on the steering wheel. Once. Twice. Three times. "I couldn't tell you even if I wanted to. I don't know where Dendoncker is. No one does."

"What do you know?"

"We were ordered to take you to the house. Someone would come and collect you from there. I have no idea where they would take you. That's way above my pay grade."

"How would they know to come for me?"

"I'd send a text."

"To what number?"

The guy reeled off a string of ten digits. It was an Alaska area code. Presumably a burner phone, used to disguise its current location.

"What message were you to send? The exact words."

"There are no exact words. Just that we have you."

"How long after you send the message would they arrive?"

The guy shrugged. "I don't know. Sometimes they're waiting when we get there. Sometimes we have to wait five minutes. The longest was maybe ten."

"Where do you wait?"

"In the house."

"Where is the house?"

The guy described the place I'd followed the Lincoln to earlier.

"Always there?" I said. "Ever anywhere else?"

"No." The guy shook his head. "It has to be there. Whoever comes, wherever they go, it's always through there. There's no other way, as far as I know."

"What's your deadline for delivering me?"

"No deadline. We have as long as it takes to catch you."

"Put your foot on the brake."

The guy didn't move.

I tapped the canister.

The guy sighed, stretched out his foot, and pressed down on the pedal.

I took off the mask and slipped it into the pack. Dropped the gas canister in after it. Leaned through the gap between the front seats. Cupped the side of the guy's head with my left hand and pressed it into the window. Used my right hand to slide the key into the ignition. I turned it. The big motor coughed into life. Then I slid the lever into Drive and dropped back into my seat.

I said, "Take me to the house. The sooner Dendoncker's guys arrive, the sooner I'll let you go. If you don't try anything stupid."

The guy wrapped his fingers around the wheel. The zip ties made it awkward but I figured he could get a good enough grip. And it would give him something to think about other than trying to escape. He switched his foot from the brake to the gas and pulled away from the curb. He steered straight along the front of the hotel. Turned left at the end of the building. Toward the town center. Slow. Steady. Not trying anything stupid. He continued for fifty yards, until we drew level with the mouth of a road on our left.

"No. I can't do this." The guy spun the wheel. He crossed his arms at the elbows and twisted his wrists as far as they would go. Held on until we were facing the opposite direction. Back toward the border. Then he straightened up. Leaned harder on the gas. Picked up speed.

I pulled my gun, leaned around the side of his seat, and held it to his temple.

"Go ahead," he said. "Shoot me. Please. I want you to."

We were back level with the front of the hotel. The guy didn't turn. He kept going straight and bumped up the curb onto the rough sandy scrub. A cloud of dust was thrown up behind us. We slowed a little. We were pitching and bouncing. The car was not ideal for that kind of terrain. It was too long. Too low. But we kept going. The guy showed no sign of stopping. We were heading directly toward the steel barrier. The needle was a hair above twenty. The car was heavy but there was no chance of it busting through at that speed. The spikes were solid metal. Thick. No doubt with deep foundations. Designed specifically not to get breached. It wasn't likely that either of us would get hurt. Not badly, anyway.

I leaned back and worked the seatbelt, just in case. I guessed the guy was aiming to disable the car. The radiator was sure to rupture on impact. Which would be a problem in that kind of climate. The engine would overheat in no time. It would never make it all the way to the house.

I considered knocking the guy out. Or crushing his windpipe until he lost consciousness. But whatever I did it was most likely we would still hit the fence. Which wouldn't be a major problem. Sonia said Michael had two cars at the hotel. That was only yards away. I could use one of them. With this guy in the trunk. He could still be useful. Just not as a driver.

Twenty yards from the border the guy pulled back with his left hand. Hard. The steering wheel twitched. Blood started to ooze from where his skin had been broken by the edge of the zip tie. Fifteen yards from the border he pushed his arm forward through the tie as far as it would go. Then he snatched it back again. Harder. With more determination. This time a flap of skin over his thumb joint tore loose. He cried out in pain. I could see bone. And tendons. Blood gushed from the wound. Maybe that helped to lubricate the plastic. Maybe it was just brute force. But somehow he got his hand free.

Ten yards from the border he shoved his hand into his pocket. He pulled out a quarter. Held it between his thumb and index finger. And rested it at the center of the steering wheel.

Five yards from the border he leaned forward. Tilted his head up. Exposed his throat. And pressed harder on the gas.

We hit the barrier square on and instantly about a dozen airbags deployed. The sound they made was louder than the crash. One sprang out of the door next to me. It hit my arm. It was hot. It al-most burned my skin. My view of the outside world was blocked out. It was like being inside a cloud. The bags started to subside. The air was thick with white powder, like talc. There was a smell like cordite. I released my seatbelt. Opened my door. And climbed out.

The engine had stopped. There was a hissing sound. A cloud of steam was escaping from under the hood. I pulled the driver's door open. The guy had been thrown back in his seat. His face was black-ened and burned. His eyes were wide and sightless. One side of his jaw was dislocated. It was hanging down at a drunken angle. The front of his shirt was soaked with blood. And there was a gaping hole in his throat. It was like he'd been shot. Which he had, in a way. He'd used the coin as a bullet. It had been propelled by the explosive in the airbag. Probably not what the NHTSA had in mind when they mandated the technology.

I reached in. Took the guy's phone from his pocket. Collected his backpack. And started to walk to the hotel.

Chapter 31

I made it five yards, then stopped. Because of the guy's phone. I was going to need to use it. Which meant I would have to unlock it. Which could be a problem.

The phone was the kind with just a screen. There were no numbered keys. No button to press, to read a fingerprint. I raised it and its screen lit up. The whole thing buzzed angrily in my hand. A message appeared. It said, "Face ID Not Recognized. Try Again?" Heaven help any phone that recognized my face, I thought. Then I turned back to the car. Returned to the driver's door. Opened it, and held the phone level with the guy's nose. It buzzed angrily. I lowered it and tried again.

No success.

I figured the problem must be the guy's jaw. It had been broken by the airbag. The phone must keep a record of the shape of its owner's face. That was different now. Its outline had changed. I tried pushing the guy's chin up with my fingers, then lined up the phone. No luck. I shifted his jaw a little to the side. Tried the phone again. It still wouldn't unlock. It buzzed again, more angrily than before. A new message appeared. "Passcode Required to Enable Face ID."

Six circles popped up below the text. They were small and hollow and bunched up together in a horizontal line. Below them there were ten circles with the numbers 0–9. They were arranged like a conventional keypad. I touched the zero. The first small circle turned gray. So, the phone had a six-digit PIN. Far too many combinations to have a reasonable chance of cracking it. Not without knowing something about the dead guy. Something to narrow the odds. I hit the zero five more times, just in case. The other small circles filled in. The phone buzzed angrily. "Passcode Incorrect. Try Again?" I thought, *Maybe.* But not there. Not standing in the sun next to a car with two dead bodies inside it. And not when there was another avenue I could try.

I walked around to the rear of the car and popped the trunk. The other guy's body was all the way forward, piled up against the seats. It must have slid there with the force of the collision. I reached in, grabbed the guy's belt, and pulled him back. I checked his pockets. Found another phone. Another one with no keys. It also asked for a Face ID. I wrestled the guy onto his back. Shuffled him down so that his face wasn't in the shadows. Held the phone level with his nose. It buzzed, and unlocked itself.

Getting one of the phones unlocked was good. But not perfect. I had no idea how long it would be until it locked itself again. Thirty seconds? A minute? Ten? However long it took it was no problem while I was near the car. I could use the guy's face to reactivate it. The issue was I didn't want to stay near the car. And I didn't want to use the phone near the car. I wanted to get into position at the house before sending the text and summoning more of Dendoncker's guys. I wanted to watch them arrive. To see how many there were. What kind of weapons they brought. It would take me a while to get there. Half an hour, probably. At least. The Chevy was at Fenton's hotel. I had walked to the Red Roan from there. And then on to the Border Inn. I would have to retrace my steps to collect it. Or get hold of the keys to one of Michael's cars. And there were a couple of other things I wanted to attend to on the way.

Under the circumstances, I could see no alternative. I had to send the message and let the chips fall how they may. If I arrived second to the house, no real harm would be done. I could surveil the place. Make a plan. It might impact the details. But not the outcome. The way I was feeling it didn't matter how many guys Dendoncker sent or what they brought with them. They were all going to be taking a trip to the hospital. Or the morgue.

I touched the icon for messages and entered the number the guy had given me when he outlined his orders. He said no exact wording was required so I tapped out, "Prisoner Secured. Heading to House." Then I added, "ETA 40 Minutes." I figured that might make a difference. Or it might not. But it was worth a try.

I didn't know if the phone would be usable for long so I dialed Wallwork's number as I walked to the hotel. He answered on the first ring.

"This is Reacher. The clock's ticking on a lead so I've got to be brief. I have an update. I interrogated someone connected to a member of Dendoncker's crew. She admitted there's a plot to plant a bomb at a Veterans Day ceremony. She claimed the bomb only releases smoke. For some kind of publicity stunt."

"Do you believe her?"

"We know Dendoncker's guy built a real bomb. Fenton's work at

TEDAC proved that. So, either the woman I spoke to has been duped and the harmless bomb will be switched, or there's a second plot."

"Where's the target?"

"The woman didn't know."

"OK. Better play it safe. I'll put out a general alert."

"Good. Anything for me?"

"The address you gave me? I traced the owner. It's a shell corporation. Another one. No connection to Dendoncker or any of his other companies. No other assets. And there's something else weird. It changed hands ten years ago. Right after Dendoncker showed up in the town. I found a report in the local press. It says the previous owner was a nice old guy. He lived there for years and pretty much got driven out. The house wasn't on the market. He hadn't wanted to sell. Then some unnamed newcomer—presumably Dendoncker—came after it. Aggressively. Like it had been targeted specifically."

"Why? No one lives in it now. It's empty. Dendoncker's guys use it as a cutout. There must be dozens of places they could have picked. The town feels like it's on life support. Why go after that house in particular?"

"Maybe Dendoncker planned to live there, and changed his mind? Or had some other scheme for it that didn't pan out? There could be dozens of reasons."

"Could be, I guess. But do me a favor. Check who owns the neighboring houses. Check the whole street. See if anything else jumps out."

The call ended just as I reached the steps to the hotel's main entrance. The blood trail was still there. It was dry now. It had turned brown and crusty. The surviving door was closed. Someone had retrieved the other. They'd propped it up against the wall. I went in through the gap it left. Scanned the foyer. Saw that the cowboy boots were back, propped up on the reception counter. They were the same ones. Snakeskin. Holes in their soles. I was glad they were there. It meant ticking the next item off my list would be nice and easy.

The guy was lounging back in his chair. His vest was still unbuttoned. His hat was pulled down over his face again. And he still wasn't really asleep. His whole body stiffened as I came close. He wasn't expecting to see me again. That was clear. He'd probably thought the blood on the ground outside was mine.

I said, "How much?"

The guy fumbled with his hat, pushed it back, and did his best to look like he was only flustered because he'd suddenly woken up. "How much? For what?"

"Calling Dendoncker. Telling him I was here. What did he pay you?"

"Nothing. I mean, I don't know what you're talking about."

I grabbed the guy's ankles and pulled. His ass slid off the chair. He crashed onto the floor and squealed as he hit the tile. I vaulted over the counter and landed straddling his legs. He reached up toward a little shelf that wasn't visible from the other side. A shotgun was balanced there. It was an ancient thing. An L.C. Smith. Its barrel had been sawn down to about six inches. That would make it easy to wield. And it would still be plenty lethal at close quarters.

I said, "Leave it."

The guy kept on trying to grab it so I kicked him in the face. Not hard. It was more of a push. Just enough to knock him onto his back. Then I stamped on his hand. To discourage him. In case he felt the urge to go for the gun, again.

I said, "How much?"

The guy was rolling from side to side, clutching his crushed hand to his chest. "Nothing extra. He pays me every month. Five hundred dollars, cash. I report anything unusual. Or anything weird his people staying here get up to. Sometimes he puts out an alert. Like this morning. I got a text with a description of you. I had to call when I saw you. I had no choice. Mr. Dendoncker—he's a bad man."

"You always have a choice. Right or wrong. It's clear-cut. You just thought you wouldn't get caught. You chose greed. You used poor judgment. So this is what's going to happen. When you wake up, you'll leave town. Immediately. And you'll never come back. I'm going to check. And if I find you here, I'll make Dendoncker look like the Easter Bunny. Are we clear?"

"When I wake up? What, like, in the morning?"

"In the morning. The afternoon. Whenever it happens to be."

I grabbed him by the front of his shirt and hauled him into a sitting position. Then I kicked him in the face again. A little harder that time.

Chapter 32

I tapped on the door to room 212. Gently. I was trying to sound friendly. There was no reply, so I tried again.

"Go away." It was Sonia's voice, but there was an edge to it. I couldn't tell if she was angry. Or sad. Or scared. Then a thought crossed my mind. An unwelcome one. Maybe one of Dendoncker's guys was in there with her. Someone could have sneaked up while I was dealing with the pair downstairs. Who knew what the reception guy had reported. Sonia might have a gun to her head. Which meant I couldn't risk breaking down the door. Which severely limited my options. Until I remembered what Fenton had said about the routine she and Michael had with names. Sonia and Michael had been a couple. Maybe they did the same thing.

I stood to the side and knocked again. "Heather? You in there? You OK?"

I waited. I heard footsteps from inside the room. They were light, but slow. A moment later the door opened. It was Sonia. She was still in her yellow sundress. And there was no gun in sight. She leaned out into the corridor. Looked left and right, and spotted me. Her eyes were red. Her cheeks were damp.

"Reacher?" she said. "Thanks for checking in. But I'm fine. I just want to be on my own. So please go, OK?"

"I'm not checking in. I need your help."

"Oh. OK. With what?"

"Have you got a car?"

"Of course. Do you want to borrow it?"

"Where is it?"

"Parked out back."

"Good. I want you to drive me someplace."

"Where?"

"Have you got a go-bag handy?"

"Of course. Why?"

"Grab it. And your keys. I'll explain in the car."

Sonia's car was tiny. It was called a Mini, and with good reason. I barely fit inside even with the passenger seat cranked all the way back. It was red with white wheels, and decals of Old Glory on the roof and the curved front edges of the door mirrors. I wished she drove something more discreet, in the circumstances. But at least it fit in the hotel parking lot. It was in another courtyard, this one contained within the building itself. It was a small cramped space with a low arch leading to the street on the east side. I guess it was originally for receiving deliveries and allowing light into the rooms on the inner side of the corridors.

The street that ran from the arch led to the road the guy in the Lincoln had taken before making his final U-turn. Sonia turned left, toward town, and I brought her up to speed with events since I left her in her room. She saw the opportunity right away.

"I'll watch the back of the house," she said. "That way no one can sneak out unnoticed. Or in. I just have one question. If I see anyone, how do I warn you?"

"Honk your horn."

"Wouldn't it be better for me to call you? Or text? Otherwise I'll be warning them, too."

"I don't have a phone." I pulled out the one I'd taken from the guy in the Lincoln's trunk. The screen had locked itself. "Not one I can use."

Sonia reached around, took her purse from the Mini's token backseat, and balanced it on her lap. She rummaged inside with one hand, took out a phone, and passed it to me. "Here. You can use this."

The phone was old school. I flipped it open. There was a keypad on one side. A real one. And a screen on the other. It was small. Black and white. And it didn't even ask for a PIN.

"It's the one Michael used to call me on." Sonia closed her eyes for a moment. "He had a matching one. I guess he was getting paranoid, too. He didn't like the idea of lots of calls between numbers Dendoncker could find out about."

Sonia took me to Fenton's hotel. I switched to the Chevy and she followed me around the maze of streets until we reached the turn just north of the house. She peeled off and I continued to the street to the south. There were no cars parked at the far end. There were no cars anywhere in sight. That could mean Dendoncker's guys had fallen for my ETA ruse. Or they hadn't arrived yet for some other reason. It also meant I would have to find somewhere else to dump the Chevy. It was too conspicuous to leave on the route Dendoncker's guys would take.

I turned around, drove back to the bigger road, and tried the residential street on the far side. There was an RV parked halfway down. It was an antique. It looked like it hadn't moved in years. Its tires were flat. Its windows were opaque with grime. Its paintwork was a mess of beige and brown stripes, all crusted over with sand and dirt. The only thing going for it was its size. It was easily big enough to conceal a regular sedan. I tucked the Chevy in on the far side and made my way back to the house on foot.

There were still no vehicles nearby. I approached slowly and pushed through the tangle of twisted trees between it and its neighbor. I peered in through the first square window. Saw no one inside. Tried the other windows in turn. There was no sign of anybody. I crept around to the front and shimmied under the large window, past the door, to the far side of the building. Checked the smaller bedroom's window. There was no one. The bathroom window was frosted so I couldn't make anything out. I ducked below it and tried the larger bedroom. No one was there, either.

I figured that according to the plan, if they were already inside and somehow concealed, they would be expecting the door to open so that their buddies could deliver me. So I went back around, making sure not to pass in front of any windows. Slid the key into the lock. Turned it. Crouched down, and pushed. I figured that if anyone was attracted by the movement they would expect whoever was coming in to be standing. They would be aiming at head height, if they were over-endowed with caution. But no one was there to stare in my direction. No one was there to point a gun. So I went in and checked the house from the inside. I looked in every room. Looked down through the hole in the floor. Made absolutely certain. The place was deserted.

I had no car to take cover in. There were no buildings or natural features to give me shelter. So I went outside and pushed my way back into the thicket of trees. I sat and leaned against the wall of the house. The leaves and branches were dense enough. As long as I didn't move and didn't make any sound, a person could pass within a few feet and not know I was there. The clock in my head told me that if Dendoncker's guys were aiming to synchronize their arrival with my bogus ETA, they should be there within five minutes.

Five minutes crawled past. No cars arrived. No one walked up the path. There was no word from Sonia. I stayed where I was. Didn't make a sound. Another five minutes ticked away. And another. The guy in the Lincoln said he'd never had to wait more than ten minutes. I waited another ten. And another. That was thirty minutes. Half an hour after the implied RV. The waiting didn't bother me. I'd be happy to wait for the rest of the afternoon if it brought the right result. I'd wait all night. But what I didn't want to do was waste time. There was no point sitting around the water hole if the big game had been scared off. I checked the windows again, just in case. There was no one inside. So I made my way to the parallel street. I spotted Sonia's flag-on-wheels right away. I walked across to it and folded myself into the passenger seat.

I said, "It was a bust."

"Shit." Sonia frowned. "What now?"

"Any chance they approached from this side and saw you?"

"No." Sonia shook her head. "Nothing's moved the whole time I've been here."

I couldn't see what had gone wrong. The plan should have been sound. Maybe the text should have come from the other guy's phone. Maybe there had been special wording. Maybe the guy had been flat-out lying. Which was why I had wanted to bring him. But that hadn't been possible, so there was no point dwelling on it. If Dendoncker's guys wouldn't come out on their own terms, I figured it was time to make them come out on mine.

Chapter 33

Sonia said, "It won't work. You won't be able to get in. You need a transponder. I know because Michael had one. He left it behind one day. It got him into hot water. There's no lock. No keypad. The only alternative is the intercom. You have to ask someone to open the gate. You think they'll open it for you?"

"You think I'll wait for permission?"

I left Sonia to watch the back of the house and walked to the street where the giant RV was parked. Climbed into the Chevy. And headed west.

Dendoncker's company building was on its own at the end of a straight road, just as Wallwork had described. It was a simple square shape. Steel frame. Brick infill. Flat roof. Plain. Functional. Cheap to construct. And cheap to maintain. It was like the kind you see in business parks all over the country. There was a parking lot laid out in front. It had spaces for twenty cars. None were taken, and there was no movement behind any of the windows. There was nothing to suggest the place was owned by a murderer. That it was the hub of a smuggling operation. Or that it was about to be used to distribute bombs. There was just a sign on one side of the main door saying *Welcome to Pie in the Sky, Inc.* and a picture of a cartoon plane on the other. It had eyes in place of cockpit windows, a broad smile beneath its nose, and it was rubbing the underneath of its bulging fuselage with one wing.

I pulled up to the gate, which was just two sliding sections of the fence that surrounded the site. Chain link, twenty feet high. The wire was a decent gauge. The metal posts supporting it were stout. They weren't spaced too far apart. But it was only a single barrier. There was no inner layer. It would provide adequate security at best. Which was understandable. Health inspectors could show up. Clients. People could evidently look at images of it on the Internet, like Wallwork had done. If Dendoncker wanted to avoid attracting attention he couldn't afford for the place to look like Fort Knox.

I wound down my window. Next to me there was a metal pole, painted white. Four boxes were attached to it. Two were level with my face as I sat in the car. Two were higher. They would be for truck drivers to use. Each pair was identical. First there was an intercom with a call button and a speaker behind a metal grille. Then a thing the size of a keypad, but with no buttons. Just a plain white rectangle. Presumably part of the transponder system. Nothing I needed to be concerned with.

I reached out and triggered the intercom. I didn't expect to be let in. I didn't expect an answer. And I didn't need either. What I was hoping for happened right away. A camera mounted on its own pole on the other side of the fence panned around until it was pointing right at me. I stared into its lens and hit the call button an extra time.

I said, "I'm here. Come and get me."

I made a beckoning motion to the camera to make sure the message got through. Then I reversed for ten yards and turned the car around. I doubted anything incriminating would be left lying about inside the building. Or that there would be any clues as to Dendoncker's other locations. But over my years as an MP I learned never to rule out stupidity. And never to rule out luck. Guys who went AWOL turned up under the bed at their girlfriend's house. Stolen equipment was stashed in the trunks of personal vehicles. Plus, I was already there. I figured it wouldn't hurt to give Dendoncker something more to worry about.

I made sure the rear of the car lined up with the center of the entrance. Selected Reverse and pushed the gas pedal to the floor. The impact tore both gates clean off their runners, but the Chevy hardly felt a thing. I could see why they had been so popular with the police. I continued across the compound. Across the two rows of parking spaces. Slowed to check I was on target. Then accelerated again and plowed into the building's main doors.

The Chevy punched straight through. I hit the brakes and shifted into Drive. Pulled forward. Stopped. Left the car facing the exit. Got out. And listened. There was silence. It was unlikely a place like that would be wired to a police station. But not impossible. I figured I'd better work fast and keep an ear open for sirens.

I started in the office. There were desks against three of the walls. Each held a computer. They were all switched off. Each had one pedestal with regular drawers and one with a deeper drawer for files. They were all locked so I took two paperclips from a pile of old letters in someone's filing tray. Straightened them. Slid one into the lock on the nearest desk. Raked it back and forth until I felt the pins engage. Used the other to put pressure on the cylinder. Turned it. And opened the drawer. There was a bunch of regular clerical stuff inside. Quotations. Invoices. Records of other innocuous transactions. I flicked through the papers and only one thing stood out. The dates. There was nothing less than three weeks old.

There was no sign of the police. No sign of Dendoncker's guys. Yet.

The front left corner of the building was a receiving area. It had a roll-up door. A raised platform for trucks to back up against. And metal counters around three sides. Presumably for checking whatever got delivered. They would need ingredients for any meals they made from scratch. And from what Fenton had seen, plenty of high-end delicacies and beverages. There were no goods there that day. The bay was completely empty.

No sign of the police. No sign of Dendoncker's guys.

A door led to a storage room. It was next in line on the left-hand side. It had floor-to-ceiling shelves against every wall. Some had labels with different product names. Others had bar codes. There were only a few things there. A box with tiny packets of sugar, like some people use with their coffee. Some potato chips. A bunch of little bags of peanuts. Nothing to make it feel like the hub of a vibrant business.

The kitchen was at the back left corner. It was small. Clean. Sterile. There was nothing on the counters. Nothing in the fridge. The room to its side was a preparation area. It was full of shelves and packaging materials and boxes. I guessed it was where the orders for the different flights were assembled before getting loaded into containers for transport. There was a line of whiteboards along one wall. They were all wiped clean. It didn't look like there were any jobs in the pipeline.

No sign of the police. No sign of Dendoncker's guys.

The whole place seemed well set up. The different areas were lined up logically. They would make for an efficient workflow. There was nothing suspicious. Nothing out of place. But there was no reason for anything to be. According to Fenton the outgoing contraband was brought in from elsewhere by Dendoncker's guys and loaded straight onto the trucks. Any illicit incoming goods were collected and carted away immediately. The absence of anything incriminating didn't mean the place was innocent. Just that Dendoncker was smart.

The trucks were the only things I hadn't seen. I found the corridor that led to the garage and followed it into a large rectangular bay. There were six panel vans. Neatly lined up. Nose in. They were like the kind I'd seen parcel delivery companies use, only these were white with red and blue trim and a cartoon plane painted on each side. I picked one at random and checked the cargo area. It was immaculate. It looked like it had recently been hosed out. Like it belonged to a catering company with both eyes on hygiene.

Or someone who didn't want to leave any physical evidence.

The trucks' cargo areas were fitted out with racks. They ran all the way along both sides. The tallest space was at the bottom. It would be big enough for the wheeled trolleys with drawers I'd seen flight attendants use on commercial flights. Above there was plenty of room for containers that could hold the kinds of food and drink Fenton had described. Or sniper rifles. Or land mines. Or bombs. I wondered where the containers were kept. If they used standard sizes for that kind of cargo. Maybe they picked the closest fit and shoved a bunch of padding in any extra space. Or perhaps they had custom ones made. Maybe with foam inserts to ensure nothing got damaged.

Another thought struck me. The kind of container would be irrelevant if there were no serviceable trucks to carry them. I was at a caterer's depot. There was a food store nearby. There was plenty of sugar. I could pour it in the gas tanks. Or grab a wrench and smash up the engines. Cut the cables and the wires. Slash the tires. Then I thought, no. This was Dendoncker's operation. Dendoncker, who had sent guys after me with CS gas. It was time to turn up the heat. Literally.

Chapter 34

I retraced my steps to the kitchen. There was a paper-towel dispenser on the wall. The cylindrical kind, packed with a continuous roll so you can tear off whatever amount you need. I took six pieces. Each six feet long. I brought them back to the garage. Removed the cap from each truck's gas tank and fed the strips inside. Pushed them all the way into the necks and left the excess hanging down to the floor. Then I went to the office. I grabbed the chair from the desk nearest the door and used it to smash the window. Took the chair and broke the windows in all the other rooms. Went back to the office. Opened the file drawer I'd broken. Pulled out half a dozen sheets of paper. Took them to the kitchen. Lit one of the burners on the stove. Rolled the papers into a cylinder. Lit it on fire, like a torch. Carried it to the garage. Held it to the strip of paper towel sticking out of the nearest truck's tank. Waited for the flame to jump across, and double-timed it to the exit.

The first truck exploded as I was opening the Chevy's door. I heard the hiss of the sprinklers springing into life. A bunch of floodlights lit up. They were mounted on the fence poles, facing the building. I jumped into the car and started the engine. A second truck exploded. I pulled away, drove across the compound, and stopped in the middle of the road on the far side of the fence. Daylight was fading fast and fat fingers of angry orange flame were stretching up into the sky. They sent shadows of the trees and cacti dancing wildly across the rough ground. I got out and walked back to the pole with the low camera attached. I grabbed hold and wrenched it around. I kept going until it was pointing at the building. I didn't know what kind of alarms Dendoncker had and I wanted to make sure he didn't miss the show.

I heard sirens after four minutes. I looked in the Chevy's rearview mirror. The right-hand side of the structure was consumed by flames. There was no chance any of the trucks could be saved. I was confident about that. It was possible some things could be salvaged from other parts of the building. I wasn't too worried on that score so I turned my headlights on bright. Made a note how far the beams reached on either side of the road. Doubled the distance to give myself a margin of error. Then I set off slowly to my right and bounced and weaved diagonally across the scrubland, away from the road, until I figured I'd gone far enough to not be seen by any cop cars or fire trucks that went barreling past on their way toward the inferno. I found a spot I was happy with and switched off the Chevy's lights. Then I felt a buzzing in my pocket. It was the phone Sonia had given me. I flipped it open and held it to my ear.

She said, "Contact. A man just came out of the back door of the house. He's huge. Bigger than you, even. He looked like he was in a hurry. He went to the next-door house, opened its garage, and drove away. In a Jeep. It was old, like the one Michael had. Guess he could be heading your way."

I thanked her and hung up. Less than a minute later an emergency convoy rumbled by. A Dodge Charger was in the lead. It had black-and-white livery and the light bar on its roof was flashing and whooping. Then there were two fire trucks. They looked like museum pieces, but in good shape. They were all shiny red paint and brass dials and valves. They all drove through the gap I'd made in the fence, then the police car pulled away to the left. Two cops got out and stood together, watching the flames. The fire trucks turned so they were facing away from the building. Crews jumped down and started swarming around. They got busy with their hoses and nozzles and pumps. It looked like a well-practiced routine.

I turned away and focused on the road from town. A couple of minutes later I spotted another pair of headlights. They were a pale yellow color. Feeble. They drew closer and I confirmed they were on a Jeep. It was a similar age to Fenton's but cleaner and in better shape. As it drew level I could see jerry cans strapped to the front and back. A spade and an ax hanging from the side. Mansour was behind the wheel. I watched the Jeep enter the compound. It stopped between the fire trucks. Mansour climbed out and headed for the building. A firefighter tried to stop him. He shoved the guy aside and kept going. The cops ignored him. Then he pulled his shirt up over his face and disappeared through the hole in the wall where the main entrance had been.

He emerged after two minutes. He strode over to the fire truck and grabbed the firefighter he'd just shoved. It looked like he was demanding information. The cops made their way toward him.

Slowly. He let go of the firefighter and turned to face them. He barked out more questions. The cops shrugged and shook their heads. He moved across to the Jeep and climbed in. The cops trailed along in his wake. It was like they were thinking about detaining him. But it was a halfhearted move. Mansour paid them no further attention. And they made no serious attempt at stopping him.

The Jeep sped back out of the compound. It passed me and I saw Mansour was on the phone. Probably reporting what he had found. I waited until he was fifty yards clear of me then started the Chevy rolling forward. I made it to the road. Picked up speed. Followed the Jeep's taillights. They were like faint red pinpricks. I kept the Chevy's lights off. The road was a straight line all the way into town. I'd be fine as long as no animals ran out.

Mansour took a left in the outskirts of the town, then two rights. I moved in closer to be sure not to lose him. A couple of minutes later I saw him turn into the street to the north of the house. I continued and took the next right. After a moment my phone buzzed. It was Sonia again.

"He's back. He pulled into the neighboring garage. Now he's out. He's on foot. Heading for the house. Unlocking the back door. OK. He's inside."

I hung up and pulled over to the side of the street. I stopped in a pool of shadow between two streetlights, ten yards from the house. There was a light on inside. But no other vehicles outside. He must have had one in another garage. I scanned the nearby houses. There was nothing to suggest which one it could be. I took the gun from my waistband and focused on the front door. Nothing happened for twenty seconds. Then the lights went out in the house. I wound down my window, ready to shoot if the guy ran. But he didn't appear. The door didn't open. Ten more seconds passed. Another ten. I opened the phone. Found the button to return the last call I received. Hit it. Sonia answered on the first ring.

I said, "Anything?"

"The lights went off. Did he come out your side?"

"No. Did he come back out yours?"

"No."

"Sure?"

"A hundred percent."

"OK. Keep your eyes open. If he approaches, shoot first. Questions afterward."

Chapter 35

I closed the phone, slipped it into my pocket, and got out of the car. Mansour must have seen me tailing him after all. Or maybe he spotted Sonia's car. But whatever it was, something had spooked him. That was clear. Because he was staying inside. I could wait him out. There were no creature comforts in the house. And he didn't strike me as a patient kind of guy. Not as patient as me. I was pretty sure of that. But appearances can be deceptive. I had no idea how long he would stay. Every minute he lay low was a minute Fenton might not have. And there was no guarantee he would come out my side. He could sneak out of the back. Make me get involved with chasing him. Or he could go after Sonia. I didn't want to end up with two hostages to rescue. So I decided on a different approach.

I cut across diagonally from the sidewalk to the front right-hand corner of the house. Ducked down. Crept beneath the window. Past the door. Around to the far side. Ducked below the first bedroom window. And stopped outside the next room. The bathroom. The best room to break in through. The place you're least likely to find anyone hanging around. And if someone does happen to be there, they'll be in the least favorable position to fight back.

I took the knife I'd captured from the guy at the Border Inn out of my pocket. Discarded its sheath. Found its largest blade. Unfolded it. Heard it click into place. It felt solid so I reached across and worked the blade up into the gap between the two sash panels. I found the lock. It was stiff. I increased the pressure until it rotated far enough to disengage. I put the knife away. Switched the gun to my other hand. Raised the lower pane. Just an inch. And peeked in. It was dark. The room seemed empty. There was no movement. No breathing. No running water. Just a regular *drip, drip, drip,* like I'd heard earlier.

I opened the window the rest of the way and climbed through. I stood and listened. I couldn't hear anyone. Couldn't sense anyone's presence. I didn't move for five minutes. I needed my eyes to adjust to the dark as fully as possible. Then I moved to the main room. No one was there. I tried the large bedroom. The small bedroom. The kitchen. No one was in any of those places. I tried the external doors. They were locked. I found a light switch. Flicked it on. Saw nothing that helped. Which just left one place to check.

I went back into the bathroom and pulled the front off the medicine cabinet. The whole thing was a mirror. It was old. Its silver was tarnished in places. But it was good enough for what I needed. I approached the hole in the main room's floor. Stopped three feet from the edge. Used the mirror to look down. Saw the furnace. The water tank. But not Mansour. I worked my way around the circle. Started to the left of the ladder. Moved clockwise. Examined the space below. Inspected it from every angle. All the way around to the right of the ladder. No one was there. The guy had disappeared. There was no trace of him at all.

He must have heard me breaking into the bathroom and used the opportunity to escape. I figured I'd better check in with Sonia in case he went out the back and found her. I put the mirror down and reached for my phone, and I noticed something on the floor. It was faint, but definitely there. A footprint. It was large. Size eighteen, at least. Maybe twenty. Pointing toward the front door. I scanned the path whoever left it should have followed. But I couldn't see any other prints. I crouched down and looked from every angle. And realized why. The trail stretched in the opposite direction. The guy had come in through the back door. He'd walked around the hole. Got to the top of the ladder. Turned around. And gone down. His feet must have gotten soaked at Dendoncker's building. By the sprinklers, or all the water the firefighters had hosed in. They must have still been damp when he climbed down. They must have dried out the rest of the way while he was in the cellar. Then when he came back up, they left no more prints.

The drying-out part was fine. But I couldn't understand why he'd gone into the cellar in the first place. There was just a furnace down there. And a water tank. Maybe, when he heard me breaking in, he decided to hide. It was possible. But the guy didn't strike me as the hiding kind. There must have been some other reason. I wasn't thrilled at the idea of going belowground but whatever drew the guy down there was my only clue as to where he might have gone. I stood up, grabbed the ladder, and started to descend. I went faster this time. I figured that if the rungs could take his weight, they could sure as hell take mine.

I found a footprint at the bottom of the ladder. Another big one. I could see where the guy had turned. And walked over to the wall. To the section directly below the door to the bathroom. Then he'd stopped. And stood still. There was a pair of prints, side by side.

But I couldn't see where he went next. I crouched down and checked the floor from every available angle. There was nothing. The trail had vanished.

I spun around, gun out in front. I had a sudden vision of the guy charging at me from behind the furnace or the water tank. I figured he could have made the footprints as a lure so he could attack me from behind. But there was no one racing toward me. No one was there at all. It was like the guy had just walked through the wall.

I turned back and rapped the wall with my knuckles. Maybe there was a hiding place behind it. Or a safe room. But the wall wasn't hollow. It was the opposite. It sounded dense. Solid. Far more so than I would have expected for such an old structure. I moved to the side until I was beneath the smaller bedroom. I rapped again. The note was different. It was lighter. Emptier. I tried beneath the larger bedroom. That also sounded thin and flimsy. I went back to the center. Tried again there. I hadn't imagined it. It was like a castle wall in comparison. I took out the knife. Extended the biggest blade. Stabbed the surface. The wood was old. It looked desiccated and weak. The knife penetrated. But not far. Only three quarters of an inch. Then it hit something hard. Some kind of metal. I tried six inches to the right. The result was the same. I shifted another six inches. And another. I hit metal every time. The tenth spot I tried was different. The knife sank in all the way to the handle. Six inches beyond there, it sank in again.

I moved to a thin gap between the panels near the third and fourth places I'd hit metal. I jammed the blade in as far as it would go, then pushed to the side and tried to lever the wood forward. The surface layer separated. It came off in a jagged hunk, but a strip was left behind. I tried a foot lower and got the same result. It was the original wood. I was sure of that. But it was stuck to something with incredibly strong glue. Something metal. It must be a door. I couldn't see any other explanation. But I also couldn't see any handle. Or keyhole. Or any method of opening it at all.

I started at the top left and worked systematically across and down. I was pushing with my fingertips, checking every square inch. Looking for a concealed button. Or a secret flap. Or anything a lock could be hidden behind. I found nothing. I tried the sections of wall on either side. Had no luck there, either. I tried kicking the wall. There wasn't a hint of movement. Not even any noise. It was muffled by the wooden skin. I turned, raised my knee, and drove my heel back like I had done at Fenton's hotel. It didn't even make a dent.

I began to search the walls farther to the side, then stopped. Putting the controls so far away didn't make sense. I had no experience with safe rooms but I assumed that if someone like Dendoncker had one, he would want to be able to get in it quickly. The whole point was to use them in an emergency. That implies a high degree of urgency. You wouldn't want to go to the far corner of the cellar to operate some kind of elaborate mechanism. Even keying in a PIN could be too much of a delay. Plus PINs can be guessed or discovered or betrayed. Some kind of remote control would be a better solution. Like cars have. Then another thought struck me. Sonia said the gate at Dendoncker's plant was operated by a transponder. And if that was a technology Dendoncker trusted in one key area of his operation, why not in another?

If a transponder was needed to open this hidden door, Mansour must have one. I didn't know what they looked like. I thought back to that morning, when I searched his pockets at the morgue. To his keyring. Transponders serve the same function as keys. That would be a reasonable place to keep one. And Mansour's had one thing that stood out. The square piece of plastic. I had dismissed it at the time as a fob. The guys at The Tree also had them. I pulled out the Chevy's keys. There was nothing similar on its ring. I guess the guy I took it from wasn't senior enough. Which left me with a self-defeating proposition. The only way to get a transponder was to take one from Mansour. But if I could get my hands on him to take his transponder, I wouldn't need it anymore. I figured the best option was to wait for him to come back out. Or to trick him into coming out. Or to lure another of Dendoncker's stooges down there. And hope he had enough juice to warrant a transponder.

Juice. Aka power. Status. And in some places, slang for electricity. If the door lock was remotely triggered by a signal from a transponder, it must run on electricity. I crossed to the wall by the water tank. Where the fuse box was mounted. It was a decrepit-looking thing. Dark wood. Scuffed and battered. Like an electrocution waiting to happen. I opened its door. There was a row of insulators inside. Old school. Made of porcelain. Six of them. Each cradling an exposed section of fuse wire. They all looked intact. They all looked equally obsolete. There were no labels. No markings. Nothing to indicate which circuits they served. I figured I could pull them, one at a time, and see what happened. But it would be quicker to hit the switch at the top that controlled them all. I reached for it, then stopped. At the bottom, tucked away in the right-hand corner, there was a pack of matches. I was amazed how often people put matches and flashlights in their fuse box. It made no sense. It was the wrong way around. The fuse box is the destination in a power failure. Not a starting point.

I took the pack, struck a match, and flicked the switch. The bulb on the first floor blinked out. The cellar shrunk until it felt no bigger than the flickering pool of light from the flame. I couldn't see much. I couldn't swear to it, but I thought I heard something. Behind me. From the wall below the bathroom. A click. Soft. But definitely mechanical.

I moved back to the section I'd been gouging with the knife. I took out my gun. Leaned against the wall. And pushed. It didn't move. I slammed my shoulder against it. And felt it give. Just an inch. I figured it wasn't only the lock that was electric. The door itself was motorized. The mechanism wasn't designed to work without power. So I pushed harder. The panel swung back another inch. And another.

A crack appeared and light shone through. It wasn't bright. It had kind of an orange tone. But the other side was definitely illuminated. I dropped the match and crushed out the flame with my shoe. I stepped aside. Listened. I picked up no sound at all. No movement. No breathing. I waited a minute. Then I threw my full weight at the door. I kept shoving. The crack stretched to four inches. I dropped into a crouch. My gun was ready. I peered through the gap. I could see a wall of bricks to the right. They were slightly uneven sizes. They'd been whitewashed at some point and now the surface was flaking away. The mortar was crumbling. The floor was covered with the same tiles as the main part of the cellar. There was no sign of Mansour. I braced myself. I expected him to try to push the door back and knock me flying. Or pull it open and send me sprawling at his feet. But nothing happened. There was no movement. No sound. None of the subliminal vibrations emitted by another living creature. I was left with the feeling of being alone. I waited two minutes. Just to be sure. Then I pushed the door until the gap was big enough to squeeze through.

Chapter 36

The room on the far side was empty. There were no people. No things. The other walls were also brick. They had the same peeling surface. But the one ahead of me, at the west side of the house, below the bathroom window, was mainly missing. There was a hole, six feet tall by five feet wide. The top was straight. A steel girder had been installed. Presumably to reinforce the structure. And to stop the whole thing from collapsing. The edges were like cartoon teeth where the bricks had been removed. They'd been knocked out neatly, one by one. On the far side there were more bricks. These were pale yellow. The wall they were part of was curved. It was like looking into a circular passage. Or a giant pipe. But dry. A cable ran down the center of its ceiling. It connected a daisy chain of lightbulbs. They were naked, and threw a subdued golden glow. There was a track set into the floor, like the kind trolleys run on in mines. The passage continued on the level, to the left, for a hundred yards. Then it begin to climb, gradually, until it disappeared from sight. It looked like it originally extended to the right, as well, but now that side was all bricked up.

I had to go back to the main part of the cellar for my phone to pick up any signal. As soon as it was happy, I called Wallwork.

I said to him, "I need a map of the town's water system."

Wallwork was silent for a moment. "I might be able to find something online. What exactly do you need to know?"

"I'm in the basement of the house I told you about. The one owned by Dendoncker's shell company. I found a way into some kind of hidden passage. An old storm drain, maybe. Or a sewer. The guy I was chasing escaped down it. I want to know where it goes."

"All right. This drain. Does it look old? Or new?"

"Not new. That's for sure. How old, I couldn't say. Maybe seventy-five, eighty years. Could be more. I'm no expert."

"OK. That kind of age, it was probably built by the WPA. From what I read about the town, the WPA did a whole bunch of work there. Back in the 1930s. Buildings. Roads. Amenities. And particularly improvements to the sewers and drains. That's why they originally went. The town had two parts. There was a gap between them. Something weird about how it grew from a trading post, or whatever. Anyway, the southern half is higher. After a big storm the drains couldn't cope. They overflowed and the water ran downhill and flooded the northern half. It messed things up real bad. Sometimes the sewers overflowed, too. That was even less pleasant. The southern half is part of Mexico, technically, but the problem impacted the US side. And the government was less parochial in those days. If the United States saw a problem, it fixed it. Wherever it was. And everybody was happy."

"If the WPA did the work, there should be records."

"For sure. That's the government for you. Someone probably kept track of how many paperclips they used. The question is, where are the records? Did they survive? Only on paper? Or digitized and put online? I'm not sure anyone would invest the time and effort."

"They must exist. Dendoncker had to have seen them. You said he made an effort to get this particular house. There has to be a reason for that. And it's not the view. Trust me. He must have realized it gave access to what's essentially a system of tunnels."

"Seems likely. But there's no guarantee he found the information online. That's the problem. If it was on paper, in a book, he had a year to sniff it out. Your missing woman doesn't. He could have been poking around in libraries. Municipal archives. Do you have time for that? And wherever it was, how many copies were there? He could have stolen them. Or destroyed them to protect his secret."

"You're saying it's hopeless?"

"No. I'm saying I'll try. Just don't hold your breath."

I went back outside and crouched at the side of Sonia's car. She rolled down her window and I saw that her eyes were red and swollen again.

She said, "I'm sorry. I just had a crazy vision of you coming out and saying you'd found Michael. That he was OK after all."

I said nothing.

"You haven't. Have you?"

"No. I wish I had."

"Did you find anything?"

"The entrance to a tunnel. I don't know where it goes. Yet."

Sonia reached for the door release. "I'll come with you."

"No. It looks like the kind of place you go in, you might not come back out."

"I don't care."

"I do."

"But you're going anyway?"

I nodded. "I have to. Michael's sister could be at the other end."

"Michaela?"

"Right."

"I hope you find her. I hope she's OK."

"Do you know her?"

"No. We've never met. But I heard all about her. I hoped one day she'd be my sister-in-law."

I waited until Sonia's taillights had disappeared around the corner then went back into the house. I paused at the top of the ladder. Felt a prickle spread between my shoulder blades. Ignored it. Climbed down. Went through the concealed door. And looked into the tunnel. It seemed like the rails were pointing into the distance. It was an illusion, of course. A trick of perspective. But I still wanted to know where they went. And why they were there at all.

Dendoncker must have installed them. There was no place for them in a functioning sewer. Or drain. Plus they looked new. Newer than the surrounding brickwork, anyway. There was no sign of rust. The steel was shiny. It had recently been used. Polished by metal wheels running along it. Probably some kind of truck. Probably carrying Dendoncker's smuggled contraband. In which case it must link to a storage facility. Another house he took over. Or an abandoned pumping station. Someplace like that.

Which didn't make sense. Why not just drive the stuff to and from the depot from there? Why move it around underground and load it up here? It called for extra effort. Extra resources. Extra time. I couldn't see how it reduced the risk. But whatever the reason, I wanted to know where the other place was. I would rather ambush Mansour there, where he felt safe. From a direction he wasn't expecting. I didn't want to stalk him through the tunnel. That option didn't appeal to me at all. But the only alternative was to wait for Wallwork. To see if he found a map. He wasn't confident. There was no guarantee it would be conclusive. And there was no way of knowing how long it would take him.

I checked that the pack of matches was in my pocket. Retrieved the tarnished mirror. Stepped through the hole in the wall. Into the tunnel. And started to walk.

Chapter 37

The temperature in the tunnel was cool. It was surprisingly comfortable. But the air quality was a different story. It was foul. Stale. It felt thick and dusty as I breathed it in. I fought the urge to turn back. Or if I had to keep going, to cover the ground as fast as possible. I forced myself to move slowly. To make as little noise as possible. I finally got into a rhythm, stepping on every third tie and pausing in the relative shadow between each pool of light thrown by the bulbs on the ceiling. I kept going for a hundred yards. To the point where the gradient increased. Then the presence of the rail track suddenly made sense.

From the base of the incline I could see how far the tunnel continued. Another four hundred yards. At least. It climbed all the way. But it was dead straight. I pictured the position of the border in relation to the house. Calculated the distance to the buildings on the far side. The ones I'd seen when I first entered the town with

Fenton. It all added up. I thought about the WPA guys arriving all those years ago. How they must have seen things. They faced two challenges. Too much water. And gravity. They couldn't make the water disappear. They couldn't make it run uphill. And they didn't want it to keep flowing down and flooding the northern part of the town. So they must have gone lateral. Recruited gravity as an ally. Turned it to their advantage. And joined up the drainage systems.

To guys in the 1930s it must have seemed like a practical solution to a natural problem. They were engineers, not politicians. Not border guards. The world was different in those days. Before they had to worry about drugs. Cartels. Border walls. Back then they would have seen two halves of a town separated by an arbitrary line on a map. They would have thought their work was making life better for the people who lived there. Now it looked more like they were setting up a smuggler's dream. No wonder Dendoncker chose that town. And that house. He was no fool. That was becoming clearer all the time.

I kept going up the slope. At the same speed. With the same rhythm. The farther I went the more obvious it became that this underground supply route hadn't just fallen into Dendoncker's lap. As I gained height I passed a bunch of newer sections of brick. The patches were circular. And dished. They followed the contours of the wall. There must have once been lots of smaller channels that were now blocked off. Dendoncker must have done his homework. He must have come across the records of the work. Including a diagram. The system would have looked like a tree. A broad, straight trunk with thinner branches sprouting off right and left. The branches would run beneath the southern part of the town. Collecting the excess water. And carrying it to the trunk. That was the key. None of it originated in that central section. So, when Dendoncker chopped off the branches, he was left with a dry tunnel. I don't know what other impact it would have had. Maybe the population had shrunk to the point there was no longer enough water to be a problem. Maybe it rained less these days. Maybe the floods had started happening again. But whatever the outcome, I doubted Dendoncker cared. Not as long as he could roam back and forth beneath the border, carrying anything he wanted in his little railroad between two parts of a sleepy town that no one paid any attention to.

The original tunnel ended after four hundred and twenty yards. Or maybe it began there, as that was its maximum height and water ran downhill. I came to a wall made of the same pale yellow bricks. It had the same flaky surface. But the tracks veered to the left. They turned ninety degrees and disappeared through another hole. There was another steel girder at the top. And more jagged edges down both sides where the bricks had been chipped away.

I moved in close to the wall and used the mirror to look around the corner. The track only continued for ten extra feet. A rail truck was parked at the end in front of a concrete wall. It was long enough for four people to sit, single file. Or for a decent amount of cargo to be carried. There was room for a variety of sizes of boxes and containers. Like the kind Dendoncker transferred to private planes under cover of his business. A cable snaked away from the side of the truck. It was thick. Heavy-duty. Plenty of amps could flow down it. Plenty of power. It stretched all the way to a gray box on the far wall. I figured the truck was battery-powered. That was smart. It was much easier to press a button than push something that size up the grade. Empty, let alone fully loaded.

I caught movement in the mirror. It was a man. He was familiar. But he wasn't Mansour. He was the second guy from last night.

Under the streetlight, by the border fence. Whose ankle I had broken. He was sitting behind a desk. It reminded me of the kind teachers in grade school used to have. I could see his foot. It was in plaster, sticking out of the gap between the twin pedestals. A clipboard was lying flat on the surface in front of him. There was a chessboard next to it. The pieces were laid out for the start of a game. The guy was paying it no attention. His arms were crossed. His head was back. The tendons were tight in his neck. He was fidgeting. He looked tense. Nervous. I put the mirror down before he spotted it. Took my keys out of my pocket. Picked one at random. Used it to scratch the wall. I started with a short, quick movement. Then I scratched again. A longer motion. Then another short scratch. I couldn't hear any response from the guy. So I kept going. I scratched out the letters to four words in Morse code. *Run for your life.* Maybe that was unfair under the circumstances. Maybe it was impractical. Maybe *hobble for your life* would have been more appropriate.

In the end, whether he understood or not, he came to investigate. I heard him crossing the space between us. He was using crutches. I could tell from the sound he made. He came closer. His head appeared around the corner. His chest. His face registered surprise. But only for a moment. Because as he stepped forward I took a handful of his shirt, just below his neck. I twisted for a better grip and slammed him back against the wall. The wind was knocked out of him. He slumped forward, gasping for breath. Dropped one crutch and cradled the back of his head with his hand.

"Let go." He could barely manage a whisper.

I twisted the shirt harder, increasing the pressure on his throat.

"I'll yell." He summoned a little more volume. "Get help. Others'll be here in two seconds."

I said, "Really? How many? There were four of you last night. How did that work out?"

The guy tried to suck in some breath.

"Go ahead. I hope your buddies do come. I hope Dendoncker comes. I wonder if he'll be impressed? Only, the way I understand it, when you're on sentry duty you're supposed to stop intruders. Not let them in and then start crying."

The guy breathed out, slowly. He made a mean hissing sound, but he didn't shout.

"Smart move," I said. "Let's do this instead. I'll ask you a couple of questions. You answer. And Dendoncker never finds out how useless you are."

"No way. I won't tell you anything."

"OK." I hooked my foot behind the guy's standing leg and swept it out from under him. He crashed down next to the track, in the gap between the rail and the wall. I grabbed his right pants leg, just above the ankle, and hauled it up to waist height. Pulled out my knife. Found a blade with a serrated edge, like a little saw. And slid it between the plaster of paris and his skin. "Time for a new plan. Get rid of the bandage. Remember how it felt yesterday? When the bones broke? You screamed pretty good. I bet it was louder than you can shout. That should bring Dendoncker and his boys running. Save me the trouble of hunting them down later."

"You wouldn't."

I went to work with the blade. It cut through the powdery material with no effort at all. The guy was mesmerized for a moment. He was staring at the cloud of white dust puffing out and floating down to the ground.

"Stop." His voice had risen an octave or two. "OK. What kind of questions?"

"The woman Dendoncker took. Michaela Fenton. Is she here?"

"I think so."

"You think?"

"I haven't seen her. But I heard some other guys talking. It sounded like she was here."

"Where, exactly?"

"Dendoncker's half of the building. I think."

"What kind of building is this?"

"I guess it's a school, from the way it looks. Was a school. There are no kids here now. I don't know much else. This is my first time here. I was never allowed through the tunnel before."

"What does Dendoncker use it for?"

"Like, a warehouse, I think. For his merchandise. The stuff he takes on the planes. I saw the containers. I think there's a workshop here, too. Maybe an office."

"What gets made in the workshop?"

The guy looked away. He didn't answer. I started sawing the plaster again.

"Dendoncker had someone working there. That's all I know."

I paused with the knife. "Making bombs?"

"Maybe. Probably. Look, I made sure not to find out. Some things, it's better not to know."

"OK. How many people are here?"

"There's Dendoncker. There are three guys with him. At least. A bunch of locals. Maybe half a dozen. I don't know them. Haven't seen them before. I don't think Dendoncker trusts them all the way. They just do the cooking and the fetching and carrying. Plus the three guys who went to the town. We're still waiting for them to get back."

"No need to wait." I folded the knife and put it back in my pocket. "They won't be coming."

I let go of the guy's leg. He managed to stop his ankle crashing into the ground, but only just. Then he rolled onto all fours and struggled up onto his good foot.

"What happened to them?" The guy hopped around for a minute while he retrieved his crutches.

I shrugged. "Your friends are an accident-prone bunch."

The guy made a move around the corner. He acted like he was heading back to the desk. Then he spun around. He raised the crutch in his right hand and lunged. He was trying to spear me in the gut. I moved six inches to the side. Grabbed hold midway between the rubber tip and the handle. Stepped forward. And punched him. An uppercut. It lifted the guy right off his feet. His remaining crutch clattered to the ground. His body followed, completely inert. He landed on his back, neatly between the rails. I flipped him over. Secured his wrists with a zip tie. Took his pistol from his waistband. A 1911. It was old, but well maintained. I bent his good leg at the knee. Used another zip tie to fasten it to the belt loop at the back of his pants. Picked him up. Tossed him in the rail truck. And threw his crutches in after him.

Chapter 38

The desk the guy had been using was at the side of a boiler room. It was a giant place. There were four huge furnaces in a line along one wall. Four huge water tanks opposite them. The ceiling was hidden by a tangle of massive pipes. Some were lagged. Some were painted. They snaked away in every direction. There was a door in the far corner. It was the only way out I could see, apart from the tunnel. I crossed the room and opened it.

The door led to a staircase. It was made of wood. It had originally been painted white but patches of bare timber were peeking out from the center of each tread. I guess Dendoncker's operation generated more traffic than the architect originally anticipated. I climbed up. Slowly. I kept my feet near the sides to avoid creaking. There was another door at the top. I stopped. Listened. And heard nothing.

I tried the handle. It wasn't locked. It swung open easily and let me out in the corner of a kitchen. It was a huge industrial-scale place, all stainless steel and white tile. There were stoves. Ovens. Microwaves. Preparation areas. A line of giant fridges along one sidewall. A line of cupboards along the other. I picked one at random. It was full of cans of baked beans. There were hundreds of them. They were tiny. Single servings, maybe, for children with no appetite. It seemed like a weird choice, given the scale of the equipment.

The kitchen was separated from the dining hall by a serving counter. It was low. A suitable height for kids, I guess. It ran the full width of the room. A section at the left was hinged. It was folded back, so I went through. The rest of the space was dim. It felt cavernous. The ceiling was high. Maybe twenty feet. Only one bulb was working, roughly in the center. I could barely make out my surroundings. The floor was made of rectangular wooden blocks. They were fitted together like herringbones. There was just one table. It was round. Made of white plastic. There were six plastic chairs in a scruffy circle around it. They seemed lost. The place looked like it was designed for long, solid refectory tables, lined up in neat parallel rows. Not cheap garden furniture. There was a set of double doors to the right. They were closed. And they were solid, so I couldn't see where they led. The rest of the wall was glass. Narrow metal frames divided the panes. They stretched from floor to ceiling. Harsh white light was spilling out from somewhere nearby. I moved forward to see what was causing it. Then I stopped dead in my tracks.

It was the lack of light in the dining hall that saved my bacon. It prevented the two guys from spotting me. The guys in suits who had accompanied Dendoncker to the morgue. They were at the far end of the corridor that led away from the other side of the double doors. They were sitting on stools in front of another, identical set of doors. The corridor was eight feet wide. It was twenty feet long. It had glass walls and a glass ceiling. Three raised vents, evenly spaced. And a double line of fluorescent tubes. They ran the whole length. They were powerful. And bright. The human eye can't see from a brightly lit area into a much dimmer one. Which was fortunate for me. Because the guys were each holding a gun. An Uzi. An interesting choice of weapon. Not the lightest. Not the fastest cyclic rate. Not the greatest amount of rifling inside the barrel. There are better options out there. Any of the Heckler & Koch MP5 derivatives, for example. That's what I'd have picked, in their shoes. But in mine? Alone? Against two Uzis? I wouldn't have liked my chances.

It looked like the glass corridor led to a mirror image of the part of the building I was in. On the outside, anyway. Inside it most likely had a different setup. I couldn't see why a school would need two kitchens and two dining halls. Given the guards with the Uzis, it seemed like a safe bet this would be what the guy with the broken ankle had called *Dendoncker's half*. It would be suicide to approach it along the corridor. I needed to find another entrance. I would have to loop around the exterior. Which meant finding a way out.

Ahead, at the end of the dining hall farthest from the kitchen, there were two doors. The one on the right had a sign that said *El Maestro Principal*. The one on the left, *El Diputado Maestro Principal*. I checked them both. They were both empty. There was no furniture. Nothing on the walls. No closets or storage areas. And neither had an external door.

There were three sets of doors in the wall opposite the windows. I tried the closest. It opened into another large space. It was equally badly lit. It was the same width, but longer because it had no kitchen. To the right, adjacent to the offices, there was a raised area like a stage. On the far side there was another expanse of floor-to-ceiling windows. There was a pair of doors in the center, leading outside. The other two walls were covered with climbing bars. Three ropes were suspended from a central ceiling joist. They were coiled up, ten feet from the ground. I guessed the place was a combined assembly hall/performance space/gymnasium. Originally. Now it was a storage area. For Dendoncker's aluminum containers.

The containers came in all sorts of shapes and sizes. Some had wheels. Some had none. Most were jumbled up at the far end of the hall. A few were lined up in some taped-off sections of floor. There were four rectangles. Each was labeled with a word made out of white duct tape. The first said *Out*. Then there was *Prep*. Then *In*. Then *Onward*.

The *Out* area was empty. There was one container in *Prep*. *In* was empty. And there were two containers in *Onward*. I opened the container in *Prep*. It had wheels. It was six feet long by three deep and four high. And it was empty. I moved along to *Onward*. These containers were smaller. They were both four-by-three-by-one. And they were both sealed.

There were little metal tags attached to wires that looped through their catches. I broke open the nearer one. I lifted the lid. It was crammed full of cash. Bundles of twenty-dollar bills. They were used. They smelled sweet and sharp, which made me think they were real. The second container was lined with blue foam, shaped into protective peaks. It was also full. Of cardboard boxes. All the same size. All the same shape. They were plain beige. There were no markings of any kind. I picked a box at random and looked inside. It was full of plastic bottles. Thirty-two of them. White, with child-safe lids. I took one out. There was a label stuck to its side. Printed in black and purple ink. There were logos and symbols and bar codes. And some text: *Dilaudid (Hydromorphone) Instant Release, 8mg, 100 tablets.*

There was nothing I could use so I crossed to the doors in the glass wall and headed outside. Orange light was spilling around the side of the building. Ahead was a parking lot. There were spaces for forty vehicles but only two were taken. By a pair of SUVs. Cadillac Escalades. They were black and dusty and kitted out with dark glass. They were sitting low on their suspension. But evenly, front to back, which probably meant they were armored to some degree. Beyond them was a fence. It was twenty feet high. Made of stout chain link. There was another one, running parallel, the same height, the same material, twenty-five feet farther out. That meant twice the amount of cutting for anyone looking to break in. Twice the time. Twice the exposure.

I checked for cameras. There was one on every other fence post. They were all facing out. None were moving so I followed around the building. I went to my left. When I was near the corner I heard a sound. Someone was running. More than one person. But not continuously. They were starting and stopping and sprinting and turning. And there was another noise. A hollow thumping. I crouched down and peered around. I saw where the weird light was coming from. There was a pair of floodlights on tripods, like you see at construction sites. They were mainly illuminating a long rectangular patch of dirt. It stretched along the side of the building, all the way past the gap that was filled by the glass corridor. There were four guys on it. Playing soccer. They were probably in their mid-twenties. They had bare feet, baggy shorts, and no shirts. I took out my gun, held it behind my thigh, and stepped into the light.

The guys stopped and looked at me. The nearest one beckoned for me to join them. I waved, *Thanks, but no.* And started moving again. I skirted around the far side of the pitch. They started playing again. One guy tried an extravagant flick. It didn't work. The ball bounced away, off the dirt and between the two halves of the building. It rolled toward the glass wall of the corridor. He ran to fetch it. The guys inside with the Uzis didn't react. Maybe they didn't notice, because of the light imbalance. Or maybe they were used to it, and didn't care.

If you looked down on the school from above it would have looked like a capital *H*. The assembly hall and dining hall would be one of the uprights. The glass corridor would be the crossbar. And the other upright would be Dendoncker's half. I was hoping that half would have plenty of doors and windows. And it did. There was a door in both of the short sides. Four doors in the long side. As well as four windows. They were big. Six feet high by twenty wide. But none of them were any use to me. They were all boarded up. With steel plates. Half an inch thick. With tamper-proof bolts. The kind that are used to keep thieves and squatters out of high-value construction sites. There was no way to break through them. No way to pry them off. And no way up to the roof.

All the down pipes had been sawn off fifteen feet from the ground. There was no way to smash through the side of the building with a vehicle. Giant dollops of concrete had been dumped all the way around. They were four feet in diameter, on average. Reinforced with steel rebar. With a gap between them of no more than three feet. The only way to breach the place would be with a tank. Or explosives. I didn't have either. Which left the glass corridor as the only possible way in. I figured I'd have to rethink my approach. It was time to get a little more creative.

There was nothing interesting between the long side of the building and the fence. Just a big patch of ground covered with weird, rubbery asphalt. Maybe the site of a playground, back in the day. Now it was empty so I followed around the next corner. I came upon a kind of rough shed. It was built of cinder block, painted white, with a corrugated metal roof. It had a wooden door, secured with a padlock. A new one. Hefty. There was one window. At head height. It was barred, but there was no glass. I struck a match. Stretched in. Took a look. And instantly blew out the flame. The interior was packed full of cylindrical objects, sitting on flat bases with sharp noses pointing up to the ceiling. Artillery shells. Twenty rows of fifteen. At least. They looked in bad shape. Their cases were rusty and corroded. Some were dented and scraped. Not the kind of things I was in any hurry to get involved with.

I found another structure ten feet farther on. It was smaller. Cube-shaped. And slightly irregular. Each side was no more than three feet long. It was all metal, including the roof. Or the lid. There was a row of holes punched along the top edge of the sides. Maybe an inch diameter. The front was hinged. It was standing open a little. I opened it wider. Risked another match. And looked in. It was empty. It had been used recently, though. For something. Maybe animal related, judging by the stench. Or maybe part of Dendoncker's interrogation setup. It was the kind of place no one would want to be cooped up in. Especially not in the midday sun.

Chapter 39

I completed my circuit of the building and went back inside. I made my way through the assembly hall. Across the dining hall. And crouched in front of the doors leading to the glass corridor. I knocked. MP style. I figured one of three things would happen. The guys on the other side would ignore me. They would call for reinforcements. Or they would investigate.

The first option would be no help. The second could work out OK. But I was hoping for the third. I was hoping that one guy would stay back, and one would approach. He'd open the door. The one on my left, judging by the way they fitted together. He would pull it back into the corridor. Then either his gun would appear, or his head. I didn't care which. I would grab whatever I saw. Yank the guy through. Break his neck. And I'd do it quickly, before the door swung closed again. I'd take the guy's Uzi and fire it through the gap. When the clip was empty I would follow up with a pistol. If that was still necessary. If the guy who'd stayed back didn't resemble Swiss cheese. After that it would be a question of taking his key or his transponder or whatever was needed to open the other pair of doors. Then I could find out what the guys were guarding. Or who. Probably Dendoncker. And hopefully Fenton.

There was no response to my first knock so I tried again. After a moment I heard footsteps. They were heavy. Deliberate. The door opened. The left one, as I'd thought. Then Mansour appeared. Not as I'd thought. He didn't pause. He didn't peer out. He just came striding through.

I straightened up. The door was already closing, but that was the least of my worries. Mansour spun around to face me. He was grinning. His left cheek was blue and bruised and swollen. A souvenir from my elbow, that morning. I threw a swift jab, looking to add to the damage, but he read it. He dodged sideways and right away he came back at me. He was fast. Crazy fast, given his size. He raised his knee. High. Almost instantly his massive foot flicked out. He was going for my stomach. It would have been like getting hit by a bowling ball if he'd connected. My organs would have been mashed. I'd have been thrown against the door. Maybe through the door.

It would have been game over, right there. No way was I going to let that happen so I danced to the side. Slipped around his kick and launched myself forward. I grabbed his thigh. Pinned it to my side and drove the heel of my hand up and into his chin. His head rocked back. It was a solid hit. Not the best ever, but it would have knocked most guys on their ass. I had no doubt about that. I felt him begin to topple backward. I thought the job was halfway done. Loosened my grip on his leg. Shaped up to kick him as soon as he was down. Which was a mistake. The guy was falling. But deliberately. He threw both his arms around me. Locked his hands behind my back and pulled me over with him. There was no way I could resist. He had at least a hundred pounds on me. And momentum was on his side.

We landed in a tangle, face-to-face, with me on top. But the moment his back hit the ground the guy levered with his legs. He twisted at the waist. My arms were trapped. I had nothing to brace against. Just empty air. A moment later our positions were reversed. I was under him. I couldn't move. I couldn't breathe. I was in serious trouble. I knew it. He could sense it. All he had to do was hold on. Let his bulk do the work. But he was impatient. Or he wanted to show off. He pulled his arms out from beneath me. Slid his knees forward and raised his chest off mine. I sucked in air. He leaned forward. Grabbed my head, one hand either side. I felt his thumbs moving around. Homing in on my eyes. I didn't know if he was just aiming to blind me. Or if he had something else in mind, like trying to crush my skull or lift my head and slam it into the floor.

I didn't wait to find out. I gripped his wrists and whipped my arms down toward my waist. The same time I pushed down into the floor with my feet, driving my hips up into the air. A normal opponent would have been catapulted right over my head. He'd have landed winded and surprised on his back. This guy barely rose at all. Six inches at the most. But that was enough.

I rolled out, got onto all fours, and sprang up onto my feet. Mansour was already halfway up so I kicked him in the gut. The kind of kick that would send a football out of a stadium and clear across the parking lot. It flipped him onto his back. He sat right up so I kicked him again in the side of the head. He went over. Rolled away. I followed. He tried to get back on his feet. No way was he going to succeed. It was the first rule. When you get your opponent down, you finish him. No hesitation. No second chances. No mistakes. One more kick was all it would take. I pulled my foot back. Picked my spot. And heard the door open behind me.

"Stop." It was a man's voice. Raspy. Whispery.

It was Dendoncker.

The voice came closer. "Move, and she dies. Then you do."

I glanced over my shoulder. Dendoncker was there, and he wasn't alone. The guy in the pale suit was at his side, with his Uzi. Fenton was on Dendoncker's other side. She was using an old-school wooden crutch to keep her balance. The cuff of her right pant leg was hanging loose and empty. She had a rope around her neck. The other end was in Dendoncker's right hand. He was pinching it with his remaining finger and thumb. And holding a knife in his left. It had a long, narrow blade. Like the kind British commandos used in WWII. Designed for one thing. Killing. With maximum efficiency. He was pressing its tip into Fenton's throat.

"Don't listen to him." Fenton's voice was hoarse. "Kill the bastard."

"He won't." Dendoncker's eyes were glistening. "He went to a lot of trouble to find you. He wants you alive. And even if he changed his mind and decided you're not worth it, he's not a fool. He knows he's quick with his feet and his fists. But he knows he's not as quick as a 9mm bullet. And anyway, there's no need for anyone to get killed. I have a proposition. Something very simple. Very straightforward. Agree, and we all get to walk away without a scratch. No one else will get hurt, either. So what do you say, Mr. Reacher? Would you like to hear my terms?"

Chapter 40

The truth was I had no interest in hearing Dendoncker's terms. None at all. But I had negative interest in getting shot by his stooge. And I didn't like seeing Fenton trussed up and held at knife-point. I didn't like that at all.

"Lose the rope," I said. "Lose the knife. Then you can say your piece. Beyond that, I'm making no promises."

Dendoncker wanted to talk in what he called his office. Getting there involved going through the double doors, along the glass corridor, and through the doors at the far end. The guy in the dark suit unlocked them. He held his keys up to a white square attached to the frame. I guess he had a transponder hooked onto his keyring. Probably like the one Mansour had when I searched him at the morgue, but I was too far away to be certain.

The guy didn't go through. He stood to the side and Dendoncker stepped past him and pushed the right-hand door open. He went first. I followed, with the guy in the pale suit behind me. He was close, but not so close I could easily grab him. Or the Uzi. We stepped into another corridor. This one ran at ninety degrees. It stretched away, left and right, running the whole width of this half of the building. There was an exit door at each end. Their handles were missing. I guess they had to be. To allow for the steel plates that covered them on the exterior. One side of the corridor was floor-to-ceiling glass, facing the dining hall. There was a wall on the other side. It was plain white, with four doors. Two to the left of the junction with the glass corridor. And two to the right. Each door had a window. The glass was laced with steel wires and covered on the other side with newspaper. It was turning yellow with age. All the text I could see was in Spanish.

Dendoncker led the way to the right. Behind me I heard footsteps peeling off in the opposite direction. I looked over my shoulder and saw Mansour with his hand wrapped around Fenton's elbow, guiding her away. It made her arm look like a tiny stick. She was moving freely enough, though. There was no sign that they'd hurt her. Which was fortunate. For them.

Dendoncker ignored the first door he came to. He stopped outside the next one. Worked the lock with a regular key. Went in and hit the light switch. Six pairs of fluorescent tubes flickered into life on the ceiling. There was a walled-off section to the right. It was square. There were two doors, marked *Niños* and *Niñas*. There was a wide window and another door straight ahead. Both were boarded up on the outside. There was a chalkboard on the left-hand wall. It had been wiped clean. The place had been a classroom. That was clear. I could trace where the kids' desks had been from the scuff marks on the floor. They had been arranged in a horseshoe, with the open end in front of the chalkboard. It looked like there had been five pairs on each of the other sides.

The teacher's desk had survived. It was set at an angle in the far-left corner. A dining chair was next to it with metal legs and an orange plastic seat. There was another half dozen of the same kind of chairs in a circle in the center of the room. A beaten-up leather couch by the wall on the right. A low bookcase at its side. It was full of textbooks. About physics. A couple of French novels were lying on top. On the other side there was an army cot. It had a metal frame, painted olive green. There was a pillow in a white cotton pillowcase. Just one. A white sheet, pulled tight. And a footlocker on the floor. There was no natural light. No fresh air. It wasn't much of a place to work or sleep.

Dendoncker headed to the right. "Against the wall. Feet apart. I'm sure this won't be the first time you've done this."

"One minute." I made it through the door to the boys' bathroom before the guy in the pale suit could stop me.

Inside there were two stalls. Two urinals. Two basins. And two hand dryers. Everything was small and chipped worn, but it was clean. Nothing offered many options for concealing things. I had two guns and a knife. I wasn't too concerned if they got taken. I could easily replace them. I was more worried about the phone. I had called Wallwork from it. And Sonia. I didn't want Dendoncker trying those numbers.

I thought about breaking the phone and flushing it away but I didn't know if the water pressure would be up to the job. If it wasn't I would just be drawing attention to the fact I had something to hide. So I reconsidered. All the phones I had taken from Dendoncker's guys were blank. He was used to that kind of discipline. So he wouldn't see anything unusual in it. I hoped. I made sure the phone was set to silent. Worked my way through the menu until I found the option to delete all call records. Put the phone away. Waved my hand under the dryer to trigger its motor. Then went back out into the classroom.

Dendoncker was standing between the pair of doors. He was fidgeting like a five-year-old. I turned and rested my hands on the wall and stood still while he searched me. He did a competent job. A little slow, but thorough. When he was done he handed me back my passport and my cash, but he kept my toothbrush and the other things.

"Come." Dendoncker headed to the ring of dining chairs. "Sit." I strolled across and took the seat opposite him.

Dendoncker didn't speak. He just sat and stared at me. His knees were pressed together. His hands were resting on his thighs. His head was tipped to one side. He looked like an inmate at a senior center, waiting for an encounter group to get started and curious to find out all about the new arrival. But if he thought his silence would fill me with the urge to share, he had picked the wrong guy.

Dendoncker gave up after two minutes. He ran the remaining finger and thumb on his right hand through his wispy hair and wet his lips with his tongue. "So. To business. But first, a question. Who do you work for, Mr. Reacher?"

"No one."

"OK. So you're freelance. Who hired you?"

"No one."

"Someone did. And I know who it was. You can say his name. You won't be breaking any confidences. Just confirming what I already know."

"No one hired me."

Dendoncker looked me straight in the eye. "Nader Khalil. Yes? You can nod your head. You don't have to say a word."

"Never heard of the guy."

Dendoncker didn't respond for a moment. His face was blank. I couldn't tell if he was relieved or disappointed.

"All right." Dendoncker shook his head. "Let's get back on track. My proposition. It's very simple. Easy to carry out. No one gets hurt. You and your friend walk away scot-free the moment it's done. How does that sound?"

I said nothing.

"All the job involves is driving. And a little lifting. Easy for a guy your size. It'll only take three days. I'll give you the route to follow and pay for your meals and a hotel for both nights. Nice places. Then when you reach the destination you'll drop off an item. Just one. See? Nothing could be easier. I take it you agree."

"I do not."

"Maybe I wasn't clear about the alternative?" Dendoncker nodded toward the guy with the Uzi. "There's a lot of desert around here. A lot of scavengers. They'd never find the bodies. Yours. Or your friend's."

"My answer's still no. I'm not your delivery boy. And it's better for two lives to be lost than fifty."

"I don't follow." Dendoncker pretended to look confused. "How would fifty lives be lost?"

"The item you want me to deliver. I know what it is."

Wrinkles furrowed Dendoncker's forehead. "The item is harmless. I give you my word."

I said nothing.

"I don't know what you heard, but if you think the item is dangerous you've been given bad information." Dendoncker stood up. "Come. See for yourself."

Chapter 41

Dendoncker led the way to the next room along the corridor. Another former classroom. It was the same shape as Dendoncker's office. The same size. The same layout. It had the same
kids' bathrooms. The same broad rectangular window and exit door,
sealed up tight with steel plates. The same harsh lighting. Another
army cot, against the wall. This one had a green blanket over its
sheet, and two pillows. And in place of the circle of chairs in the
center of the room it looked like the contents of a mobile workshop
had been unloaded. There was a folding metal workbench with a pair
of goggles hanging over the handle of its vise. It was next to a trolley
with two gas cylinders attached with chains. One was larger than the
other. Oxygen and acetylene, I guessed. They were connected by a
flexible pipe with a nozzle at one end. There were four tool chests on
wheels with all kinds of drawers and doors and handles. They were
made of metal. Painted olive green. They were all scuffed and dented.
This wasn't their first tour of duty. That was obvious.

Dendoncker crossed the room and stood against the left-hand wall, next to the chalkboard. He was at the end of a row of artillery shells. There were nine altogether. Divided into three groups of three. One in the center of each set was pointing straight up. One was angled to the right. One was angled to the left. Each of the trios was fixed to a metal base, like a tray. The sides were four inches high and there was a wheel at each corner.

"This is what we're talking about." Dendoncker pointed at the shells. "One of these. They generate smoke. That's all. Nothing harmful. Nothing dangerous."

I stayed near the door.

Dendoncker blinked a couple of times then stared off into the distance as if he was struggling to complete a complex calculation in his head. "OK. I see the problem. This is what we're going to do. Pick one."

I didn't move.

"The original plan was to go with three, but we decided a single one would get the point across better. Less is more. Isn't that what people say? So, pick one. We'll take it outside and trigger it. You'll see for yourself that it's benign."

I figured that if Dendoncker was prepared to sacrifice one of his bombs it would be crazy not to let him. That would be one fewer to deal with later. I made my way over to the line of devices. Examined them each in turn. Saw that the shells all had a series of holes drilled around their bodies just below the point where the nose cone was attached. Each hole was half an inch in diameter. Each shell had a tube sticking out of one of the holes. The tubes were made of black rubber and they snaked down to a pump mounted at the center of each tray. Each pump was wired to a battery. The kind that might be used in a small car, or a lawnmower. Each battery was also wired to a watch and a cellphone. The watches were digital. Just the bodies. No straps. Some ancient Casio model. I remember my brother, Joe, had one just like it in the early '90s. They were secured to the left-hand shell of each device. The phones were taped to the shells on the right. They had real keys and small screens. They looked basic. Old-fashioned. But solid. Reliable. And presumably redundant if the watches did their jobs.

I had thought I would maybe see something different in one of them. Something small and subtle that showed it had been set up specially for the demonstration. Or that Dendoncker would try to trick me like a hustler who needs their mark to pick a particular card. Either way, I would go for one of the others. But there was nothing. The devices were identical as far as I could tell. Dendoncker stood back. He stayed still. His body language was silent. His expression was neutral.

"What are you waiting for?" Dendoncker swept his hand along the line, but without emphasizing one device over another. "They're all the same. Just pick one."

When in doubt I always let the numbers guide me. There were three devices. There are two prime numbers between one and three. So I pointed to the second device.

Dendoncker pulled out his phone and told whoever answered his call to report to the workshop right away. Two minutes later Mansour appeared in the doorway. Dendoncker pointed to the device I'd picked and said he wanted it taken outside. Mansour loped across the room and studied it for a moment. Then he grabbed it by its central upright shell. He dragged it away from the wall and steered it back toward the door. The whole time he was dealing with it he was ignoring me. Actively, the way feuding cats pretend not to notice one another.

We must have made a strange-looking procession. First Mansour wheeling the bomb in front of him. Then Dendoncker. Then me. And finally the guy with the Uzi, farther back, keeping what he probably thought was a safe distance. No one spoke as we went through the first set of double doors. Along the glass corridor. Through the second set of doors. Across the dining hall. Through the assembly hall. And out into the parking lot. Mansour continued until he was level with the pair of SUVs. It was almost fully dark by then. His outline started to fade as he reached the limit of the glow that was spilling out through the tall windows. The orange light was no longer visible from around the corner of the building. There was no sound, except for the device's wheels skittering across the asphalt. The soccer players must have called it a night.

Dendoncker made another call. He said he wanted the flood-lights switched on. A moment later the whole perimeter of the building lit up. It was like a castle moat, only made of light rather than water. Ahead of us Mansour prodded the device's wheels with his toe. One at a time. Engaging their locks. Then he made his way over and stood at Dendoncker's side.

Dendoncker dialed another number and held the phone out to me. "Want to do it?"

I shook my head.

"OK." Dendoncker hit the green button, closed the phone, and slid it back into his pocket. "Just watch."

Nothing happened for ten seconds. Twenty. Then I heard three beeps. From the device. High-pitched. Electronic. The pump began to hum. It built up to a steady drone. Smoke appeared. Just a wisp at first. White. From the holes in the central shell. It grew into a steady stream. It was thick. Dense. Like steam from a kettle. Blue smoke began to pour from the right-hand shell. It mingled into a single plume but maintained the two distinct colors. Finally the left-hand shell got in on the act. Red smoke gushed out. It was at full force right away, billowing upward and quickly matching the other shades for volume.

"See? Smoke." Dendoncker walked forward until he was a couple of feet away from the device. He flapped his left arm and made a show of wafting some of each color into his mouth and nose. He kept it up for ten seconds then coughed and retreated to his previous spot. "It burns the throat a little. I can't deny that. But it's not poisonous. There are no explosions. And there's no danger. So, are you satisfied?"

I waited another minute until the last of the smoke had petered out. The blue lasted longest, but all three shells had produced a prodigious quantity. The space between the wall and the fence along the whole width of the building was filled with a swirling patriotic cloud. I was impressed. When Sonia first told me about Michael's plan I was dubious. I pictured a tiny spurt. Pale colors. A blink-and-you-miss-it kind of deal. Nothing to impress an audience. Live, or on TV. But if a thing like this went off in the middle of a ceremony there was no way the crowd could fail to notice.

"Satisfied?" Dendoncker glared at me. "Good to go?"

I was starting to think I'd been wrong. Maybe I should have been more interested in Dendoncker's proposal after all.

I said, "You want me to take one of these things, drive for three days, then leave it somewhere?"

"Precisely." Dendoncker nodded. "That's all you have to do."

"Where do you want me to leave it?"

"You'll be given directions, one day at a time."

Three days' drive. Enough time to get all the way up into Canada. Or down into Central America. But realistically, given that kind of distance, the target would be on the East Coast. D.C., maybe. Or the White House. Or the Pentagon.

I said, "OK. But why do you want me to leave it anywhere? What's the point?"

"I have my reasons. You don't need to know them. And they're not up for debate. The only question is who drives the truck. You can do it and walk away when the job's done. Or you can choose a different outcome and I'll find someone else to do it."

"And the woman?"

"Her fate is your fate. You choose to live, she lives. You choose not to . . ."

"OK. She can come with me. In the truck. Share the driving. Help with the navigation."

Dendoncker shook his head. "She's going to remain our guest until you complete the mission."

"In other words, you don't trust me."

Dendoncker didn't reply.

"That's OK," I said. "I don't trust you, either. How do I know you won't kill the woman the moment I'm out of sight?"

Dendoncker took a moment to think. "Fair point. Before you leave I'll return your phone. I'll give you a number. You can call it anytime. Talk to her. Confirm she's OK."

"You let a captive sit around all day with a phone?"

"Of course not. One of my guys will bring her the phone when you call."

I would have been happier if I was sure which of his guys would answer the phone. If I could guarantee it would be one guy in particular. But I had a good idea who it would be. What role he would play, anyway. And in the circumstances I figured that was good enough.

Chapter 42

My mother was French. I was born in Germany. I've lived on bases in dozens of countries. I've listened to people speak all kinds of languages. Some sound familiar. Some I can make sense of pretty easily. Others, not so much.

The words I heard come out of Dendoncker's mouth sounded just like they were English. Only I knew they meant something else altogether. Something I could understand with no trouble at all. He wanted me to do his dirty work. To plant the device for him. He would keep Fenton alive until it was in place. Then he would kill her. And me. Maybe the truck he'd supply was booby-trapped. Maybe he'd have someone lying in wait with a sniper rifle. But one way or another there was no scenario in which he could let Fenton or me survive.

I understood Dendoncker's words when he laid out his plan. I was sure I did. But whether he understood mine when I agreed was a whole other question. One he wasn't going to like the answer to.

* * *

The demonstration was over. Terms were agreed. The wind was picking up. It was tugging at our clothes. The desert night was growing chilly. There was no reason to stay outside so we headed back into the building. We trooped along in the same order as before. But two things were different this time. The first was that Mansour wasn't wheeling a bomb in front of him. He just left its spent remains outside in the parking lot, still shrouded in the last traces of smoke. The second came when we reached the far end of the glass corridor. We passed through the double doors and Mansour turned left. Dendoncker went to the right and headed for his office. I stopped and stood still. The guy with the Uzi almost clattered into me.

"This way, asshole." Mansour stopped outside the first door he reached and worked its lock.

I let a moment tick past then moved up alongside him. The guy with the Uzi trailed along behind.

"In." Mansour pushed the door open.

I stepped through and he shoved me in the back. Hard. His fingers were spread. His hand landed square between my shoulder blades. He put his full weight into it, like he was trying to launch me through the back wall. A little payback for earlier, I guessed. Probably hoping I'd at least end up flat on my face and look stupid in front of the guy with the Uzi. In which case he must have been disappointed. Because I saw him move. He was reflected in the glass. So I planted my foot. Leaned back into the pressure. And barely broke my stride.

The room was just like Dendoncker's office and the workshop, only it was laid out the opposite way around. The bathrooms were on the left and the chalkboard was on the right. There was only one piece of furniture. An army cot. It was in the dead center of the room. It was bolted to the floor. And Fenton was sitting on it. She grabbed her crutch, stood up, and took one step in my direction.

The door slammed behind me. Footsteps stomped away down the corridor. Thirty seconds later they stomped back again. The door opened and a mattress came sailing in through the gap. I stepped to the side to avoid it landing on me. It was thin with cream and olive-green stripes. And it had more than its share of marks and stains. It was probably the one from the bed in the workshop. Minus its sheets and blanket. And pillows.

"Sleep well, assholes." Mansour slammed the door again. I heard the key turn. And this time two sets of footsteps clattered away into the distance.

Fenton hustled around the crumpled mattress, closed the gap between us, and threw her free arm around me. She pulled me close and pressed her head against my chest.

She said, "I can't believe you're here." Then she let go and took a step back. "You shouldn't have come. You know that, right? What were you thinking?"

"I'm like the proverbial bad penny. You can't get rid of me."

"This isn't funny. Now we're both in trouble. Deep trouble. Honestly, there might be no way out of this. For either of us."

I shook my head. "Don't worry. Everything's going to work out fine. Give it three days, and we'll be home and dry."

Fenton held up her free hand, then pointed to her ear, then made a circular gesture indicating the room in general. "All I can I say is thank you. And I'm sorry I got you involved in all this."

"Don't mention it." I picked up the mattress and set it on the floor about six feet away from the bed. "And seriously, don't worry." I copied her *someone might be listening* signal. "I've made an arrangement with Dendoncker. I do something for him, and he lets us both go."

"Oh." Fenton rolled her eyes. "Good. That's reassuring."

I used the bathroom and when I came out I saw that Fenton had moved her mattress off her bed frame and laid it on the floor next to mine. She'd spread her sheet out so that it covered about half of each side, and had given us one pillow each. "Want to get the light?" she said.

I hit the switch and made my way slowly through the darkness until my foot found the side of my mattress. I lay down and put my head on the pillow but didn't take off my shoes. I wanted to be ready for whatever might be in store before morning. I didn't trust Dendoncker one inch. And I could easily imagine Mansour and his buddies hatching some dumb scheme with me in their crosshairs.

A moment later Fenton sat down. I heard her crutch rattle against the floor. I felt her stretch out. She was still for a moment, then she wriggled across onto my half of the makeshift bed. She snuggled in close. Her breath was warm on my neck. Then she was twisted like she was having some sort of convulsion. Something landed on my head. It was rough against my cheek. And it stank. Like a mixture of diesel fuel and mildew. It was her blanket. Judging by the weight, she'd folded it multiple times. To muffle the sound.

She whispered, "Where are we?"

"You don't know?" I whispered back.

"They threw a hood over my head. Made me go down a ladder. Felt like maybe through a tunnel. There were stairs at the far end."

"We're in Mexico. The tunnel is actually a drain. It goes right under the border."

"How did you know?"

"I'm good at finding people, remember?"

"You said you were good at catching people. Seems to me we're the ones who've been caught."

"Don't worry. It's a temporary situation."

"Why did you come?"

"I heard you were in trouble. Figured you'd do the same for me."

"You came to help?"

"And to deal with Dendoncker."

Fenton sighed. "It's just, I was hoping . . . No. Forget it. I'm being stupid."

"About what?"

"I was hoping you were bringing news. About Michael. That he was alive."

I said nothing.

"So," Fenton said after a moment. "What happens next?"

"Dendoncker lets me go in the morning. I come back for you."

"Think he'll let me live long enough?"

"I guarantee he will."

"Why would he?"

"He thinks he has to. In order to get what he wants."

"Just what kind of deal did you make?"

"One that won't turn out the way he thinks it will."

"Why not?"

"Because I'm going to cheat."

Fenton didn't reply. She rested her head on my shoulder but I knew she wasn't about to sleep. I could feel the tension in her.

"Reacher?" She lifted her head. "Will you really come back?"

"Count on it."

"I have no right to ask, but when you do, will you help me with one more thing?"

"What?"

"Michael's body. Help me find it. I want to take him home. Give him a proper funeral."

I didn't answer right away. It was an understandable request. I didn't see how I could say no. But the body could be anywhere. Buried in the sand. Burned beyond recognition. Blown to pieces. I didn't want to commit to a never-ending, hopeless quest.

"Don't worry." It was like she'd read my mind. "I know where it will be. The guy at The Tree said, 'the usual place.' I know where that is."

It was getting stuffy under the blanket. Fenton raised her arm to push it away, but I stopped her.

I whispered, "Wait. I have a question for you. About Michael. Is it true that he liked puzzles? Cryptic clues?"

"I guess. I never paid much attention to that kind of thing. I'm too literal. Too analytical. It's the one thing we don't have in common. Take crosswords, for example. Michael loved them. I hate them. I'm too pedantic. I can always give you ten reasons why the answers don't make sense. They drive me crazy."

Fenton didn't wait for me to ask her anything else. She just flung the blanket aside. We lay still, side by side, breathing the slightly fresher air. Then she put her head on my shoulder. Rolled onto her side. Stretched her left arm out across my chest. And she was still again, except for a little shiver that ran down her spine. I brought my arm up and cupped her shoulder in my hand. She snuggled her face into my neck. Her hair smelled of lavender. All of a sudden I didn't care about the lumpy pillow. Or the paper-thin mattress. Or the hard floor beneath it. Spending the night there with Fenton was an upgrade on the morgue and the dismembered guy. That was for sure. Though I would have been even happier if we were somewhere else altogether.

"Reacher?" Fenton's voice was even quieter than before. "Will this really turn out all right?"

"Absolutely," I said. "For us."

Chapter 43

I felt Fenton's body relax and her breathing grow slower and deeper. But when I tried to follow her off to sleep I had no luck. Not right away. My head was too full of questions. And doubts. About Dendoncker. About the whole charade we were playing out. I'd almost caused him to get kidnapped. And I had killed a bunch of his guys. Burned down his business. Broken into his hidden HQ. He should have been angry. Resentful. Outraged. But instead he'd laid out his proposal like he was interviewing me for a job in a candy store. I was missing part of the picture. There was no other explanation. I just didn't know how big a part.

Dendoncker could have had someone from his regular smuggling crew deliver the bomb. The long-standing team Fenton had been allocated to backfill when she infiltrated his organization. That would have been the easy thing to do. The straightforward thing. But he hadn't gone down that path. He'd gone out of his way to avoid it. Twice. First when he tapped Michael to transport the bomb, even though that wasn't his specialty. And now with me. He was determined to compartmentalize. To insulate the rest of his operation from this one job. And he was desperate to see it through to completion. Both those things were clear. But neither was consistent with helping Michael make an innocent protest.

My guess was that there was an additional layer to the scheme. That someone else had approached Dendoncker. Someone with an agenda that involved wreaking havoc on Veterans Day. And with deep enough pockets to convince Dendoncker to play ball. Or with a big enough stick to force him to. Dendoncker already had Michael on board. Fenton's contact said Dendoncker hired Michael to help with the land mines he was selling. Michael was on shaky ground, psychologically, at that time. I doubt it would have been too hard for Dendoncker to finesse him into believing the protest was his own idea. So Michael designed the devices. Built them. Tested them. Then something happened. He got cold feet. And sent an SOS to his sister.

I didn't know Michael. I'd never met him. But I couldn't imagine anyone in his position wanting to pull the plug on an operation he'd worked so hard to create. Not unless something about it had fundamentally changed. Or had been fundamentally misunderstood from the outset. Like the ingredients of the smoke. Maybe Dendoncker was planning to add something to the final mix. Or maybe his paymaster was. Dendoncker had a bunch of artillery shells crammed into the shed beyond the school building. Three hundred of them. At least. Some of them could contain chemicals. All of them could. Mustard gas. Sarin. All kinds of nasty things. That could be what Michael had discovered. What brought him to his senses. What ultimately got him killed.

If I was right, Dendoncker and his guys were in for a busy night.

The device wouldn't just need to be moved through the tunnel and carried up to ground level. It would need to be doctored. Filled with poison or loaded with extra explosives or made lethal in some other way. All without their resident bomb maker's help. But whatever Dendoncker had in mind it wouldn't make any difference. Not anymore. Not combined with the demonstration. Because he hadn't just agreed to prepare another bomb for transport. He'd also promised me the keys to its truck. That meant two-thirds of his immediate arsenal would soon be neutralized. Which left only one device to deal with. And it would be. Just as soon as Fenton was out of harm's way.

I slept for five hours, in the end. My eyes opened again at seven. Half an hour later I heard the key turn in the lock. The door was thrown open. Fenton woke with a start. She rolled back onto her own mattress. The lights flickered into life. And the guy in the pale suit stepped into the room. He covered us with his Uzi. The guy in the dark suit moved in behind him. He was carrying a tray in each hand. He set them down on the floor between the bathroom doors. Each had a plate covered with some kind of orange mush, and a cup of coffee.

"Thirty minutes," the guy in the pale suit said. His words were slurred. I guess his jaw still wasn't working quite right. "Be ready. Don't keep us waiting."

The two guys backed out into the corridor and locked the door. I collected the trays while Fenton hauled her mattress up onto the bed frame and then we sat together and drank our coffee. It was weak and lukewarm, and someone had put milk in both cups. Not a promising start. And things got worse with the food. The stuff on the plates turned out to be baked beans. They must have been microwaved to death, but now they were cold. They had started to congeal. Fenton balked at hers so I ate both platefuls. It was the golden rule. Eat when you can.

The guys came back after twenty-eight minutes. I was lying on my mattress, pretending to doze. Fenton was in the bathroom.

"On your feet." The guy in the pale suit held the door open. "Let's go."

I stretched and yawned and stood up and ambled toward him. "See you in three days," I called as I passed the bathrooms. Then I left the room. The guy in the dark suit led the way. I was the meat in the sandwich, with the other guy following with his Uzi. We went through the double doors. Along the glass corridor. Diagonally across the dining hall. And into the kitchen.

The guy pointed to the door in the far corner. "You know the way."

Mansour was waiting for me at the bottom of the stairs. He didn't say anything. Just set off into the tunnel and beckoned for me to follow.

We walked in silence, side by side, breathing the stale air. We followed the rails, in and out of the pools of yellow light, until we reached the hole in the wall that led into the house. Mansour went through first. It was darker in the little anteroom. The motorized door was closed. There was a button on its frame. A small thing, like a bell push. Mansour pressed it. A motor rumbled and the door started to move. It cranked its way through ninety degrees. We went through into the cellar. Mansour waved his keys near a spot on the rough wooden wall and the door started to close again. Then he nodded toward the ladder. I climbed up first. He followed, pushed past me, and led the way through the door to the side of the kitchen.

A U-Haul truck was sitting out on the street. It had been left in the spot Sonia had parked in the day before. It was a regular size. Not shiny. Not filthy. It had pictures of national park scenes on both sides. It was a good choice of vehicle. It was so ubiquitous as to be practically invisible. The guy walked over to it then reached into his pocket and pulled out Sonia's phone.

"Here." He handed it to me. "There's a number in the memory. Call it, and you can talk to the woman. Nothing will happen to her. Nothing bad. Not as long as you follow your instructions."

Chapter 44

I opened the phone Mansour had just returned to me and worked my way through the menu. I located the memory. There was one entry. I called it, and after a couple of rings a man answered. I hadn't heard his voice before.

"What's up?" the new voice said. "Why are you calling so soon?"

I said, "Put Fenton on."

"Already? You've got to be kidding."

"I was told, *anytime.* Do you have a different understanding of the word?"

"Fine. Give me a minute."

I heard a sound like a chair being pushed back on a wooden floor. Then footsteps. Five. Not hurried. Probably an average length stride. A door opened. There were more footsteps. Another eight. Some keys jangled. Another door opened. And the guy called out, "Hey. Phone call. Make it quick, will you?"

The door didn't close. The guy didn't move. After ten seconds I heard a squeak and hop, squeak and hop as Fenton crossed the floor with her crutch. After another ten seconds her voice came on the line. "Yes?"

I said, "Miss me yet?"

"I'm learning to live with the disappointment."

"Outstanding. Hang in there. I'll call again soon."

I ended the call and slid the phone into my pocket.

Mansour passed me a bundle of twenty-dollar bills. "For food and gas. There's five hundred dollars. Should be plenty. The hotels are already paid for."

I put the money in my pocket.

Next he gave me a piece of paper. There were some directions written on it. By hand. First giving the route to I-10, heading east. Then continuing to a motel near a place called Big Spring, Texas. "There's a room booked in your name. A fax will be waiting when you check out in the morning. Tomorrow's instructions will be on it. Keep your head down. Stay out of trouble." He handed me a key. "One last thing. If I ever see you again . . ."

"You'll do what?" I walked around to the back of the truck and rolled up the tailgate. "Hand me your ass so I can give it another kicking?"

There was one item in the load bay. An aluminum container. It was on wheels. It looked like one that had been in the area marked *Prep* in the school assembly hall the day before. It was the same size. Six feet long. Three feet wide. Four feet tall. The only difference was that it had stenciled words painted in black on its long sides. *Premier Event Management.* I reached in and touched the letters. The paint was dry.

Above the words, in the top right-hand corner, there was a line of digits. They were in the same font, but the size was smaller. There were six of them, then a hyphen, then four more. Maybe a serial number. Or an inventory reference of some kind.

The container was large enough to hold a device with three artillery shells. I was sure of that. But I couldn't verify that anything was actually inside. The lid was fixed down. With padlocks. Eight of them. Heavy and shiny and new. A line of holes had been drilled in the sides, near the top. An inch and a half in diameter. And the whole thing was secured to anchor points on the floor of the truck with orange straps. Six. Heavy duty. Cinched down tight. It looked like checking the contents was going to be someone else's problem.

"You need to get going." Mansour was pacing up and down alongside the truck. "And remember. If you stop, we'll know. You deviate from the route, we'll know. You mess with the device, we'll know. Do any of those things and there'll be a price to pay. Only you won't pay it. The woman will. I'll see to it. Personally. I'll make a video and send it to you."

I couldn't help wondering how important this guy was to Dendoncker. How he would react if I took a minute to finish what I started the day before. I was tempted to find out. Very tempted. But I forced myself to leave the guy alone. For the time being. There was no sense in jeopardizing the mission. Not with Fenton still behind enemy lines. And anyway, good things come to those who wait.

I rolled down the tailgate and latched it in place. "In that case there are two things you need to know. First, I stop for coffee. Frequently. That's not negotiable. And second, I'm taking a detour. A short one. Down the street on the other side of the house. I parked my car there, yesterday. There's something in it I want."

"What?"

"Fenton's suitcase."

"Why do you need that?"

"I don't. But she will. When I've delivered the package and Dendoncker lets her go, we're going to get together."

Mansour thought for a moment. He must have realized he was in a bind. He couldn't admit that Dendoncker had no intention of releasing Fenton or he knew I wouldn't do what they wanted me to. He said, "The street parallel to this one?"

"Correct."

He started toward the passenger door. "All right. I'll come with you."

The driver's seat was already pushed all the way back. The mirrors were fine. The controls seemed straightforward. So I fired up the engine and pulled away from the curb. I took it easy on that first street. Negotiated my way around the next couple of turns. Continued to the end. Lumbered back and forth across the fishtail until I got the truck turned around. Then I pulled in behind the Chevy and climbed down. I didn't have the keys so I couldn't unlock the trunk—Dendoncker had kept them after he searched me—so I opened the driver's door and found the release lever. Mansour lifted the lid. He reached in and already had Fenton's case unzipped by the time I got to the back of the car. He rummaged around, messing up her neat packing and spilling the odd item, but he seemed satisfied there was nothing in there he needed to worry about. Nothing I could use to defuse their bomb or derail their scheme. He ran his fingers around the outside of the case one last time then closed it up, lifted it out, and set it on the sidewalk.

He said, "OK. You can take it. Better get moving."

I stepped around the case and opened the car's back door. "There's one other thing she's going to need." I picked up the backpack I'd retrieved from the Lincoln after the crash outside the Border Inn.

"Wait." Mansour scowled at me. "What's in there?"

"Just this." I pulled out Fenton's prosthetic foot and shoved it in his face. "Hard for her to walk without it."

The guy jumped back. "Fine. Take that, too. Now get out of here."

I guess Fenton was right when she said people were freaked out by anything to do with wounds or injuries. Mansour certainly was. Enough not to find out if anything else was in the bag.

I left Mansour to walk back to the house and started out following Dendoncker's directions. They led me through the final few mazy streets on the outskirts of the town and onto the long straight road that went past The Tree. The spot where I first met Fenton. No one was staging an ambush there that day. No one was there at all. Alive. Or dead.

I drove slowly and steadily, like an old geezer taking his antique car for its weekly outing. I was mindful of the cargo in the back of the truck. I didn't want it blowing up if I hit a pothole. And I didn't want to get pulled over with it on board. I figured it was unlikely there would be any police patrols around those parts. But it's the things you don't expect that bite you in the ass.

I kept an eye on my mirrors the whole time. I wanted to know if I was being followed. I couldn't see anyone. No black Lincolns. No worn-out Jeeps. So I also scanned the sky. For small planes. Or helicopters. Or drones. And again I came up blank. Which wasn't a surprise. I believed Mansour when he said they'd be monitoring me. But it was more likely they'd have put a GPS chip in the bomb. Or in the truck. Or both. Which would be fine. That wouldn't hurt me at all. In fact, I was relying on it.

Chapter 45

The small roads led me through scrub and desert for forty minutes, then I merged onto the highway. Traffic was light. I let the truck settle down to a steady fifty-five. I checked the mirrors. I checked the sky. No one was following. Nothing was watching. After twenty minutes I came to a truck stop. I pulled in. Topped off the truck's tank. Then headed into the little store to pay. I filled a to-go cup with coffee. Hot, this time. With no milk. And I asked the clerk for change for the pay phone. The guy looked like I'd asked for a date with his mother. He must have been in his early twenties. I guess it wasn't a request he heard very often. Maybe it was a request he'd never heard at all.

There were two pay phones. Both were outside, attached to the end wall of the building. They were covered with matching, curved canopies made out of translucent plastic. Maybe for protection from the weather. Maybe for privacy. Either way, I wasn't too concerned. It wasn't too hot. It wasn't raining. And there was no one around to overhear anything I said.

I ducked under the nearer canopy. The wall beneath it was plastered with business-card-sized pieces of paper and cardboard. Adverts for escort services, mainly. Some were subtle. But most, not so much. I ignored them, picked up the handset, and dialed Wallwork's number. Nothing happened. The phone was dead. So I tried the second one. I was in luck this time. It had a dial tone. I tapped the digits in again and Wallwork answered on the second ring.

"Sorry, Reacher," he said. "The map of the drainage system? I've tried, but there's nothing."

"Don't worry about it," I said. "The research phase is over."

I brought him up to speed with how I came to have the truck. Its cargo. And my destination for the night.

"My ETA is around 2100, local," I said. "Can you meet me there?"

Wallwork was silent for a moment. "It won't be easy. I'll have to pull some strings. But to secure the device? Sure. I'll find a way."

"You'll fly out?"

"I'll have to. I'm in the middle of Tennessee. Too far to drive to Texas in time."

"OK. When you land, make sure the chopper doesn't leave right away. And tell the pilot to refuel. Fill the tanks to the brim."

"Why?"

"I'm going to need a ride someplace."

"Can't do that, Reacher. You're a civilian. The Bureau's not a taxi service."

"I don't need a taxi. I need to get to Fenton before Dendoncker kills her."

Wallwork went silent again.

"And I need to get Dendoncker. I'm the only one who can. Unless you'd rather he walks?"

"There might be a way," Wallwork said, after a long moment. "On one condition. When you get Dendoncker, you hand him over to me. Alive."

"Understood. Now, two other things. You can't move the truck until the morning. That's critical. Fenton's life depends on it. And there are some items I need you to bring for me. Five, altogether."

Wallwork wrote down my list then hung up. I refilled my coffee, climbed into the truck, and got back on the road. The truck wasn't fast. It wasn't fancy. But it was surprisingly relaxing to drive. It just did what it was designed to do. Ate up the miles, hour after hour, no fuss, no drama. I rolled along, nice and steady. Arizona gave way to New Mexico. New Mexico gave way to Texas. The pavement stretched away in front of me. It seemed to go on forever. The sky above was vast. Mainly blue, with occasional smudges of wispy white clouds. An ocean of gray-green scrub extended all around. Sometimes flat. Sometimes rising up or falling away. Sometimes with jagged peaks on the horizon, never coming closer, never getting farther away.

I stopped for gas whenever the needle dropped below halfway. I kept an eye open for anyone who might take too much interest in me. No one did. And I called Fenton at random intervals. The same guy answered every time. And he followed the same routine when he brought the phone to her. His chair scraped back. He took five footsteps. He opened a door. He took eight footsteps. Then he unlocked Fenton's door. I figured he had to be coming from the next room. The one at the end of the corridor. The only one I hadn't seen the inside of. Yet.

I arrived at the hotel at 2105. It was the first in a line of four. It was identical to the others except for the sign announcing which chain it belonged to. The building was rectangular. It had two stories. Small windows. A flat roof. The office was at one end. A bunch of air-conditioning machines was clustered at the other, half-hidden behind a line of spindly bushes. There were parking spots all along one wall, with an overflow lot between the building and the next hotel. It was empty, so I took a space at the far end of the last row. I climbed out. Stretched. Made sure the truck was locked. And made my way back to reception.

A woman was sitting behind the counter. She didn't notice me for a moment. She was too engrossed in a book she was reading. Her concentration didn't break until the phone rang on the desk in front of her. It was a complicated-looking thing all covered with buttons and lights. She stretched out to pick up the receiver, then stopped when she realized I was standing there.

"They can call back." She smiled at me. "Or leave a message. Sorry to keep you waiting. Can I help?"

"I have a reservation. Name of Reacher."

The woman woke her computer and tapped on some keys. "Here we are. Already paid for. An online booking. Just the one night?"

I nodded.

"Could I see some ID, please?"

I handed her my passport.

She flicked through to the information page, then narrowed her eyes. "This is expired, sir."

"Correct. No good for international travel. But still valid for identification."

"I'm not sure . . ."

I pointed to her computer. "Go online if you don't believe me. Check with the federal government."

She paused with one hand hovering above the keyboard. She didn't believe me. That was obvious. I guess she was weighing the consequences of proving me wrong. The paperwork involved with issuing a refund. Explaining to her bosses why she'd turned away a customer. The impact on occupancy statistics. "No need, Mr. Reacher. I'm sure you're right." She passed the passport back to me. "How many room keys will you be needing?"

"Just one."

The woman opened a drawer and took out a piece of plastic the size of a credit card. She fed it into a machine on her desk and tapped some more computer keys. A little light turned from red to green. She retrieved the card and handed it to me. "Room 222. Would you like me to write that down for you?"

"No need."

"OK, then. The breakfast bar's in the lobby and it's open from six until eight. Any questions, dial zero on your room phone. I hope you enjoy your stay with us, and visit again soon."

The woman went back to her book. I went back to the truck. I sat on the rear fender, leaned my head against the tailgate, closed my eyes, and felt the cool evening breeze on my face. Ten minutes ticked past. Fifteen. Then I heard a vehicle approaching. More than one. I looked up and saw a line of silver sedans. Five of them. All identical. Chrysler 300s. The lead car swooped into the parking lot. The others followed, then fanned out and stopped in a row in front of me. The guy who was driving the nearest car climbed out. It was Wallwork. He hurried across, passed me a white plastic sack, then shook my hand.

"Reacher. Good to see you." He nodded toward the truck. "The device. It's in there?"

"As promised."

"Excellent work." Wallwork gave a thumbs-up to the guys in the car next to his. "Thank you. We'll take it from here."

I unlocked the door, took out the backpack, and handed the key to Wallwork. "I've left a suitcase in there. It's Fenton's. Look after it until tomorrow?"

"Sure." Wallwork took me by the elbow and led me away from the other vehicles. "Listen." He lowered his voice. "I think we trust each other, so I'm going to be totally honest with you. After we spoke I called my old supervisor. The one who's at TEDAC now. He's on his way out here. We're going to secure the area, and he's going to examine the device. In situ. I know I said we wouldn't move it until tomorrow. But unless he's certain there's no risk to the public, I'm going to have to break that promise."

I said nothing.

"Think about it, Reacher. What if the device explodes? If it spews toxic gas into the atmosphere? If it's radioactive? We have those risks on one hand. And a woman who put herself in harm's way on the other. A woman you might not even be able to save, whenever we move the truck."

Chapter 46

"Impossible." The pilot looked at the place I was pointing to on the map and shook his head. "No. I refuse. I can't do it. I cannot cross into Mexican airspace. Not without authorization. It's out of the question. It's not going to happen. Not under any circumstances. Do you understand?"

I was surprised. A little disappointed. But not in any way confused. So I didn't feel the need to reply.

A pair of mechanics was watching us. So was the agent who had driven me from the hotel to the airfield. They were hanging around, not so close that the pilot might feel inhibited about yelling at me. But not so far away they would miss anything he said. The mechanics were apparently studying something on a handheld computer screen that didn't have a keyboard. The agent was fiddling with his phone. All of them were overcompensating. Pretending not to be aware of us. But clearly listening to every word. And enjoying the confrontation. The pilot was belligerent. Unnecessarily so, I thought. The three of them had picked up on that, too. They were waiting to see where things went from there. Whether the pilot would be satisfied with a verbal argument. Or whether an escalation was in the cards. To something physical. Something to spice up their evening.

"I'll take you as close to the border as you like," the pilot said. "Right up to it. But we will stay on the US side. I will not be party to an illegal border crossing. So do not ask me again. Are we clear?"

I said, "Fine. Los Gemelos it is. The US side. Let's just get going."

When I came up with this plan I figured I would have until at least 8:00 A.M. to carry it out. Maybe 9:00 A.M. at a stretch. That would be plenty of time. But if Wallwork's guy insisted on moving the truck before morning, Dendoncker would know. I was certain of that. So he would also know that I'd double-crossed him. Not a problem for me. But a death sentence for Fenton. There was no longer a second to spare.

The mechanics quit gazing at their computer and drifted away toward the only hangar with an open door. The agent put his phone away and jumped in behind the wheel of his silver Chrysler. The pilot climbed up into the cockpit of the helicopter. Its silhouette was familiar. It was a Sikorsky UH-60M. The civilian version of the Black Hawk that the army uses. This one had more antennae than I remembered. It had wheels rather than skids. And it wasn't dusty green. It was gloss black. Long and sleek and menacing. Like a predator rather than a workhorse. There was an index number on its tail but nothing to indicate which agency owned it. Just a discreet *United States* in gray letters toward the rear of its fuselage. I lifted my backpack into the rear compartment, climbed in after it, slid the door closed, buckled myself into one of the rear-facing jump seats, and put on my headset.

The pilot went to work on his preflight procedures and once the rotors were whirling and the aircraft was starting to hop on its suspension, eager to get off the ground, I heard his voice through the intercom.

He said, "Sorry about that little show. I needed to make sure those guys will remember me refusing to cross the border. Just in case."

"In case of what?"

"You getting caught. Here's what's going to happen. I'll attempt a landing, right by the barrier, just like I said I would. But we'll be in the desert. The wind is unpredictable. At the last minute I'll get blown off course. To the south. Just a few yards. The thermals happen to be patchy right there so we'll drop. To about three feet off the ground. Then I'll recover. Hold position for a couple of seconds. My wheels will never touch Mexican soil. No harm, no foul. But if you, without my prior knowledge or consent, take advantage of the situation and spontaneously jump out of the aircraft, there'll be nothing I can do about it."

"Will that work?"

"Of course. It's the way we always do it."

Including the walk through the tunnel it took a whisker over twelve hours to get from Dendoncker's school HQ to the hotel in Big Spring. Including the two-mile walk from the illicit drop zone, it took a shade under five hours to get back. The time in the air was uneventful. The pilot knew what he was doing. He flew fast and smooth and straight. And I dozed as much as the rattling of the fixtures and fittings and the throbbing of the rotors and engines would allow.

I woke when we plunged down twenty feet. The pilot was something of a Method actor, I guess. That gave me my cue to unstrap my harness, abandon my headset, and haul back the door. The cabin filled with noise. The downdraft almost pulled me out. I couldn't see the ground. Three feet, the guy had said. The prospect of leaping into the darkness didn't appeal. However far there was to drop. Then I felt the helicopter begin to rise again. There was no more time. I stepped out. My feet touched the ground. I ducked down. And stayed that way until the roaring and the noise and the wind were no long directly overhead.

The next thing I did was check my phone. There was nothing from Wallwork. They must not have moved the truck.

Not yet.

I took a black hoodie out of my backpack—the first of the things I'd asked Wallwork to get for me—and pulled it on. Partly for concealment. Partly to ward off the chill of the desert night. Then I started to move. Quickly. But carefully. The ground was all sand and grit and gravel. Hard to cross without making a lot of noise. It was dark. And the surface was uneven. It rose and fell at unpredictable intervals and it was studded with holes and channels and cracks. The whole place was a broken ankle waiting to happen. And I didn't know what kind of company might be out there. Snakes. Scorpions. Spiders. Nothing I was interested in having a close encounter with.

I was coming from the west so the glow of the US half of the town was away to my left. I kept moving until I was as close to the school's outer fence as I could risk, due to the cameras. The building was dark. Both halves. So were its grounds. Everything was wrapped in shadow except the glass corridor. It was ablaze with light. There was no way to approach it that wasn't transparent. And no other way into Dendoncker's side of the building.

I checked my phone. Nothing from Wallwork.

Not yet.

It was five to two in the morning. Normally I would have preferred to find some shelter and lay up for a couple of hours. Launch my attack at 4:00 A.M. The time the KGB had always used to stage their raids. When people are at their most vulnerable, psychologically. That was their scientific conclusion. Based on a whole lot of data. But that night I didn't have the luxury of waiting. I couldn't hold out until every detail was ideal. Two hours was plenty of time for the TEDAC guy to insist on moving the bomb. Plenty of time for Fenton to run out of luck.

I pulled out my phone and called the number in its memory.

The usual guy answered. His voice was thick and heavy with sleep. He just said, "No."

I said, "I haven't asked you to do anything yet."

"You want to speak to the woman. Again."

"Correct. Put her on."

"No."

"Put. Her. On."

"Are you crazy? It's the middle of the damn night. Go to sleep. Call back in the morning."

"*Anytime,* remember? Has the word been redefined in the last twenty-four hours? Do I need to wake Dendoncker and ask him?"

The guy grunted, then I heard a rustling sound. A bedsheet being flung aside, I guess. Then footsteps. Seven, this time. Not five. Then a door being opened.

I moved forward until I reached the fence. I stopped at the foot of one of the posts with a camera mounted on it and set my back-pack down on the ground.

The guy continued down the corridor. Eight more steps. He opened Fenton's door and yelled for her to come and take the phone. Her voice came on the line after another minute.

"Reacher? Why aren't you asleep? What's wrong?"

"Nothing's wrong," I said. "I need you to do something. It's very important. In a second I'm going to put the phone down, but I'm not going to hang up. I need you to keep talking like we're having a regular conversation. I'll be back in a flash. Can you do that?"

"Sure. I guess. Why?"

"Don't worry. It'll be clear soon."

Chapter 47

I put my phone down on my backpack and began to climb the post. It was easy to grip with my hands. I could just hang on to the fence where it was attached on either side. But it was another story for my feet. The diamond-shaped gaps in the wire were not big enough for my shoes. The toe caps were too wide. Just a fraction. But enough to be a problem. I started with my right and my foot slipped straight out and slapped down onto the ground. I tried again. Slipped again. Then I found that if I pushed my toe in extra hard and pulled my foot up to a steep angle I could just about make it stick. I repeated the process with my left. Raised my right. Kept going. I didn't fall. But progress was slow. Painfully slow. Precious seconds were slipping away. I had no idea how long Fenton would be able to keep up the ruse with the phone. But then, if I was wrong about the guy who'd brought it to her, it would already be too late.

I kept climbing until my chest was level with the top of the fence.

My calves were burning from supporting my weight at such a weird angle. I gripped the wire with my left hand and stretched up with my right. I took hold of the camera. I tried to rotate it. Counterclockwise. But it wouldn't move. It was jammed solid. I twisted harder and my right foot slipped. My left foot followed. I wound up hanging by my left hand. I grabbed the fence with my right. Jammed both feet back into their gaps. Straightened up. Took a fresh hold of the camera. Twisted again. And felt it give. Just a little. But there was movement. I was sure of that.

I didn't let up on the pressure. The camera shifted an eighth of an inch. Another eighth. I kept going until it had crept through twenty degrees. Then I climbed down. Slowly. I made it to the bottom without falling. Retrieved my phone. Held it to my ear. And heard Fenton's voice. She was mid-anecdote. Something to do with her aunt, a jar of marmalade, and a TSA agent. I moved to my left until I was halfway across the section of fence. Put the backpack and the phone on the ground. Continued to the next post. And began to climb again. It was as awkward as with the first one. My right foot slipped twice before I made it to the top. My left, once. I grabbed the camera. Twisted it. This one moved more easily. I rotated it twenty degrees, clockwise. Then climbed down. Moved to my right. Picked up my phone. And heard nothing. Not Fenton. Not the guy. Just silence.

I put the phone in my pocket and tried to pick up any sound coming from the building. Maybe the guy had seen through Fenton's act. Maybe he just got tired and snatched the phone so he could go back to bed. But the important question was, *when*? How long ago did he get back to his room? If he'd made it before I was done with the cameras there would soon be footsteps. Guys getting into position with their Uzis. Then the floodlights would come on, silhouetting me against the desert like a target at a shooting range. I crouched down, legs tensed, ready to run.

Nothing happened.

I took my phone out and checked for messages. There was nothing from Wallwork.

Not yet.

If my estimate was accurate I should now be in a dead zone between the cameras I'd moved. Just as long as no one had been watching the monitors when they were turning. And if not, then they wouldn't pick up on the slightly different view of the desert they were now getting. I stayed in a crouch and took Wallwork's second item out of my backpack. A pair of bolt cutters. I removed a section of wire. A square, just broader than my shoulders. But I didn't crawl through. Not right away. I lay down and looked along the surface of the ground between the inner and outer sections of fence. I wanted to see if it was flat. Or if there were any telltale humps. Dendoncker had been selling land mines. If he'd kept any for himself, this would be an ideal place to use them.

The verdict was inconclusive. The land wasn't flat. It wasn't even close. But there was nothing to say that the undulations weren't natural. Or random. The work of the wind. Or the rain. Or the original construction crew. So I took out Wallwork's third item. A knife. It had a long, broad blade. Ten inches by two, at its widest point. I slid the tip into the sandy surface and pushed it out ahead of me. Slowly. Gently. I kept it as horizontal as possible so that no part of the blade was more than an inch or so underground. It didn't come into contact with anything so I pulled it out and repeated the process six inches to the left. Nothing obstructed it, so I tried again. I kept going until I had defined a two-foot-wide section I could be sure was safe. I crawled forward, placed my knees on the line my test holes had made, and probed the area six inches farther forward.

It was a time-consuming procedure. I was moving forward at around a foot a minute. Around fifteen thousand times slower than when I'd been in the helicopter. I was expecting a text from Wallwork at any second. And I was completely exposed in a fenced-in no-man's-land. Completely at the mercy of anyone who came out on patrol. The only upside was that I hadn't come across any land mines. I was beginning to think I was being overcautious. I made it ten feet. I had fifteen to go. Then the tip of my knife hit something. Something hard. Something metal. I froze. Didn't breathe. Pulled back on the handle. The first fraction of an inch was the most critical. When the contact was broken. If the thing was a mine.

Whatever the thing was, it didn't explode. But I wasn't out of the woods. The knife still had to be removed the rest of the way. Shock waves could still be transmitted through the dirt. The tiniest movement could still be fatal.

The thing did not explode.

I forced myself to take a breath then started again, a foot to the right. I moved even more slowly after that. Found three more potential mines. But made it to the inner fence in one piece. I cut a hole. Crawled through. And hurried to the long wall at the back of Dendoncker's side of the building. I moved to the boarded-up window belonging to Fenton's room. I doubted anyone would be inside with her, and she was hardly likely to raise the alarm if she heard me. I took Wallwork's fourth item out of my backpack. A weighted hook. It had four claws, covered in rubber. And it was attached to twenty-five feet of rope. I stepped back, took hold of the rope three feet from the hook, twirled it around a half-dozen times to gauge the way it would fly, then launched it up toward the roof. It cleared the top of the wall. Disappeared. And landed with a dull *clunk*. I pulled my end of the rope. Gently. I teased the hook back toward the wall. It kept moving. Coming closer to the edge. Then it caught on something. I pulled harder. The hook held. So I started to climb. Hands on the rope. Feet flat on the wall. Like rappelling, but in reverse. I made it to the top. Scrambled up onto the roof. Pulled the rope up behind me. And started toward the far side of the building. The side that the glass corridor joined onto.

Chapter 48

The guys in the suits with the Uzis were there. Both of them. I hoped that meant Dendoncker was in his office. I hoped they were like the Royal Standard the Queen of England flies above whichever palace she's at, announcing her presence. I like efficiency. Two birds with one stone would suit me fine.

I could see the tops of the guys' heads through the glass roof. They were sitting on their stools, each leaning against one of the double doors. They were very still. Maybe in some kind of exhausted trance. Or if I was very lucky, asleep at the wheel. There was a gun in my backpack. Two, in fact. The Berettas I had captured at the Border Inn. It would have been convenient to just shoot these guys. But that was a high-risk strategy. They were on the other side of a pane of structural-grade glass. It was thick. Strong. My first shot would most likely penetrate. But its trajectory was bound to be affected. It would almost certainly miss. And with it would go my element of surprise. All I would be doing was advertising my presence to two men with Uzis. I would probably still get one of them. But the other would probably get me. Not the kind of odds I liked. So I took out Wallwork's final item. A pair of wire cutters. I gripped the handle in my teeth and lowered myself down onto the glass roof. And stood completely still. I checked on the two guys. Neither of them stirred, so I inched forward. Kept going until I reached the vent. Snipped around the edge of the mesh bug screen. Checked on the guys again. Took the mask from my backpack. Put it on. Took the canister of DS gas. And pulled the pin.

The spoon kicked back. The metal skin started to get hot. The device was real. Not a prop. Which was fortunate in the circumstances. But I still hesitated. I didn't know how fast the guys would react. How quickly they would move. If they were able to get through the double doors I would be left with a major problem.

Five seconds ticked away. Then wisps of white gas started to appear. I dropped the canister through the vent. It clattered against the floor and started to roll. The guys jolted upright. Jumped to their feet. A moment later they started grabbing their throats and clawing at their eyes. One tried to run. He was disoriented and crashed into the glass wall. He fell backward. The other guy started to writhe and scream. I switched the wire cutters for the bolt cutters. Severed the metal posts at each corner of the vent's roof. Pulled it off and flung it away. Then leaned in through the hole and shot each of the guys in the head. Twice. For insurance.

I tucked the gun into my waistband, lowered myself down, and dropped the last few inches into the corridor. Moved across to the nearer guy's body. Took his keys and his Uzi. Collected the second guy's Uzi. Slung it over my shoulder. And used the transponder to unlock the door. I pushed it open. Stepped through. And pushed the mask up onto the top of my head.

Eight seconds had passed since the first gunshot. Nine at the most. Not much time to react. And yet there was Mansour, in the next corridor. There was a chair outside Dendoncker's office door. One of the orange ones. Mansour must have been stationed there, like a guard. But now he was coming toward me. Charging. Head down. Arms wide. Moving fast. Already too close for me to bring the Uzi to bear. So I stepped forward. I figured I could grab some part of him, move to the side, pivot, and use his weight and speed against him. Launch him into the window. Or the wall. Or at least send him sprawling on the floor. But the space was too narrow. He was too broad. His shoulder caught me in the chest. It was like being hit by a cannonball. I was knocked off my feet. I landed on my back, half propped up by the pack, and slid along the shiny floor. One of the Uzis clattered into the glass. I lost track of the other. All the breath was knocked out of me. I couldn't suck any more in. My ribs felt like a million volts had been run through them. All I knew was that I had to get up. Get off the ground before the guy closed in with his feet or his fists or his overwhelming bulk. I clawed my way upright. And saw Dendoncker. He was disappearing into the glass corridor. He was wearing a gas mask. I realized it was mine. It must have fallen off when I fell. Mansour was following him. With no mask. Dendoncker had a way of inspiring loyalty. I had to admit that.

I retrieved the Uzis and started to chase after them. I reached the double doors. Then I heard a sound behind me. A guy had come out of the room at the far side of Fenton's. Someone I hadn't seen before. Presumably the guy I'd spoken to on the phone. He had already reached Fenton's door. He must have tiptoed along while I was reeling from the impact with Mansour. The noise was his key working the lock. He opened the door. Stepped inside. With a gun in his hand. I turned and ran back. The door swung closed. I couldn't see into the room because of the newspaper over the glass. But I could hear sounds from inside. A scream. A crash. And a shot. Then silence.

I kicked the door open and strode inside, ready to empty the Uzi's magazine into the guy who had just entered. And I came face-to-face with Fenton. She was standing near the bed, without her crutch. She was pointing the guy's gun at me. The guy himself was on the floor. He was slumped half on the mattress I'd used the night before and half on the wood. His right wrist was twisted around at a crazy angle. It was broken. That was clear. And the top of his skull was missing.

"Guess we'll need new accommodations tonight." Fenton lowered the gun.

"Guess we will." I came farther into the room. "You all right?"

She nodded and sat on the bed. "More or less."

I opened my backpack and handed her the prosthetic foot. The one that Dendoncker's guy had brought to the café. Then I turned and headed for the door.

"Thanks," she said. Then, "Where are you going?"

"To get Dendoncker. If he's still here."

Chapter 49

I paused in front of the double doors. Took a couple of deep breaths. Then went through, raced to the far end of the glass corridor, and burst into the dining hall. There was a breeze blowing over the roof now. It was helping to suck the gas out through the gap left by the vent. But Dendoncker's formula was potent. My eyes were stinging and raw even after such a tiny exposure. I resisted the urge to rub them. Made myself stay still and wait until my view of the world was less blurred. Then I started to search.

I didn't bother with the kitchen or the offices. I figured Dendoncker wouldn't want to hide. He would want to get out of the place. There were two ways to do that. The tunnel. Or the SUVs. I crossed the assembly hall and looked through the window. The parking lot was empty. There was no sign of the Cadillacs. And no sign of Dendoncker or Mansour. I went outside and crossed to the gates. Both were still and closed and solid. But on the rough road beyond them, I could make out four red pinpricks. Two pairs.

The same configuration. The Cadillacs' taillights. The lead vehicle looked like it was riding lower on its suspension. Like it was carrying something heavy. But that was just an impression. I couldn't be sure. Not at that distance. Not with the way they were bouncing through the gloom. It didn't matter anyway. They were heading for the horizon. And there was nothing I could do to stop them.

Fenton was in the corridor when I got back to the far side of the building. She was moving gingerly as if her refitted foot was causing her pain. She had already passed the door to the next room and she stopped when she heard me catching up to her.

"Someone else is here." Her voice dropped to a whisper. "Another prisoner. I don't think he's in good shape."

I said, "How do you know?"

"When you called me the guy who brought the phone always stood in the doorway while we talked. With the door open. One time when we were done I was taking the phone back to him and I saw two people in the corridor. Walking together. Coming from the right. One was Dendoncker's sidekick. The enormous guy. The other was a stranger. He was carrying a bag. A black leather one, all beat-up, like doctors use. He was speaking. In Spanish. He said something like, 'You have to dial it down. He can't take much more. Leave him alone for a while. Forty-eight hours. At least.'"

"Who was he talking about?"

"I don't know."

"How did Dendoncker's guy react?"

"He sounded annoyed. Said Dendoncker would never go for a delay. That he needed to know where *it* was, and there wasn't much time."

"*It?*"

Fenton shook her head. "I don't know what they meant."

"So where are they holding this other guy?"

"I thought he would be in the room next to mine. But I just looked. No one's there. Just a bed and a bunch of security monitors. Nowhere to keep a prisoner. So there must be somewhere else."

Fenton started moving again. With some difficulty. I followed, keeping to her pace. It seemed futile. The corridor must be a dead end. Like beyond Dendoncker's office. The exit was boarded up tight. I'd seen it when I was searching for an alternative way in. But as we went farther I realized there was a difference. The final classroom's wall didn't run straight. Not all the way to the perpendicular wall. The was a recess at the very end. A setback of about a foot. To draw attention away from another door. A solid wooden one. With a sign attached. It said El Conserje. *The Janitor.*

The door was locked. But not in any serious way. It only took one kick to open it. Inside a set of stairs led down to another basement. They were wooden. Painted white, but less worn than the ones running from the kitchen down to the tunnel. I turned on the light and started to descend. Fenton followed. The space at the bottom was divided into two areas. One-third was for cleaning equipment and supplies. Two-thirds were for maintenance and repair. Or they had been. Now the tool benches and equipment lockers had been pushed to one end. Another army cot had been set up in the space that had been created. There was an intravenous drip stand next to it. A tube ran down from a bag of clear fluid. It was hooked up to the arm of a guy on the bed. His body was covered by a sheet. So were his legs and his other arm. But his head was visible. His face was swollen and cut and covered with scabs and bruises and burns. There was a huge lump on his forehead. Big chunks of his hair were missing. Fenton screamed. She pushed past me. Rushed to the bed. She looked like she was going to pull the guy into her arms. But she stopped herself. Took hold of his hand. And said one word. Softly. With a voice full of guilt and pain.

"Michael."

Chapter 50

I moved closer to the bed, too. I thought maybe the guy in it was dead. I was worried about how to get Fenton out of there if that was the case. But after a moment one of his eyes flickered open.

"Mickey." His voice was dry and scratchy and barely audible. "You got my warning. You came?" Then his eye closed and his head rolled to the side.

Fenton checked his pulse. "It's OK. He's still with us. Help me get him up."

It was a tough call. Michael didn't look in any kind of shape to be moved. I would rather have brought the medics to him. But Dendoncker was on my mind. He couldn't know that Fenton had found out about Michael. And evidently Michael had information that Dendoncker wanted. So Dendoncker would come back for him. Or he would send some guys. Either way, we were in no position to defend that cellar. Not for any significant length of time. Which made evacuation the lesser of two evils.

I picked Michael up and carried him to the stairs, still wrapped in the sheet. Fenton followed with the IV bag. We moved slowly and gently, trying not to shake or jostle him, and we paused when we reached the corridor. We detoured into the room she'd been kept in and I laid Michael down on the bed. Fenton stayed with him while I went back to the glass corridor. I used one of the Uzis to blast out the windows. Half a magazine on each side. To allow the gas to dissipate faster. Then I went back to the room and called Wallwork. He answered immediately. There was no hint of sleep in his voice. I guessed he was with the TEDAC crew and they were pulling an all-nighter. I told him Fenton was safe so they were clear to move the truck whenever they wanted. I told him we had recovered a casualty, and asked him how long it would take to send some agents to the medical center in Los Gemelos. When Dendoncker discovered Michael was missing he wouldn't take it lying down. He would send out a search party, and knowing the condition Michael was in, the closest hospital was the obvious place to start.

Wallwork took a minute to figure the timing and distances. Then he said, "I'll have to make some calls. But best guess? A couple of agents could be there inside four hours. If you're worried about the guy, can you babysit until then? Unofficially?"

"I don't see why not." Maybe my luck would change, I thought. Maybe Dendoncker would show up in person to look for Michael. Mansour, too. I hated to think of them walking around free. "How's it going at your end?"

"Good. Just got off the phone with Quantico. After what I told them they're putting a major effort together to bring Dendoncker in. A full-court press. Worldwide, if necessary."

"And the bomb?"

"My guy's just finishing up. He's done inspecting. Now he's getting the device ready for transport. We're flying it out first thing."

"Did you take any flak for dragging him out there?"

"No. The opposite, actually. He's in hog heaven. Keeps taking photos and videos and emailing them to his lab. Says it's one of the most interesting things he's seen in a long time."

"Because of the gas?"

"No. He doesn't have a definitive on that yet. Says it's too dangerous to mess around with the shells while they're in the field."

"He doesn't think they're harmless?"

"He knows they're not. Because of what they were coated with. VX."

VX. The most deadly nerve agent ever invented. Developed in Britain in the 1950s. I don't recall everything about the chemistry. But I remember what the V stands for. Venom. And the name's not misplaced. A few years back two women wiped a little on Kim Jong Nam's face while he waited for a flight at the Kuala Lumpur airport. He was Kim Jong Un's half brother. Maybe he was making moves behind the scenes. Maybe someone just said he was. But either way, he was dead before he reached the hospital.

I said, "Does your guy think Dendoncker added VX to the smoke?"

"He'll find out for sure at the lab. But look. All the shells had signs of recent tampering. And VX isn't like sarin. It's not a gas. It's a liquid, like oil or honey, so it would be easy to pour inside. Then it needs a heat source to vaporize it. Like the reaction that would produce the colored smoke. And the smoke would then help to dissipate the poison. You couldn't find a system better suited to dispersing VX if you spent the rest of your life searching. Is that a coincidence?"

"Seems unlikely. No wonder your guy is excited."

"I can see the cogs going round in his head. He's thinking about the papers he's going to write. The law enforcement conferences he's going to speak at. But that's not all that got his bell ringing. He also found something hidden away in the electronics. A third way to detonate the bomb. On top of the timer and the cellular."

"What kind of a third way?"

"A transponder. A common enough doodad, apparently. But not generally used this way. I know he's an asshole. But this Dendoncker must be a hell of a creative guy. And thorough. A defensive coating of VX and three systems to do one job? Talk about leaving nothing to chance."

Wallwork hung up, leaving me feeling a little guilty for not telling him that Dendoncker didn't build the bomb. Michael did. He was the thorough, creative one. Ordinarily the TEDAC guys would have figured that out when they fed the details into their database. Aside from the last-minute addition of the VX, the components and the construction techniques would match the ones from the first bomb Michael had made. Which also had a transponder. With his fingerprint on it. Only TEDAC wouldn't make the connection this time. Because Fenton had destroyed the older evidence. I guess keeping quiet made me an accessory to some kind of federal crime. I didn't think it mattered too much, though. Michael's bomb-making career was over. And if the FBI followed through, Dendoncker's soon would be, too.

Fenton was anxious to get moving but I convinced her to wait while I made one more call. To Dr. Houllier. On his cell. I didn't know if the medical center was staffed 24/7 and I didn't want to show up with Michael and find there were no doctors in the place. Dr. Houllier said he would make sure someone was there. He sounded cagey so I pressed him and he admitted he would come and treat Michael himself. He confessed he was already back in town and offered to come for us in an ambulance. That was tempting. My only concern was the risk involved. Someone could see him and inform Dendoncker. Reprisals could follow, depending on how long he remained on the loose. But a more immediate problem was that we had no other transport. Only the Chevy that should still be parked outside the house. Which we had no keys for. So I told Dr. Houllier about the place. Gave him the address. And said I'd call him when we were ready to be picked up.

Dr. Houllier set us up on the pediatric floor. That was a thoughtful move. Instead of regular rooms they had a series of little suites. The kind of places that enable parents to stay with their sick kids. A couple of nurses helped Dr. Houllier get Michael squared away in the hospital bed. They hung extra IV bags. Took his temperature. Blood pressure. Peered into his eyes and ears with special machines. Daubed him with creams and lotions. And prodded and poked him in all kinds of different places.

Eventually Dr. Houllier said he was happy. He said it might take a while but he was sure Michael would be OK. He warned us that someone would come by every hour to do some observations. Then he left us to get comfortable. Fenton took an armchair. She shoved it close in at Michael's side and curled up, knees to chest. I took the other bed. It was close to five A.M. I'd been up for twenty-two hours.

I was exhausted. But I was feeling quietly satisfied. Fenton was safe. Michael wasn't dead. The bomb was defused and on its way to be studied by the experts. I figured that things were basically good in the world.

It's funny how wrong a person can be.

Chapter 51

I got woken up at a minute to seven. By my phone. I was dead asleep one moment. Wide awake the next. Like a switch being thrown. Some kind of instinctive response to anything unnatural. Or threatening.

I figured the electronic howl qualified as both.

I answered the call. It was the FBI. One of the special agents who Wallwork had rounded up to guard Michael. Her team had reached the outskirts of town and she wanted to know where we should rendezvous. I gave her directions. Then lay back down and closed my eyes. An argument was brewing in my head. The thought of taking a shower on one side. The appeal of not moving on the other. Both were persuasive. But neither got the chance to carry the day. Because my phone rang again. It was Wallwork this time.

"News," he said. "Huge. The pictures and samples my guy sent in from Dendoncker's bomb? One already hit the jackpot. The transponder? There was a fingerprint on it. They have an ID. The TEDAC guys say it's solid. Good enough to survive any test in court."

I said, "Michael Curtis, right?" I figured the day was about to go downhill for Fenton and her brother. Fast. So I might as well get out ahead of it.

"Who? No. It was Nader Khalil."

"I don't know who that is." That was true. Although I had heard the name. Dendoncker accused me of working for the guy.

"Khalil's a big fish. Very big. I'm told the system lit up like a Christmas tree when it came back with his name. He's a terrorist. Out of Beirut. One of a family of terrorists. His father was one. He got killed by the police. His brother was one. He got killed, too. A more notorious death. He was driving the truck that carried the Marine barracks bomb. Nader himself has been linked to a dozen different atrocities. But there was never any evidence. Until now."

It was a strange detail from the past. That Khalil's brother was driving the barracks truck bomb. He must have died yards away from me. But there was something about the present that didn't add up. If Michael made the bomb, I couldn't see how someone else's fingerprint wound up on part of it.

Wallwork wasn't done. "A manhunt has started for him. World-wide. Unlimited resources. The guy's toast. It's just a question of when."

Maybe Khalil had supplied the parts Michael had used, I thought. That could be how his fingerprint got to be there.

Wallwork kept going. "The manhunt is worldwide. But there's another concern. Closer to home. The TEDAC guys are worried that Khalil is still in the States."

Or maybe Dendoncker had stolen the parts, I thought. Or refused to pay. Or ripped off Khalil in some other way. That could be why he was expecting a reprisal.

Wallwork continued. "The TEDAC guys are scared that Khalil is ramping up a bombing campaign. Here. And they figure Dendoncker's helping him. His family was from Beirut, too, remember. His mother was, anyway."

"They think this on the strength of one fingerprint and a vague connection to a foreign city?"

"No. On the strength of this being the second of Khalil's bombs that they found."

"Where was the other one?"

"I'm not sure where it turned up. It was a dud. It was taken to TEDAC. A few weeks ago. It was analyzed. And it had enough identical features for them to be certain it was made by the same person."

"Did it have a transponder?"

"No. And it didn't emit gas. But the components came from the same source. The wiring techniques were the same. The architecture was the same. There are enough hallmarks for them to be convinced. More than enough."

This is the problem when a lie gets too much oxygen. It grows. Even a lie of omission. The smoke bomb had been made by Michael. So if the TEDAC guys had connected it with another one made by the same person, it must be the last bomb Fenton worked on. The one Michael made and sent to her as an SOS. Only the TEDAC guys didn't know there had been a transponder in that one, too. Or that Fenton had destroyed it. Because of Michael's fingerprint. If they had known, they'd have reached a different conclusion. I had no doubt about that. I was about to tell Wallwork. Ask him to bring the TEDAC guys up to speed. To correct their misconception. But something stopped me. The nagging at the back of my mind. It had started when Fenton told me about finding Michael's message. With the card and the condom. It had grown louder with Dendoncker's weird responses. Now, with all the talk about the Khalil guy, it was practically deafening.

Wallwork was silent for a moment, too. Then he said, "So, they're worried about what Khalil's up to. They think Dendoncker is helping him. And you're the only person who's been in contact with Dendoncker. Reacher, I might as well just come out and say it. The bosses at TEDAC want to talk to you."

I wasn't buying the cooperation angle. Not when Dendoncker seemed to think that Khalil could have sent me to kill him. But there was a connection between them. It was a recipe for nothing good. That was for sure. And I had seen Dendoncker. How he operates. Where he hung out. How much he needed to be taken off the street. So I said, "All right. Have them call me."

"They don't want to talk on the phone, Reacher. They want to talk face-to-face."

I said nothing.

"Think about it. If this goes south there's the potential for major casualties. Major loss of life. If that happens, and you were in their shoes, could you live with yourself if you hadn't adequately interviewed the only guy with firsthand information?"

He had a point.

"They only want you for an hour. Two, tops. So, what do you say?"

"I don't know. When?"

"Today."

"Where?"

"TEDAC. It's at the Redstone Arsenal. Near Huntsville, Alabama."

"How am I supposed to get there in a day? It must be more than fifteen hundred miles away."

"They'll send a plane. To be honest, they already sent one. It's waiting for you. There's an airfield an hour's drive from Los Gemelos. Four agents are on their way to safeguard the guy you rescued. One of them will drive you."

I wondered if it was one of the airfields Dendoncker's crew used to smuggle things through. "And afterward?"

"They'll take you wherever you like. Within the United States."

"San Francisco?"

"Sure. If that's what you want."

"It is."

"OK. I'll arrange it. Oh. One other thing. This might make you smile. A fax came for you at the hotel. At 12:34 A.M. From Dendoncker. He said the operation was on hold. You were to stay where you were. And not let *the item* out of your sight."

The conversation had woken Fenton up. She was still in the armchair at Michael's side so I went and sat on his bed and filled her in on developments.

"Well then," Fenton said when I was finished. "Looks like you'll make it to the ocean after all. A private jet. Sent by the government. Guess you're taking hitchhiking to a whole new level."

I said, "I hope Michael pulls through. And I'll put in a good word for both of you."

She shook her head. "Just for Michael. I knew what I was doing. I'll take what's coming to me."

"Can you remember a number?"

"You're keeping that phone?"

"No. The number's for someone else. A woman. Her name's Sonia. I met her when I was looking for you. She helped me. And she was close to Michael. You should call her. Let her know he's alive."

"She was close to Michael? How close?"

I shrugged. "Very, I guess. They met in the hospital in Germany. Seems like they've been together ever since."

I could see Fenton doing the math. She hadn't heard about this woman before. That was clear. And her own relationship with her brother had started to wither right around the time the two must have hooked up.

She said, "What's she like, this Sonia? Will I like her?"

"I hope so. Could be your future sister-in-law we're talking about."

Chapter 52

The plane was waiting when I reached the airport. It was sitting near the end of the runway, alone and aloof from the handful of crop dusters and two-seater trainers that were dotted around. It was some kind of Gulfstream. All sharp angles and glossy black paint so that it looked like it was going fast even when it wasn't moving. It had a tail number, but like the Sikorsky I'd flown back from Texas in, there was no agency designation. Just the words *United States.*

The agent flashed her badge at the video camera on the intercom at the gate and then drove right up to the plane. Its engines were turning over and when we looped around its tail, I saw that the steps were down. Thirty seconds later I was on board and strapped into a seat. A couple of minutes after that we were in the air. No safety briefings. No lining up to take off. And no other passengers.

The vibe inside was more mobile office than luxury club. There was plenty of blond wood with all kinds of plugs and ports and connectors for computers. There were twelve seats. They were finished in navy leather and could be swiveled around. Tables could be folded out from under the windows. There was a projector on the ceiling. A display screen. And a coffee machine. I helped myself to a cup and then settled down to doze. The flight was smooth and quiet. The pilot flew high and fast. We were in the air for less than three hours. I woke up when she began our final descent. The landing was gentle. The taxi was short. And a car was waiting for me when I climbed down the steps.

The army airfield is in the northwest corner of the Redstone Arsenal complex. The TEDAC buildings are at the southeast, more than a mile away. The Bureau driver who collected me didn't say a word as he zigzagged through the warren of NASA laboratories and army facilities and other kinds of FBI operations. I guess getting sent to ferry scruffy civilians around wasn't the plum choice of duty around there. He finally pulled up alongside a line of shiny, knee-high security bollards and pointed toward a glass-fronted building on the far side.

He said, "In there. Ask for Agent Lane."

Inside there were three security guards, all in private contractor's uniforms. The first was sitting behind a reception desk. She asked to see my ID. I handed her my passport. She didn't care that it had expired. She just laid it on a scanner and a minute later a machine to its side spat out a laminated pass with my photo, the date, and a two-hour validity period. I clipped it to my shirt and the next guy held out a bin for my other possessions. I dropped in my cash and my phone and he fed them through an X-ray machine. He asked for my shoes. I slipped them off and dumped them on the conveyor belt. The third guy then directed me through an arch-shaped metal detector. It didn't buzz or beep, and by the time I had replaced my shoes and retrieved my things, a fourth guy had showed up. He looked like he was in his early forties. He was wearing a dark gray suit with a tie and he had an ID badge on a chain around his neck.

He said, "I'm Supervisory Special Agent James Lane." He held out his hand. "Quite a mouthful, I know. I'm heading up the team we're putting together in response to these new developments. I appreciate you taking the time to talk to me. I hope you'll be able to help. Come on. This way. I'll show you what's what."

A stone path stretched away from the exit to the security building. It led up two sets of matching stone steps to a broad, flat area that was full of wooden picnic tables with gray umbrellas. There were two neighboring buildings. Lane pointed to the one on the left. It was big, gray, rectangular, and featureless.

He said, "We call that one *The Building*. Never tell me G-Men have no imagination, eh? Anyway, ever seen that Indiana Jones movie about the Ark of the Covenant? The scene at the end where they hide its crate in a warehouse? That's what it's like inside. Shelves, floor to ceiling, end to end. More than a hundred thousand containers. Every piece of every device we've analyzed over the last eighteen years. The place is almost full. We've already broken ground on another one. But that's not where we're going."

Lane started walking toward the right-hand building. This one had two distinct sections. A single-story part with a flat roof, stone walls, and tall windows. And a part with a higher, angled roof, white walls, and no windows. The way they were butted up together made it look like the second half was trying to swallow the first.

"This is where the magic happens." Lane paused at the door. "The labs are here. Plus the less interesting things. Like admin. And the meeting rooms. That's where we're going. Sorry."

Lane used his ID to unlock the door then led the way along the main corridor until we reached a room labeled *Conference One*. Inside there was a space about fifteen feet by twenty. There was a wooden-topped table in the center. It was rectangular. Surrounded by eleven chairs. They were angled toward the far wall, which was plain white. I guess it doubled as a projection screen. There were three closets built into the wall on the right. Windows to the left. And a carpet that looked like a kind of muted, textile version of a Jackson Pollock painting.

Lane took the chair at the head of the table, facing the wall. He said, "I'm sorry to be treating you like a regular visitor. I've read your record. I know all about your service. I would like to give you a full tour. But, you know, regulations. There was no time to get clearance. And at the end of the day more than two hundred people work here. We have a lot of equipment that would be extremely hard to replace. And a trove of evidence from all over the world that's vital in the war on terror. This place might not be the most glamorous target. But it's near the top of the list, strategically. It's what I'd hit if I were on the other side. So we have to take precautions. And we can't make exceptions. I hope you understand."

"Of course."

"So, down to business. Khalil's fingerprint. Finding it is a two-sided coin. The good thing is, he can be arrested now. If anyone can find him. But the bad thing is that if he's active here, currently, we must stop him. Fast. The problem is figuring out where to look. There are so many potential targets available to him. We need to narrow them down. The bomb you helped us secure will be arriving in the next thirty minutes or so. That may give us some pointers. Or it may not. We won't know until we try. Either way, it will take time. In the interim we're looking for all the help we can get. The angle

I'd like to start with is the delivery mechanism. Khalil could be working on a bomb to be carried in a car, for example. Or a truck. Or a plane. Or worn as a vest. Or even sent in the mail. Did anything you saw or heard give any kind of a clue?"

"Dendoncker was running a smuggling operation. He was piggybacking it on a catering service for private planes out of small airfields. But that's pretty much been shut down. He seemed unconcerned about it. Strangely so, like he had already planned to move on to something else. The question is, *what*? I'm not convinced Dendoncker's working with Khalil. I think he was terrified of him."

"These guys—they're weird. Paranoid, most of them. They start out as introverts, then live their whole lives doubly desperate not to draw attention to themselves. Trying not to visit the same electronics store too often. Or to buy from the same websites over and over. They wind up running from shadows. It's probably nothing. But even if they have fallen out already, there could still be useful clues from when they did work together."

"The flight thing is all I can think of."

"OK. Then the second angle is materials. Is he using precursors, for example. Things like ammonium nitrate or fuel oil or nitromethane. Or specialist compounds like TATP, or ethylene glycol dinitrate. Or even military grade explosives like C-4." Lane paused for a moment and looked right at me. "As an aside, the Beirut barracks bomb used precursors. You were there. Well, we recently recovered new evidence, after all these years. We should have good news on that soon."

There was something strange about the way Lane spoke those words. How he said, "You were there." It sounded half like a question. Half like a statement. It caused an echo at the back of my mind. I'd heard something similar recently, but I couldn't put my finger on what.

Lane said, "Mr. Reacher? Materials?"

"Artillery shells," I said. "Dendoncker had a bunch of them. At least three hundred. They were locked in a shed. At the abandoned school he was camped out in."

"Any idea what was in them?"

"No."

"You didn't see a code book? If they were recovered from an enemy they're often deliberately mislabeled. The code book is needed to confirm the contents."

I shook my head.

"OK. Let me have the location. I'll arrange collection. Now, the third angle is the method of detonation. We know Khalil used two kinds in his first device. A timer and cellular. Those are quite normal. And three kinds in the device that's incoming. A timer, cellular, and a transponder. That's unusual. But whether he was looking for another level of backup, or whether he's messing with us, I don't know. Not yet."

I said nothing.

"Do you know how transponders work?"

I said, "I have an idea what they do. Not so much how they do it."

"A good example is a car's ignition. Try to start the engine and a chip in the car sends out a radio signal. A transponder in the key automatically bounces back a reply. If the reply is correct, the chip completes the circuit. That's why you can't hotwire modern cars. Even if you join the right wires, there's no transponder to reply to the car's chip, so the circuit remains open."

"And the same thing could happen with this bomb?"

"I assume so. I haven't seen it yet, obviously. I need to examine it to be sure. But if it's a technique Khalil has perfected it could be a massive problem. Imagine you have a target with an unpredictable schedule. You plant a bomb somewhere along his route. Sneak a transponder onto his keychain or into his pocket. Anyone else could go by without a problem. But when he approaches—boom."

"OK. But you said the transponder's in the key. Not the car."

"Correct. The chip in the car initiates the communication. The key responds."

"So the chip in the bomb would be like the chip in the car?"

"Correct. I'll verify that once the bomb is here, but I don't see another way it could work."

"What kind of range do these things have?"

"They vary. Depends on the application. Planes use them for automatic identification, in which case the signal can travel many kilometers. If you use one to unlock a door in place of a key, you'd want the signal to only go a few millimeters. You put one in a bomb, you'd want it to be similar, I guess, or your target would be out of the blast zone when it detonated. Unless it was a giant bomb and you didn't care about collateral damage."

Lane had done it again. The way he spoke, I couldn't tell if "You put one in a bomb" was a question or a statement. And I suddenly realized who he reminded me of. Michael. When he briefly spoke to Fenton, right after we first found him. He either said, "You came." Or "You came?" And that was right after something else weird. He said, "You got my warning?" Fenton had described it as a cry for help. An SOS. That was nothing like the same thing. I thought about what she had found. What she had based her conclusion on. And stood up.

I said, "Excuse me. I have to make a call."

"Now?" Lane checked his watch. "The bomb will be here any minute. I'll have to step out. Can't you do it then?"

"No." I moved to the corner of the room and dialed Dr. Houllier's number. "This can't wait."

Dr. Houllier answered and I asked to speak to Michael.

He said, "Not possible. Sorry. He's unconscious again."

"Again?"

"Correct. He was awake for a while earlier, though he wasn't saying much. Nothing coherent anyway. Just rambling about finding a goal or something like that."

I thanked Dr. Houllier and hung up. Then immediately called him back and asked for Fenton.

I said, "Please hurry. This is important."

Fenton came on the line after thirty seconds. "What's up? Make it quick. I want to get back to Michael."

I said, "I need you to think very carefully about a question. Don't guess. Only answer if you are one hundred percent sure. OK?"

"Sure. Fire away."

"The condom you found in the message Michael sent. What brand was it?"

"Trojan."

"You sure?"

"One hundred percent."

Chapter 53

A condom. And a business card. A Trojan. And a Red
Roan. Which is a kind of horse. Michael had been trying to tell his
sister that the device she was given to analyze at TEDAC was a
Trojan horse. But Fenton had misunderstood from the start. She
had made two false assumptions: That the bomb containing Michael's message had been intended to explode. And that the transponder inside it was the trigger.

I was betting that neither thing was true. The bomb was just a
vehicle. Its job was to deliver the transponder. To a place where
only a bomb could go. And the transponder's job was not to trigger
the bomb it was in. It was to trigger something else. Which hadn't
happened. Because Fenton had fixated on Michael's fingerprint. She
hadn't realized it was to ensure that the bomb reached her desk. Or
that it doubled as a way to sign the warning. She hated puzzles
after all. She was too pedantic. She'd taken it at face value. As
damning evidence. So she destroyed it.

Fenton destroyed the first transponder. But another one was coming. In the smoke bomb. It was minutes away. Heading for the building I was in. Where two hundred people worked. Which was full of irreplaceable machines and priceless evidence. No wonder Dendoncker had been so desperate to push me into transporting the device for him. He had wanted it at TEDAC from the start.

Lane was scowling. "You broke off this meeting to talk about condoms? What's wrong with you?"

Michael's original bomb arrived at TEDAC weeks ago, initially with its transponder intact. But the place didn't blow up. So the thing it was supposed to trigger wasn't here at that time. It must have come in later.

I said, "The last three weeks. Have any new devices been brought in?"

Lane checked his watch again. "Of course."

"Anything particularly large?"

"I can't share that kind of information. It's too sensitive."

"Come on, Lane. This is important."

"Why?"

"It's a long story. A guy with a liking for cryptic messages sent a warning that the transponder in the device that's about to arrive is supposed to trigger something else. Not be triggered itself."

Lane smiled and shook his head. "No. That theory doesn't hold water. For it to be right, the device already here would need to have the corresponding transponder. And no such devices have been brought in. Fact."

"Are you sure? You said some evidence waits awhile before you get to it."

"We prioritize. Some evidence does have to wait for full analysis. That's true. But we don't just throw it in a closet when it shows up.

It doesn't slip down the back of the couch. Every piece that's wait-listed is examined on delivery. Photographs are taken. Components are listed. Transponders are highly unusual. If anything had arrived containing one, I would know."

"These inspections. They're done without exception?"

"Priority cases go straight to analysis planning who handle the documentation and record keeping. It's integrated into their process. Everything else gets an initial inspection. Without exception." Lane paused for a second. "Actually, there was one exception. A truck bomb. A city destroyer. It came in from overseas. The vehicle was too large to fit into a work bay here so the minute it arrived we sent it away again. To our old premises. At Quantico. A huge place. You could fit dozens of trucks in it."

"What if something arrived while we were talking?"

"That's possible, I suppose." Lane took out his phone and had a brief conversation. "No. There was nothing new today."

The prickling at the back of my neck was worse. "When M— Khalil's bomb arrives, you should stop it. Don't let it in."

"Impossible."

"Why? You didn't let the big truck bomb in."

"No. But it came by road. It already had an escort. Khalil's is being flown in. It doesn't have an escort. It can't go on the public roads without one. What if there was an accident? And it's full of chemical weapons? And people die? Because we sent it away, against procedure, and with no good reason. Based entirely on your whim."

"It's—"

There was a knock on the door and another agent stepped into the room. A much younger guy. He looked freshly pressed and eager. "It's here, sir. The device from Texas."

"Excellent." Lane stood and made for the door. "You stay here. Keep Mr. Reacher company. I'll be back as soon as the device has been processed."

I thought about the truck bomb. Lane had called it a city destroyer. That didn't sound good. Not good at all. I was happy it was no longer here. And I figured it must be the one Michael's bomb was supposed to trigger. It had to be. It was the only one that hadn't been inspected, and all the others had been free of transponders. Then I realized something else. The truck being sent away could explain Dendoncker's sudden change of heart. Why he told me to keep the smoke bomb at the hotel. If he had someone watching TEDAC, he would know there was no point sending a second transponder.

I turned to the new agent. "The city destroyer. The one that wouldn't fit in the workshop. When did it get refused? I need to know exactly. To the minute."

"Let me find out for you, sir." The agent called someone. There was a lot of nodding and gesticulating and changing of facial expressions before he hung up. "The destroyer's still here, sir. It actually never left. One of its escort vehicles broke down and they still haven't sent a replacement."

"Where is it, exactly?"

"Parked between this building and The Building."

"When did it arrive?"

"Around midnight, last night. I believe."

"OK. Call Agent Lane. Tell him not to let the new device onto the site. Not under any circumstances."

"If you're worried about the destroyer being here, sir, then please

don't. It's been made safe. Emergency procedure. It had three detonation systems, and they've all been disconnected."

"Was one a transponder?"

"No, sir. It had cellular. Magnetic. And photosensitive."

"Call Lane. Right now. No time to explain."

The agent dialed a number, held the phone to his ear, then shook
his head. "Line's busy."

"Call the driver."

"OK. What's his number?"

"No idea."

"His name?"

I shrugged.

"No problem." The agent started tapping and swiping at his
phone's screen. "I'll go on the intranet. See if I can find a roster."

"No time. What kind of truck is the destroyer?"

"It's ex-military. An M35 deuce and a half, I think."

"Which is farther? The truck, or the gate?"

"The gate."

"Then you take the gate. Go now. Run. Keep trying Lane's number. One way or the other, stop him."

Chapter 54

I rushed into the corridor. Sprinted to the exit. Burst through. Ran to the space between the two buildings. And saw the truck. Tried not to think about its cargo. Ran to the driver's door. Tugged on the handle. And couldn't get it to move. Which was weird. That kind of truck doesn't have locking doors. Then I noticed the problem. A padlock had been added. The hasp went through a hole in the door skin. It must have been attached to the inner bodywork.

I looked around. There was a border running along the bottom of the wall of the building. Filled with rocks. Some white, decorative kind. I grabbed the biggest one I could see. Smashed it down on the padlock. Hit it again and the lock sprang open. I pulled it free. Tossed it aside. Dropped the rock. Climbed up. Jammed myself into the seat. Which wasn't easy because there's no adjustment. I pushed down on the clutch. Then tried to remember how to get the motor started. It was years since I'd been in a truck like this one. I knew there was no key. There were three steps to follow instead. I scanned all the knobs and levers and gauges. Most had no markings. The few that had labels were in Arabic, which didn't help me. I spotted a lever near the center of the dash that looked familiar. I turned it. About twenty degrees, counterclockwise. Which was as far as it would go. I found a knob on the left, with a spade handle. It was sticking out. I pushed it in. Then hit a red button, low down on the right. The heavy old diesel cranked and coughed into life. I found first gear. Which is where second is on most vehicles. Released the parking brake. Lifted the clutch. And the truck shuddered forward.

Ahead there was a road that led to a roll-up door at the back of the laboratory building. There was no point taking it, or I'd wind up closer to the vehicle I was trying to avoid. So when I reached the end I swung left. Continued around The Building. Swung left again and drove back along the far side. I came to the picnic area. The place was full of tables and umbrellas. There was no way through. They were too close together. So I drove over a bunch of them. I saw a dirt road to the right. It ran along the rear of eight buildings adjacent to the TEDAC site. They were new. The road was probably leftover from the construction phase. And there were no vehicles its whole length. It was on the far side of a fence so I smashed through, straightened up, and pressed harder on the gas.

I heard sirens. Behind me. I checked my door mirror. It was shaking horribly. All I could make out was a pair of black sedans with flashing light bars on their roofs. They were catching me. Easily. But catching me wouldn't do them any good. They needed to stop me. I didn't know how they were planning to do that. Whether they knew what the truck was carrying. How reckless they were prepared to be. Or how stupid. I figured I was about a thousand feet away from the laboratory at that point. Roughly the width of the whole TEDAC campus. Probably far enough from the smoke bomb's transponder. The sedans were almost behind me. One disappeared from view. Trying to sneak up the passenger side. Then two more sedans appeared. Directly ahead. I decided that would have to do. I took my foot off the gas. Shifted down a couple of gears. Hit the brake. And coasted to as gentle a stop as possible. I took my shirt off. Hung it out of my window. It wasn't white, but I hoped the guys got the message all the same.

I spent the next hour in Conference One with two guys with guns. Neither of them spoke, which suited me fine. I sat in the same chair as before. Leaned forward. Cushioned my head in my arms. Ran through some Magic Slim. And followed up with a little Shawn Holt.

I didn't sit up until Lane came into the room. He walked to the head of the table and set down a small box. It was black. Dusty. And a bunch of colored wires were sticking out of one corner.

"Mr. Reacher, I owe you thanks. And an apology. Today was a bad day for terrorists because of you." He pointed to the box. "This was found in the city destroyer. It transmits and receives, and it's coded to the transponder in the smoke bomb. If they'd come within range of each other, there'd be no more Redstone Arsenal. No more us. And maybe thousands of other casualties."

I said nothing.

"One question." Lane sat down. "How did you know?"

Michael's warning had been the key. Along with Dendoncker's

desperate behavior. But those were all things I didn't want to get into. They'd only raise more questions. Ones I didn't feel like answering. So I said, "No biggie. Just a lucky guess."

"And motive? Khalil trying to destroy some evidence that's stored here?"

"Trying to destroy evidence, yes. Khalil, no." I had no proof of that. Only a hunch. Which meant the West Coast was going to have to wait after all.

Chapter 55

"He won't come," Fenton said. Again.

She first said it when she met me at the small airfield an hour from Los Gemelos.

She said it right after she climbed in behind the wheel of Dr. Houllier's Cadillac.

She said it three more times as the huge car wafted and wallowed along the long straight roads into town.

She said it as she parked outside The House.

She said it as we walked through the tunnel.

She said it as we checked that the money and the narcotics were still there.

She said it as we confirmed that the final smoke bomb had been removed from Michael's workshop.

She said it as we sat down against the back wall of the old school's assembly hall.

And every time she said it, I gave the same reply. "He will."

"How can you be sure?"

"He has no choice. His plan failed. That means he can't stay in the United States. He can't return to Beirut. He'll be on watch lists everywhere. So he'll have to go to ground. Forever. So he'll need every penny he can put his hands on. And every valuable thing he can sell."

"What if the FBI already caught him? He tried to destroy TEDAC. They'll have a hard-on for him like you wouldn't believe."

"The Bureau wants to find him. Sure. But they don't know where to look."

"You didn't tell them?"

I said nothing.

"Outstanding. Gold star for you. But what if they found him on their own? Or if you're wrong about his plan? What if you misunderstood? If it didn't fail?"

"Then he won't come."

Fenton elbowed me in the ribs and we settled in to wait.

It was pushing 7:00 P.M. Twelve hours since I was woken up by the phone. Six hours since I broke into the city destroyer. The sun was low. Everything its dipping rays touched turned orange or pink. The view was magnificent. If it only happened once a century everyone would gather to watch. Then rave about what they saw. The colors changed by the minute. The shadows shifted and lengthened. The sky began its final fade to gray. Then two brighter points appeared. Low down. Unsteady. But growing bigger. Coming our way. Headlights.

Fenton and I moved into the dining hall. We left the doors open, just a crack. We peered through. Five minutes passed. Ten. Then the tall windows lit up like giant mirrors. They went dark again. The outer doors opened. And Mansour walked in. He was followed by Dendoncker. They went straight for the aluminum containers. The ones that were full of cash and pills.

Fenton went first. She was carrying one of the captured Uzis. She raised it and lined it up on Dendoncker's chest.

She said, "You. Against the wall. Hands in the air."

Dendoncker didn't hesitate. He was a smart man. He did exactly what she told him to.

I took a step toward Mansour. He grinned, held out his hand, and gestured for me to keep on coming.

I said, "You don't have to do this. You know you're going to lose. You should go sit in the car. I'll send your boss out when we're done talking. Assuming he can still walk."

Mansour stretched both arms straight up above his head then started to bring them down slowly, out to each side, in a broad circle. His fingers were arrowed. It looked like the start of some kind of martial arts ritual. Maybe it was supposed to symbolize something. Maybe it was supposed to impress. Or intimidate. But whatever the purpose I saw no advantage in letting him finish so I darted forward and kicked him in the right knee. Viciously. Hard enough to shatter most people's patellas. He grunted and threw a wild roundhouse punch at my head. I ducked under it and jabbed him in the kidney. I brought my other fist up under his chin. I put all my strength into it. Pushed up onto my tiptoes at just the right moment. Timed it perfectly. Against a normal guy the fight would have been over there and then. It almost was with him. He rocked onto his heels. His neck snapped back. He started to fall. If he'd hit the ground he would have been toast. There was no way I would have let him get up again. But the wall saved him. Or the climbing bars that were attached to it did. He slammed into the center of a section of the frame. It was ten feet tall by six wide. There was plenty of spring to it. Which cushioned the impact. Allowed him to stay on his feet. He staggered forward. The bars swung after him. They were hinged at the right side. The force of the impact had unhooked their latch. They continued through ninety degrees then stopped, sticking straight out into the hall. I guess they all did that to form a series of obstacles for the kids to climb when they were doing circuit training.

The guy held up his hands in surrender. "OK. You win. I'm done."

He took a step toward me. His legs were unsteady. His breathing was ragged. He took another slow step. Then a fast one. He curled his fingers into fists. And launched a punch straight at my face with his right. I deflected it and danced away to the side. Which was just what he wanted. He was already swinging his left. I saw it late. Twisted and ducked and caught the brunt on my shoulder. It felt like I'd been hit by a train. I saw him lining up another shot with his right. I planted my foot. Twisted back in the opposite direction. Raised my arm. And drove my elbow into the side of his head. It was the kind of contact that would have split most guys' skulls. His mouth opened. His arms slumped down to his sides. I reversed direction again and smashed my fist into his other temple. He staggered to the side. His legs were turning to jelly. For real this time. It was my opportunity. I had no intention of wasting it. There was no one to intervene. I jabbed him in the face three times in quick succession with my left. He reeled back. I switched to my right and drove a huge reverse punch into his gut. He doubled over. I stood him up straight again with a knee to the face. He staggered back farther. I followed in and crashed the heel of my right hand into his chin. The back of his head cannoned into the wall. His eyes rolled up. His knees buckled. He flopped down into kneeling position. He balanced like that for a moment, and before he could fall the rest of the way I kicked him in the side of the head with my left foot. He spun around and down and wound up with his chest on the floor. His arms out to the sides. And his face jammed into a gap near the base of the climbing bars. I was pretty sure he was down and out. But I never take that kind of thing for granted. I stepped in close. And stamped on the base of his skull. I felt his spine snap. I was sure about that.

Chapter 56

Dendoncker was standing still, staring at the body. His face was pale and completely expressionless. Fenton was covering him with the Uzi. I moved in close and felt his jacket pocket. He had a tiny revolver. Another NAA-22S. I took it and slipped it into my waistband.

"I offered Mansour the chance to walk out of here," I said. "Now I'm going to offer you the same. With one condition."

"Which is?"

"You tell me the truth."

Dendoncker wet his lips with his tongue. "What do you want to know?"

"How did you get hold of a transponder with Nader Khalil's fingerprint on it?"

"I didn't. Michael and Khalil, they tricked me. They were working together, but I didn't know. I bought Michael's story about a protest with smoke. I had no idea there was anything more going on."

Fenton raised the Uzi. "Shall I shoot him?"

Dendoncker lifted his arms like they could shield him from her bullets. I grabbed his wrist and dragged him around to the other side of the climbing bars. I forced him onto his knees. Held the back of his head. And pushed his face to within an inch of Mansour's.

I said, "Think carefully. Is this how you want to go?"

"I bought the fingerprint." Dendoncker squirmed away from the body. "It took years. And lots of money. But finally I found someone who was ready to betray Khalil."

I let Dendoncker stand up. "How did you get your hands on it?"

"I used one of the women who worked for my catering company. I sent her to Beirut with the money. She brought the fingerprint back. It was fixed in sticky tape. Lifted from a drinking glass. It was easy to transfer it onto the transponder."

"When was this?"

"A few weeks ago." Dendoncker pointed at Fenton. "It's why I hired her. I actually had to send two women. One stayed behind in Beirut. She was part of the price."

"Did she know in advance? The one who stayed."

"Of course not. Neither did the one who returned. She thought there'd been an accident."

"What happened to the other women? You had six on your crew, from what I heard. Five, excluding Fenton."

"One was plotting with Michael. She ran away. Two are coming with me. The other two are going to . . . retire."

I caught movement out of the corner of my eye. It was Fenton. Heading for the exit. As planned.

I said, "You used the fingerprint to frame Khalil. He was never actually involved."

Dendoncker nodded.

"He was trying to kill you. There was some kind of feud going on."

Dendoncker nodded again.

"Which is why you always checked the bodies of anyone who came after you. You're not just paranoid."

"He sent others to kill me many times. I hoped one day he'd try in person. And fail. Then I would be free."

"What was the feud about?"

Dendoncker wet his lips. "Khalil's father blamed me for his other son's death. Khalil carried it on when his father died."

"Khalil's brother was killed. He was driving a truck bomb."

"His father and I, we were rivals. I was young. Ambitious. Looking for a shortcut to the top of our group. He stood in my way. I thought if he lost his son it would break his spirit. He would fade away. I could fill the void." Dendoncker shrugged. "I was wrong. It only made him stronger. Harder."

"You made his son drive the bomb?"

"Not made. Led him to the decision."

"Not a distinction his father was impressed by, I guess."

Dendoncker shook his head.

"So you saw the opportunity to get Khalil off your back. That's what this is all about?"

"Correct. It was the only way I could buy my freedom."

"The way I see it, you planned on three steps. First you had Michael make you a bomb. A dud. It was left where it would be found. It had a GPS chip so you could confirm it wound up at TEDAC. It also had a transponder. You knew the components would be studied. The details recorded. The pieces stored."

Dendoncker nodded.

"Step two involved the city destroyer. It was supposed to arrive at TEDAC and get triggered by the transponder from Michael's bomb."

I felt my phone buzz in my pocket. That told me Fenton had found what she was looking for in Dendoncker's SUV.

Dendoncker nodded again.

"One question. How do you get your hands on a city destroyer?"

Dendoncker shrugged. "Same way you get anything. Money."

"So the city destroyer detonates. Takes TEDAC with it. Then step three. The smoke bomb is found. It has the same technology inside it. Plus Khalil's fingerprint."

"That's the way it was supposed to happen."

"But the first transponder didn't trigger the city destroyer."

"No. It should have done. I have no idea why it failed."

I smiled. I was tempted to tell him that the transponder didn't fail. That it didn't have the chance to. Because Fenton had destroyed it weeks ago. But I resisted. I needed to keep him focused. He had some big questions coming up. So instead I said, "Then why try to stop the smoke bomb? Why not make sure it went to TEDAC so its transponder could finish the job?"

"The smoke bomb had the same transponder. It would have triggered the truck bomb. That's true. But I didn't want to risk wasting the fingerprint."

"Wasting it?"

"Right. It was damn expensive. Two million dollars and a fair employee. It might have survived. But a blast that size? It could easily have been destroyed. And think of the scene. A hundred thousand pieces of evidence are already there. The fingerprint could have survived then got mixed up with the rest. And got lost."

"OK. Tell me what you did after the demonstration I watched. What you added to the smoke bomb before you put it in the truck for me to drive."

"I added nothing. Why would I?"

"Because you didn't want the fingerprint to be wasted. The T in *TEDAC* stands for *terrorist*. Not protester. Not attention seeker. Those agents are specialists. They don't get out of bed for a pretty puff of smoke. So unless you spiced the bomb up a little it would have gone to a local field office, at best. Maybe just the police department. Where it would have sat on a shelf in the evidence room, gathering dust until long after you're dead."

"I disagree. TEDAC would have taken it. Because of all the press coverage. I didn't add a thing."

"You didn't smear the outside of the shells with VX?"

"Where would I get VX from?"

"You didn't pour VX into the shells?"

Fenton came back inside. She stayed near the exit door. She peeled off a pair of latex surgeon's gloves and jammed them into her pocket.

Dendoncker said, "VX is a weapon of mass destruction. I wouldn't touch it."

"And the third smoke bomb. The last one left in your workshop. You didn't fill it with VX?"

"I don't even know where it is." Dendoncker pointed at Mansour. "He disposed of it. He didn't say where or how."

"You didn't add anything to either bomb. You don't know where the third bomb is. That's the story you're going with?"

"It's not a story."

I waited a moment to give him one last chance to come clean. He didn't take it. So I said, "OK. I choose to believe you."

"Then I can go?"

"In a minute. There's still one thing I don't understand. You want to blow someplace up and let Khalil take the fall. But why does that place have to be TEDAC? There are plenty of softer targets out there."

Dendoncker was silent for a moment. "I thought, if I hit part of the FBI they'd take it personally. Leave no stone unturned. Make sure the fingerprint was found and—"

"No." I shook my head. "Here's what I think. You learned that there was some evidence against you at TEDAC. Something that hadn't come to light yet. But that would. Soon. Then you were offered Khalil's fingerprint. And you saw your chance. Two birds, one bomb."

Dendoncker didn't reply.

"I know what that evidence is. I've joined the dots. But I need to hear you admit it. And I want you to apologize. Do those two things, then you can walk."

Dendoncker stayed silent.

I pointed at Mansour's body. "Do those two things, or that's how you'll leave this world. Your choice."

Dendoncker took a deep breath. "OK. The Beirut barracks bomb. I didn't build it. But I taught the guys who did. They used parts I touched."

"You were an instructor? That's how you were in a position to pick the driver?"

"Correct. And it's why I recognized your name when we first met at the morgue. You won the Purple Heart that day. I read about it afterward."

"OK. And?"

"And I'm sorry. I apologize. To everyone who got hurt. For everyone who got killed."

I looked at Fenton. She nodded.

"OK." I stepped back. "You're free to go."

Dendoncker was frozen to the spot. His eyes were darting around wildly, looking for a trap. He stayed still for twenty seconds. Then he started toward the door. First walking, then scuttling as fast as he could go. He kept moving until he reached the Cadillac. He jumped in. Fired it up. And steered for the gate.

I pulled out my phone. There was a message saying I'd missed a call. I'd never seen the number before. But I knew exactly who it was from. Or rather, what it was from. Thanks to Fenton's fishing expedition.

I hit the button to call the number back.

Fenton said, "Are you sure you want to do this?"

"Why wouldn't I? If Dendoncker's telling the truth, he'll be OK."

"He lied about not knowing where the third bomb is. I doubt he's telling the truth about the VX."

"Then that's his problem. I'm still giving him more of a chance than he gave 241 Marines in Beirut that day."

Dendoncker's Cadillac stopped at the inner gate. My phone showed that my call had been answered. The gate started to crawl to the side. The gap grew wide enough to drive through. The Cadillac stayed still. The gate opened the rest of the way. The Cadillac didn't move. Then its brake lights went out. It rolled forward. Barely above walking pace. Its horn blared. It trundled on. Slewed slightly to the left. And ran into a fence post.

Its horn continued to blare.

Fenton said, "Want to check? To be sure? Confirm he added VX to the smoke?"

I shook my head. "No chance. That car's not airtight. Dendoncker's right where he deserves to be. And I have no intention of joining him."

Chapter 57

I last encountered Michaela Fenton half a day later. We met on the road outside the town. I was on foot. She was in her Jeep. She roared past me then swung hard to her left. She blocked my path. Her front fender was a hairsbreadth away from the trunk of a tree. A stunted, twisted, ugly thing with hardly any leaves. But the only thing growing taller than knee height for miles in either direction.

Fenton said, "You left without saying goodbye."

I shrugged. "Everyone was asleep."

"I tried to call you."

"I don't have that phone anymore. I dropped it in the trash."

"I figured. That's why I came to look for you. I thought I might find you on this road."

"It's the only one leading out of town."

"Still heading for the ocean?"

"Won't stop till I get there."

"Any chance you'll change your mind?"

I shook my head.

"In that case, I want to thank you. And so does Michael."

"He's awake?"

"He is. He's weak, but he's talking."

"Did he say what he had that Dendoncker was so desperate to get?"

"He called it his insurance. It was a code book. It showed what was inside all the shells Dendoncker had stockpiled. He needed it to make the maximum money when he sold them."

"Where did he hide it?"

"He said he rolled it up and shoved it inside the crossbar of a soccer goal at the school."

"Outstanding."

"And there's something else. I called Sonia. She came back. And you know what? I do like her. Maybe she is my future sister-in-law. And if she is, that's fine by me."

I said nothing.

Fenton tipped her head to the side. "You won't stay even another day?"

"No point. You'd be sick of me in ten minutes. You'd be begging me to leave."

"I doubt it."

"That's right." I turned and started walking again. "You'd probably shoot me instead."

About the Authors

LEE CHILD is the author of twenty-five *New York Times* best-selling Jack Reacher thrillers, with sixteen having reached the #1 position, and the #1 bestselling complete Jack Reacher story collection, *No Middle Name*. Foreign rights in the Reacher series have sold in one hundred territories. A native of England and a former television director, Lee Child lives in New York City and Wyoming.

leechild.com
Facebook.com/LeeChildOfficial
Twitter: @LeeChildReacher

To inquire about booking Lee Child for a speaking engagement, please contact the Penguin Random House Speakers Bureau at speakers@penguinrandomhouse.com.

ANDREW CHILD, who also writes as Andrew Grant, is the author of *RUN, False Positive, False Friend, False Witness, Invisible,* and *Too Close to Home.* Child and his wife, the novelist Tasha Alexander, live on a wildlife preserve in Wyoming. He is the co-author of the #1 bestselling Jack Reacher novel *The Sentinel.*

andrewgrantbooks.com
Facebook.com/andrewgrantauthor
Twitter: @Andrew_Grant